"Mr. Updike is predictably dazzling in his mimicry of an intelligent, witty, articulate woman with the fullest possible storehouse of gripes and perceptions about the role of women in contemporary America."

The New York Times

"*S.* is an epistolary novel, dominated by the engaging voice of Sarah Worth, distant descendant and flawed version of Hester Prynne, who, muddled by feminism and yoga, and inspired by pale religious sparks, leaves her family in New England to take up a life of meaning in the Arizona desert. . . . A wonderful comic invention."

Newsweek

"A funny, wise and finally poignant novel about a flawed but likable woman who represents the cultural confusions of our age. It's Updike's best book in years, and reveals him—once again—as one of our most brilliantly inventive writers."

The Cleveland Plain Dealer

"Outrageous . . . A very funny satirical novel."

San Francisco Chronicle

John Updike

S.

FAWCETT CREST • NEW YORK

Author's Note

Some details of this novel were suggested by reports on Rajneeshpuram in newspapers, *Oregon Magazine*, and *Cities on a Hill*, by Frances FitzGerald; but all characters and milieux are fictional and not meant to resemble any actual persons or places. As to the religious context, much is owed to Mircea Eliade's *Yoga* and *A History of Religious Ideas*, Joseph Campbell's *The Masks of God: Oriental Mythology*, and Ajit Mookerjee's *Kundalini*; the method of transliterating Sanskrit words in these works, however, has for this book's purposes been replaced by a relatively imprecise style requiring no diacritical marks. A glossary of such words used in the text has been placed at the back.

The quotations from *The Dhammapada* are from the Penguin Classics edition, translated from the Pali by Juan Mascaró. I thank Toinette Lippe, Jean Le Mée, Alistair Shearer, Janet Surrey, Steve Bergman, and Martha Updike for guiding and correcting my steps in these occult paths.

She had dark and abundant hair, so glossy that it threw off the sunshine with a gleam, and a face which, besides being beautiful from regularity of feature and richness of complexion, had the impressiveness belonging to a marked brow and deep black eyes. She was lady-like, too, after the manner of the feminine gentility of those days; characterized by a certain state and dignity, rather than by the delicate, evanescent, and indescribable grace, which is now recognized as its indication. And never had Hester Prynne appeared more lady-like, in the antique interpretation of the term, than as she issued from the prison. Those who had before known her, and had expected to behold her dimmed and obscured by a disastrous cloud, were astonished, and even startled, to perceive how her beauty shone out, and made a halo of the misfortune and ignominy in which she was enveloped.

. . .

Much of the marble coldness of Hester's impression was to be attributed to the circumstance that her life had turned, in a great measure, from passion and feeling, to thought. Standing alone in the world,—alone, as to any dependence on society, and with little Pearl to be guided and protected,—alone, and hopeless of retrieving her position, even had she not scorned to consider it desirable,—she cast away the fragments of a broken chain. The world's law was no law for her mind.

—Nathaniel Hawthorne, *The Scarlet Letter*

Dearest Charles—

The distance between us grows, even as my pen hesi-
tates. The engines drone in the spaces between words,
eating up the miles, the acres of the flat farms in big
brown and green squares below the wing as it inches
along. I close my eyes and see our white house, its two
screened porches and long glassy conservatory, its peek
at the sea and the rocks of the cove—those gray rocks
you and Pearl and I have picnicked on so many times
and that when the sun beats on their veins feel warm
even in February—and its undulating lap of lawn and
the bulb bed so happy and thrusty with leaves, now that
spring has come. Do leave a note for the lawn boys
when they come tomorrow to set their big wide reel
mower a notch higher, since last Tuesday they scalped
that area over by the roses, where the ground bulges up.
How often I've spoken to them about it, and with what
results! Of course it's not always the same boys, year
after year.

I bought two extra boxes each of your apple granola
and unprocessed bran—so you have breakfasts at least
for a month. You may wish to speak to Mrs. Kimball

about coming now more than once a week. As you know Thursday is her day and I always try to tidy up for her, especially the kitchen and our bedroom. She arrives around noon. If you can't bring yourself to make the bed at least pull the covers up and smooth the puff. The most gracious thing, the day she comes, is to air the bed for the morning with the puff and covers *down* and windows *open* to get our body smells out but possibly such refinements were wasted on her anyway. Also: she knows where the front-door key is hidden down up in under the garbage-can bin lid, the door on the right, and puts it back there when she goes home, but *don't leave the burglar alarm on* when you go off in the morning—I did once, as you may remember, absent-mindedly when Irving switched yoga lessons at Midge's to Thursday morning because the boy who helps him in the framing shop had to go to his grand-mother's funeral or something and the police came as they're supposed to (though not very promptly, she later confided) and poor Mrs. K. with that crooked heavy-lidded eye of hers that makes her look dishonest in any case had a terrible time explaining, since though I trust her with the key I could never bring myself to trust her with the code to the burglar-alarm system—it seemed too intimate. She does, incredible though it may seem to us, have a sex life and who knows with what kind of men who might casually get it out of her? Whereas it would take a real conscious betrayal for her to cold-bloodedly take a key to the hardware store and have duplicates made on that nasty-sounding little machine. You might ask her if she can give you Mondays as well. The thing about dust and dirt that men don't realize is it doesn't just sit there, *it sinks in*.

I withdrew half of our joint accounts, all the ones I could find records of—the 5½% checking, the savings account at 6½%, and the capital account in Boston at 7¼% (I think). Indeed, I took a *teeny* bit more than half since the CDs are tied up for six months at a time and you have all the Keogh and medical-partnership retirement-plan money stashed away that you've always been rather cagey and secretive about, not to mention those tax-shelter real-estate partnerships Ducky Bradford got you into years ago and that you said would be too much trouble and might alert the IRS to put into our joint name—one of the things I suppose I've always resented without admitting it to myself is how you tended to call money "yours" that we really earned together since not only was I keeping up *our* lovely home to enhance your image with your patients and fellow-doctors and raising *our* daughter virtually unassisted since you were always at the office for reasons that didn't dawn on poor innocent me for years, not to mention how while you so heroically (everybody kept telling me) slogged through medical school and internship *I* was the one who gave up two years of college and any chance of going on to graduate school—I was majoring, you have no doubt forgotten, in French philosophy, Descartes to Sartre—it's amazing to me what I once knew and have forgotten, all that being and nothingness and *cogito ergo sum*, all I remember now is essence precedes existence, or is it the other way around?—anyway I *loved* it then, and fantasized myself as Simone de Beauvoir or Simone

Weil and instead substitute-taught French and sewing at that terrifying parochial school in Somerville, those clammy-faced nuns and priests who I swear *did* act a bit lecherous even though nobody in those days believed they could, and stood on my feet all day in the boutique in Porter Square where it turned out their real business was selling pot in little Marimekko sachets. And you have also no doubt forgotten that your tuition fees were partly paid out of that trust fund Daddy had set up for *me*.

As to the stocks—I had intended to sell only half but then couldn't decide which ones and since everybody agrees the market can't keep rising like it has been I told the broker at Shearson Lehman to go and unload them all. He sent me these forms requiring both our signatures and I rummaged through your desk for one of those big black felt-tips you always use—that same imperious C-scrawl you use on prescriptions and checks and even on the love-note to that brainless LPN you were fucking that time I discovered the Christmas present you were going to give her in your golf-club closet (a Wedgwood shepherdess!—no doubt some private erotic joke in that, to your little Bo-Peep)—I know it so well, that signature, it's been branded into me, I wouldn't be surprised to see it burned into my flank if I looked down, char for Charles, it felt wonderful writing it—being *you* for a second, with all your dark unheeding illegible male authority. I had meant to divide the amount but Shearson Lehman sent it all in one big check though I had asked the young man I talked to *not* to—Midge was saying they get them all out of Tufts

and Northeastern, these baby brokers now, the smart
boys from Harvard and Brandeis go to Hong Kong or
straight to Wall Street where the huge money is—but
it came in one check anyway and I figured that if the
market goes down as it's certain to—even Irving was
saying the other day it will, according to the astrologi-
cal signs—then I'm saving us both money and maybe
should award myself a commission. So I have. Anyway,
darling, you have all the house and furniture plus the
Cape house and the acres in New Hampshire we
bought as an investment in case the Loon Mountain
condos ever spread that way. Besides taking my jewelry—you *can't* object to that, some of it was Great-
grandmother Perkins's and you *gave* me the other
things, the moonstone brooch for our fifth anniversary
and the pear-cut diamond pendant for our tenth and for
our fifteenth those rather ugly though I know expensive
rectangular emerald earrings I always thought with my
dark hair and rich complexion made me look too much
like a squaw, a Navajo in turquoise chunks—I rented a
big safe-deposit box and put in it the silver teapot with
the side-hinged lid and the oblong salver with the big
monogrammed P and embossed rim in rope motif that
came from the Prices, and the chest of Adam flatware
and those lovely fluted double-serpentine candleholders
from the Peabodys, and Daddy's coin collection and
those old editions of Milton and the Metaphysicals he
scandalized his family by spending so much money on
the year he went to London to learn the luxury-leather
business and didn't, plus some other few odd old family
things, I forget what. It's a huge box, *much* bigger than

a breadbox, and the girl at the bank and I both struggled sliding it back into its empty space, like a pair of weakling undertakers grunting and straining in the crypt. I have both keys, don't bother looking.

(Wet spot here because stewardess came with second drink. Little and giggly, just your type, a Filipino I think. The prefab daiquiri mix is not so absolutely sugary as most. Daiquiris it just occurs to me have always been my drink for "letting go"—remember that time we flew down to Saint Martin for your vacation?)

My old Charles—how much I loved you and love you still! Your cheek so excitingly rough in bed at night, that of a beast in whom time had been ticking all day, and then so excitingly smooth in the morning when I kissed you goodbye so you could go heal the world. The wonderful *worthy* way you smelled—after-shave lotion and the starch in your shirt collar and your hands all soapy and antiseptic and pink. And your sweat, your distinctly own, after we played tennis or made love. Sometimes (may I confess?), even when we were along in years and a distance had grown between us, even then I would miss you so much, the afternoons in the house alone stretching so silently long for me, and the sea that bright metallic four-o'clock blue but the rocks already in shadow, that to cure my hollowness, my dread, I would go to your pajamas on their hook in the closet and smell them—bury my face in their soft flannel in search of your faint, far stale sweat. It was most intense around where your neck rubbed: I found that touching. Somehow we American girls are raised for the smell of a man in the house. Even the scent of your urine and of that unmentionable other lingering in the bathroom into the middle of the morning was comforting—doorways into another being, another body like your own, helplessly a body.

And unlike, say, Midge and Ann Turner and even Liz Bellingham, I was never really satirical about our material advantages, the socio-economic side of it all. Our comfort did not embarrass me. I knew how hard we had worked together to make you a grand grave man, with just enough silvery hair flaring out above the ears, and how important to you the alchemy was that turned your horrible patients' complaints and diseases into our prosperity. Unlike some (Liz, who should talk, whose father never lifted a finger except to sign a bar bill) I saw nothing funny or vulgar in our matching Mercedeses, or the heated lap pool we installed in the old conservatory for your back and my figure. This was economic *health*, it seemed to me, as attractive as any other kind. The Truro house perhaps was an enhancement that didn't quite work—I could never get used to that mildewy mousy little damp stink that hangs under the pines—*so* unlike the North Shore with its stern chaste oaks and hemlocks and granite—or keep the squirrels out of the crawl spaces in the winter, or get the aura of the previous people's fried clams and onion rings out of the kitchen. And then of course Pearl and her friends rather ruined my happy early associations (when you could still go skinny-dipping in the ponds in the dunes and the roads really *were* just ruts in the sand) after they got old enough for rock and beer and cigarettes and the dreadful rest of it those last summers. For me it became like running a bus route, slithering up and down the driveway heading back into Wellfleet for one more ton of hot dogs and some pimply guest's highly specific favorite munchie called Fritos or Doritos or Cheez Doodles.

Why do Americans always think they should feel guilty about their *things*? I loved our things. Things are what we strive for, what all the waves in the air tell us to strive for—things are the stuff of our dreams and then like Eve and Adam digesting the apple we must feel so *guilty*. I didn't, I don't think. Through my thirties I was shamelessly happy about being me, being part of *us*. I loved our renovations, the amalgamated maids' rooms and the garage excavated under the porch and the marble-topped island in the kitchen and the lap pool echoing and splashing under all that whitewashed-dappled conservatory glass. I grimly enjoyed doing battle with the aphids on the roses and the chinch bugs under the sod and the garden boys with their headphones and lazy stoned smiles, their pulling up groundcover and leaving weeds and poisoning the lawn with fertilizers every summer in big brown stripes. I loved even those famously dreaded suburban cocktail parties, going in the car with you and in the door on your arm and then us separating and coming together at the end and out the door again like that Charles Addams cartoon of the two ski tracks around the tree. I loved you, my eternal date, the silent absent center of my storm of homemaking, the self-important sagely nodding doctor off in his high-rise palace of pain. I didn't mind fatally the comical snobbish brusque callousness that comes when

you've processed enough misery, or the rabid reaction-
ary politics that came with not wanting any national
health plan to cut into your fat fees, or even the nurse-
fucking when it became apparent—I could smell them
on your hands no matter how many times you
scrubbed, and there was a new rough way you handled
me—because though in some sense you were just another Boston-bred preppy brat not much older than I
in another you were my creator, you had put me here,
in this rocky grassy sparkling seaside landscape, amid
the afternoon silence and the furniture (except of
course the things Daddy wanted me to have and Mother
had to ditch, grudgingly, when she sold the Dedham
house and bought her hideous Florida condo).

Charles darling, it was not your *fault.*

(Long interruption. They brought me food on a
tray—funny chickeny sort of rolled-up thing. Fork and
knife and napkin all rolled up too. Hard to unroll and
not bother with my elbows the sleeping man next to
me. He already hates my writing, my scratching and
scratching and pausing now and then to blot my tears.
He's terrified I'm going to start confiding the reason for
my hysteria and so feigns sleep. Typical male avoidance
maneuver. Then *I* got sleepy, having consumed the
little *demi-bouteille du vin rosé californien.* Plane bounced
up and down over some white-nosed mountain range as
soon as the girl filled my coffee cup. No girl, actually—a
woman about my age, both of us too old to be bouncing
around in the sky with these mountains poking upwards at us. Then I dozed. I don't know where your
Filipino went to—she seemed busy in the first-class

section and then got absorbed into the cockpit. They say with these automatic pilots all sorts of things go on—nobody, really, is flying the plane. Just like the universe.)

Perhaps it *was* your fault. Leaving me alone so much amid our piled-up treasures, you gave me time to sense that my life was illusion, *maya*. Midge's yoga group, that I joined just for the exercises and something to do, gave me a vocabulary. My spirit, a little motionless fleck of eternal unchanging *purusha*, was invited to grow impatient with *prakriti*—all that brightness, all that flow. I would look at the rim of the saucer of my fourth decaf for the day and feel myself sinking—drawn around and around and down like a bug caught on the surface of bathwater when the plug is pulled. Pearl's going away to England was part of it. Your emotional desertion and the fading of our sex life was part of it. But there was something beyond and behind these phenomenal manifestations that was rendering even my unhappiness insubstantial. I seemed, like some dainty Japanese on the other side of the world with her rice-powdered face and pigeon-toed stockinged feet, to be living in a paper house, among miniature trees and gardens raked to represent nothingness. And into this papery world broke love.

That much you should know. I have left you out of love for another. Your own genteel atrocities of coldness and blindness toward me were not by themselves enough. I was too stoical, too Puritan, too much a creature of my society for solitary rebellion; I needed another. Who he is, and where we are together, I will trust you *not* to seek out. Your dignified useful life, of which I was an ever smaller and less significant adornment, surely will forbid any ugly vulgar furor of detectives and lawyers and warrants. Let me become truly nothing to you, at last. I will change my name. I will change my being. The woman you "knew" and "possessed" is no more. I am destroying her. I am sinking into the great and beautiful blankness which it is our European/Christian/Western avoidance maneuver to clutter and mask with material things and personal "achievements." Ego is the enemy. Love is the goal. I shed you as I would shed a skin, with some awkwardness perhaps and at first a sensitivity to the touch of the new, but without pain and certainly without regret. How can I—we—regret a phase of life that is already dead? Are not all our attachments, in truth, to things that are already dead?

If you decide to sell the house or any part of our joint holdings, I of course expect my legal half. If in time you wish to remarry (and I expect you will, not out of any great talent for uxoriousness but because the ferocious sea of seeking women will at some point overpower your basic indifference; the only bulwark against women is a woman, and a wife is *convenient*, especially for spoiled and preoccupied men of middling years) I will ask an appropriate settlement in exchange for your freedom. The affront, to your pride and convenience, of my desertion should weigh little, in any wise court, against the nearly twenty-two years of mental and emotional cruelty you with your antiseptic chill have inflicted on me. More than twenty-two—since I date my bondage not from that rather grotesquely gauzy and bubbly and overphotographed August wedding at King's Chapel the year our fathers were all for Goldwater but from the moment when you, with the connivance of my parents, "rescued" me from what was so generally deemed to be an "unsuitable" attachment to dear little Myron Stern.

But enough, my once and only husband. No grudges. Between us the scale is fairly balanced. Darkness, though the plane has moved west with the sun and given us a sunset in slow motion, has at last come, and little unknown cities twinkle below. We are descending. The human pilot has resumed the controls and the pretty little Filipino has reappeared, checking our seat belts with mock concern for our well-being. The fat man has stopped pretending to be asleep and is leaning his bulk into me, straining to see out my window. He fears for his life. In his gross voice he has the temerity to tell me I should put up my tray. I hope he reads this sentence. That is not my hand trembling, but the sudden uncongenial mixture of air and metal—the shaking of the plane. No—I am suddenly *terrified* to be without you (interruption: we have landed and are taxiing)—to be without you now that dinner hour has properly come, and our windows will be black against the yews outside, with the lights of a lone boat moving across the cove, and the automatic garage door will be grinding upward to receive your Mercedes, and rumbling down again, and the stairs up from the basement will resound with your aggressive footsteps, and there you will be, so solid and competent and trusting and expecting your quick martini before dinner. But then I realize that this happened—darkness came to you, you found the house empty, you read my horrible hasty note—hours ago, in quite another time zone.

Love,
S.

April 22

Dearest Pearl—

Perhaps by now you will have heard from your father. He was always less afraid of the transatlantic telephone—those strings of dialled numbers, those crackling foreign accents—than I was. My wiggles, you used to call my writing. When you were two, and we were still living in the little Brighton house, you would crawl up on my lap expecting to see a drawing on my desk as when we crayonned together, and were *so* disappointed to see just my wiggles, little crooked lines all in one dull color.

Well, darling, I am doing my wiggles now in a motel

in Los Angeles, and have left your father. It was nothing he *did*, or that I did, suddenly—it was more a matter of what he and I had been doing for years and years, or not doing, rather—not even paying attention. You remember how conscientiously I used to tell him, at dinnertime, of my day?—the little tail-wagging housewife-puppy, whimpering and drooling, offering up her pathetic worried bones and chewing sticks, her shopping trips to Boston and her excursions to the plant nursery in Wenham, her tennis games and her yoga lessons and her boozy little lunches at the club with the same women she played tennis with yesterday, as if to say to this big silent he-doctor, this gray eminence, "Look, dear, how hard I've been working to enhance your lovely estate!" or "See, I'm not wasting your money, I couldn't find a thing I wanted to buy at Bonwit's!" or "Every hour accounted for—not a minute of idleness or daydreaming or sleeping with all these dark handsome strangers that came today to pump out the fat trap!" Well, I recently tried an experiment. I didn't tell your father a thing about my day. And *he never asked*. Not once, day after day of biting my tongue—he utterly didn't notice. That settled it. So absent from his perceptions, I might as well be absent in fact.

Of course, there is a little more to it than that. We of the frailer sex have to have some wild hope, something *to go to*—otherwise a million years of slavery has conditioned us to huddle by the hearth, stony as it is, and pound some more millet, and get pounded in turn by way of thanks, and commune with the moon. I speak as one of my generation, that came of age just as the Fifties ended—I was nineteen when Lee Harvey Oswald shot them dead—and then by twenty I was married to your father and working too hard to support him really to notice that a revolution was going on, and all the old barriers were down. With your generation, dear Pearl, the barriers are not just down but forgotten, trampled into history. The harvest is in. How thrilling it has been for me—I almost wrote "us," still thinking in the plighted plural—to see you grow, tall and fearless and carrying your femaleness like a battle flag! Even when you were tiny I saw you as a soldier, your hair pale and straight and shiny as a helmet—magical blond child of a dark mother and prematurely gray father. I had been a tall girl too but had always to fight the impulse to hunch. Your father, to give the devil his due, loved you extravagantly. He didn't want a son—when you were born he confessed to me he couldn't have tolerated sharing me with another male. That was still in his chivalrous days. To your generation his remark will sound chauvinistic but at the time it expressed our happiness, our three-cornered joy. My own bliss, holding you even that first hour with your pulsing hot bald skull and freshly unfolded hands that even then had a bit of a grip, was that of seeing myself extended, my womanhood given a second try. My genitals had always been presented to me subtly as a kind of wound and you I vowed would never feel wounded. *Daughter*, your father liked to say. Just the word. It *is* a much more satisfying word, with those mysterious silent letters in the middle, than simple little *son*.

So now you can see how I have this fear of being

locked out by you two. I am in disgrace, I have flubbed my rôle. You have been so admirably the daughter—lisping your first words ("Dada," "Mama," and then "coogie" from the Cookie Monster on "Sesame Street"), mastering toilet-training and small-muscle motor control just when Dr. Spock thought you should, pitching for that mixed-sex softball team that went all the way to the semifinals in Danvers when you were thirteen, growing flaxen-haired and just the right amount of buxom and getting into Yale so smartly when Harvard couldn't accept any more legacies and now for your junior year abroad pondering the Metaphysicals (your grandfather would be so proud!—he doted on them, and Milton and Spenser and Marvell) in some fogey old don's musty digs with its electric fire (this is more my imagining of it than anything you've written in your I must say very few letters) and lighting up High Street and Carfax with your wide-eyed long-haired easy-striding American beauty and on weekends having champagne and strawberries with the sons of the nobility just as in "Brideshead Revisited," which you will remember we enjoyed so much, you and I together, you staying up to watch it even though it was school the next day, not so very long ago. (Am I wrong to date your passion for things English from those shows?) You have played and are playing so splendidly the rôle of Daughter and your father impeccably assumed the part of Dada but I seem to have forgotten my lines and wandered offstage. Will you forgive me? (Your father's forgiveness, oddly, doesn't interest me at all.)

Twenty is an age when your parents still think of you as a child and if you were to die or get married one would sadly say "only twenty" but as I recall that age there is little "only" about it and I must appeal to you as another woman to understand me, to simply *know*. And having so appealed I realize, or seem to realize, in this rather terrifying motel room where the air-conditioner rattles as if mounted off-center and people seem to keep bumping against the door as they go by in the hall to the ice machine, that of course there is no question of condemnation, that you and I will continue to love each other as we did that first minute, when you gripped my finger with this little violet baby hand the texture of a wilted flower, because we are aspects of the same large person, that even in that first minute all your eggs (this is an incredible physiological fact I recently read in *The New England Journal of Medicine* which your father gets) were tiny and perfect in you and you were *my* egg, tiny and perfect. I am crying as I write this and perhaps make insufficient sense in the fashion of maudlin people but do beg you to believe that I am your mother still.

Study well, my sweetheart. When I try to picture you to myself I see a shining blond head bent over a book. Your love of books, from Babar to Tolkien and romances with those embossed titles in lurid colors to Austen and Dickens on up to these unpleasant modern writers who try to make us all feel shabby was so intense your father and I used to whisper what had we done wrong, what parental failing of ours was to blame.

To Pearl

When you were in your early teens, after your softball craze but before "Brideshead" caught your fancy, I would sit and watch television—these very stupid well-intentioned shows with minority families cavorting around or police stations or high schools and the canned laughter heaving away—hoping you would be tempted to join me in that cozy. corner room upstairs, with the heavy drapes and your father's old medical books and my father's priceless editions, because I imagined this was what normal American children should be watching. But no, my dear elf-child, you stayed in your room wrapped in lovely contortions around a book, while I of course got hooked and had to watch these idiotic stories to the end. Of course I used to worry at your snubbing television and me together but now I see that the children we have are just miracles like any other, like geysers or glass skyscrapers or mountains of maple trees in fall in Vermont, and that we have nothing to do with creating them—our job is to stand and wonder. Our job is to marvel and love.

Study well, and never be tempted by drugs. *People* (which I see only in the dentist's office, but must say I do devour eagerly there) and the *National Enquirer* (which Irving my yoga instructor is devoted to for its spiritual dimensions, its ESP and UFO news) are so full of these young English nobility and their dangerous drug habits that they pick up in imitation of the rock stars, out of class guilt and a subconscious Marxist wish to destroy themselves I suppose. But there's no reason for an American girl to get involved in any of that. Your mother's not a churchgoer as you know but I do believe firmly that our body as God made it, with no additives, not only lasts longest but is most *fun*. And along the same lines don't get too infatuated with male homosexuals. I know they must seem, especially with those English accents and marvellous high rosy complexions, very amusing and charming and unthreatening but remember, dearest, they don't really *like* women. They think women are strange, too strange to deal with, and competitors furthermore. Normal men think women are strange too but they don't try to steal other men from us and at least up to your mother's generation had developed a certain delusional system around our strangeness that could be quite touching—they treated us like handicapped persons, opening doors and explaining our needs to waiters as though we couldn't talk. Well that may be gone but I'm sure that enough of something similar remains for you to concentrate on nice normal boys if you can find any in that dear decadent old country.

I must be tired all my commas are dropping away. About an hour ago there was a strange kind of rodeo in the parking lot—low-slung cars covered with glittery paint prowling in noisy circles, and then there was a quarrel just outside my door in an appalling language I realized was Japanese! In fact in the coffee shop I was surprised at how many Japanese there were, as if I had gone farther west than I wanted. Tomorrow I must head east again, driving into the desert in my rented car—not a dreadfully perilous adventure perhaps but enough to make a middle-aged lady's heart rise in her throat. I must end, darling. I must let you and me go to bed. I began by feeling quite prickly and apologetic and defensive toward you but now feel quite close. I feel you are with me. Part of you, of course, with part of me. Write me at this address: c/o Ashram Arhat, Forrest, AZ 85077. Doesn't it sound like the end of the world? Do try to be a more conscientious correspondent than you have been—I am so alone now. And *don't give the address to your father.*

Much *much* love,
Mother

April 23

Dear Dr. Podhoretz—

I am sorry, but I am going to miss my cleaning appointment next Tuesday the 29th and don't know when I can make another. As you can see from the postmark I am a long way from Swampscott. But I promise to keep flossing and using the rubber tip on my gums. I certainly don't want to undo your good work and go through all that oral surgery again! Once was enough!!

Cordially,
Sarah Worth (Mrs. Charles)

To Shirlee

April 23

Dear Shirlee—

I'm afraid I'm going to miss my hair appointment next week after all, after all the trouble we went to to find an ideal time when I wouldn't get caught in either rush hour. My husband and I are taking a quite unexpected vacation in the romantic Far West. We're about in fact to get into the car and drive hundreds of miles, right past Palm Springs where Bob Hope and President Ford have their fabulous homes! I'll phone you when I get back—by that time my hair may be down to my waist! Your rinse should be kept up and I'll pick up some Clairol at a drugstore—Darkest Brown I think is better for me than the Natural Black, which tends as we know to kill the gleam. I do hope things begin to work out better with Martin and his new probation officer, and that Eldridge's dyslexia therapy continues to work wonders. He is such a cute boy—the day he came into the beauty parlor and asked each woman in a chair if her boyfriend lived with her or just came around! As we agreed last time, it would probably be less unsettling for him if his father didn't come around at all—but then life is so complex, isn't it? It's so hard to know how totally we're supposed to live for others, and what we may do for ourselves.

Say hello for me to Marcus and Foster and Annette. Not to mention the meter maid on Newbury Street who always seemed to be there *the very moment* my meter ran out!

> Your customer and friend,
> Sally Worth

> April 23, 24

Dear Mother—

I'm *exhausted* from driving in the desert for hours but wanted to drop you a note to counterbalance whatever alarming stories Charles is pouring into your ears. It is true I've left him but for ten years more or less it's felt every morning and midnight as if *he's* left *me*. Ever since my second miscarriage and our realizing that Pearl was the only child we would ever have there's been this coldness and tension between us that you surely have noticed on your visits, though perhaps you haven't—Charles always seemed, frankly, more your kind of man than mine. You and he did use to get together with your martinis and purr, over exactly what piece of catnip I could never decide, and then decided it was *me*—me as some kind of possibly lovable but certainly messy and very likely untrainable discipline problem. You two shared a curious dry ability to without exactly saying anything make me feel *dirty*— my hair untidy, my feet too big, my skin too swarthy,

I didn't know, people don't ever know what's wrong with them, they'll believe any bad thing. Whereas Daddy, as you remember, never *did* warm to him, though he tried, with that wonderful gentlemanly nature of his, but after Charles kept questioning his calls those Sundays when they played singles on the grass courts at Longwood he really stopped trying. Also, Charles was so humorless and whatever Daddy's other faults he was just the opposite, always so sly and wry, such a tease though I'm not sure you always knew when he was teasing, as I did.

At any rate I'm not writing to justify myself—my God, I'm forty-two!—but to let you know on the wing as it were that I'm physically well and you're not to worry. There's no other man, not really, not the way you think, but I did feel my entire flight out here the day before yesterday taking place in an upholding atmosphere of *love*—love streaming against my face and chest like the sunset light in that clipper ship we had framed above the big carved mantel in Dedham. I used to look at the picture as a little girl until I felt myself to be a mermaid in the waves, looking up at this artifact of men from another world—the masts, the riggings, the portholes, the wooden woman on the prow. All the details of that picture—the froth, the clouds, their little dabbed-on crests of sunset red—seemed magical to me, a piece of a Heaven I would some day enter. Think of me as still that little girl. Think of this episode now as my continuing my education. In fact it is like that, back to school, but school where my real innermost self, my *atman*, will be taught to free itself from *maya* and *karma*, from all the trappings of *prakriti*. Trapped among trappings—isn't that what we all are? Women, especially. I loved the way you lightened yourself so drastically after Daddy died and you went to Florida, but when I was there in December you seemed to have accumulated so many glass-and-wrought-iron tables and splashy pink mildew-proof sofas and driftwood sculpture and shadowboxed paintings on black felt I felt claustrophobic again, just like back in Dedham with all of Daddy's collections and your nice things from the Prices and the dark walnut furniture, the lancet-window breakfront and Gothic sideboard, from Great-granddaddy Perkins's Medford place. Speaking of which, I had such a strange hallucination today, while driving through the desert. There *is* this shimmer, you *do* see mirages, they become very common—lakes with not just water but what look like beachfront cottages and I could have sworn sailboats and (this is the point) at one point a big rambling Victorian brown-shingled structure being reflected in the water just like that lodge in Maine we went to once or twice when I was very little to visit Great-granddaddy Perkins in the summer—this impossibly ancient man with a beard smelling of mentholated cough drops who took me by the hand to the edge of the porch to show me where the red-squirrel family lived in the hickory tree. He said the red were smaller but fiercer than the gray and drove them out. He seemed to think their being red squirrels would greatly interest me but I didn't know they were rarer than the gray and expected all squirrels to wear little trousers like in Beatrix Potter. How stupid children are.

What I want to say is, *Don't let Charles con you.* To him I was another piece of furniture and unless I got coffee spilled on me or squeaked like a rusty door he never gave me a glance. You and he have always tended to gang up on me and as Pearl would say I'm through with guilt trips. *Through*, Mother.

Next morning. The words were beginning to blur before my eyes and I could hardly hold my head up. Also there seemed to be a wolf snuffling and scratching just outside my window, trying to get some lid off something, though maybe it was a raccoon or if they don't have those out here a gopher. And what I think must be coyotes off in the distance, yipping and yowling, saying something to each other all night and being somehow ventriloquists so their voices came from all sides of me and seemed right in the room. There was a full moon last night. I shouldn't have broken off in the middle of my letter for my dreams all night were of *you*, you when much younger, moving around the Dedham place with a kind of angelic swiftness and telling me to sit up straight and *never* rest my left hand on the table while eating. I was setting the dinner table and couldn't for the life of me remember what side of the plate the fork went on—I have this problem with left-right sometimes when driving and people are giving me rapid directions, and though I know you always deny it I *still* have this feeling I was meant to be left-handed and you and Mrs. Resnick in Miss Grandison's Day School's first grade *forced* me to be right-handed; they say you're cross-wired for life if that happens. Anyway, tired as I was, I hardly slept. Dawn out here comes with a kind of snap, like those metal shutters being rolled up in Italy, and by nine-thirty it's already hot. But dry—I had that usual New England April cold when I left and after less than forty-eight hours my head feels clear. I do hope your back is better now that Boca Raton is beginning to swelter again. What you've always called rheumatism the doctors and the television commercials seem to think is *osteoporosis*, bone loss due to improper diet. You never drank milk and all that frantic dieting to keep getting yourself into your same dresses all those years must have taken its nutritional toll. It's not too late—you can buy these calcium supplements at any drug- or health-food store, and if you don't rush the dose at first, there's no constipation. Also, you *must* wear number 15—Total Protection—sun screen when you go to the beach; the buildup of actinic damage over the years is cumulative and at your age the circulation doesn't carry away the damaged DNA like it used to. In fact, at your age you shouldn't be going to the beach at all—when Charles and I were down at Christmas I was *shocked* to see how brown you were. You looked dyed, frankly, and with your tinted hair the effect was honestly bizarre. It's not as if you have naturally tanning skin, the way Daddy did and I do. Use lotions with PABA and take vitamin A, 500 mg. twice a day. Super stuff, A. Good for skin, eyes, insomnia, and cancer.

The best of the Price silver along with that serpentine candelabra Granddaddy saved from the Peabody creditors I put for safekeeping in a rented lockbox at the same bank where I opened *my own independent account.*

I'm still angry about the way my trust fund got absorbed into Charles's medical education and I can't tell you the satisfaction it gave me not to check the little box marked Joint. The Price and Peabody silver you still have (and that *precious* teeny-tiny salt-and-pepper set way back from the Prynnes) I hope you are taking out and polishing once every three months and keeping in felt bags, *not* plastic, between polishings—that Florida salt air is *death* on silver, whereas somehow in Massachusetts the salt doesn't matter so much, maybe the lower humidity doesn't hold it in such suspension. Grandmother's lacework tray for calling cards for instance I noticed looked definitely pitted, and I know that didn't happen in Dedham where all those pieces were kept in the Perkins breakfront. I don't know why you have the tray out since you have so few callers and nobody uses cards any more anyway. While we're on these materialistic subjects, I think your plan to cash in your CDs as they come due and go back into the stock market now that interest rates are down is *disastrous*. For one thing everybody is doing it and the market is inflated. For another with inflation flattening out thanks to Reagan's hardheartedness cash is as good as gold—better than gold, in fact, which slumps right along with the soft dollar our export industries are clamoring for. My advice would be to rake off the interest every six months when you roll them over if you *must* have the spending money but keep the capital in these no-risk certificates and let Daddy's portfolio—all that heavenly old IBM and AT&T he picked up for almost nothing—enjoy the bull market if there is going to continue to be one. The gain there over the years is so great that a little bearishness only dents your paper profits but if you were to enter now at the peak with real cash it would break your heart. Someone of your age or even mine trying to select stocks tends to be disastrous because we have no real grasp of this new world of services and computer communication and go for solid old things like steel and rivets and coal oil and GM that are losers. *Real* things nowadays are losers. Things like fast food and videotapes that people use only for a minute and then forget are where the money is, somehow. But not all the companies doing that are doing well either.

I guess this is what they call parting advice. Today makes me nervous. I'm making my leap into a new life. For breakfast, this Mexican girl brought a tray to the room in worn blue jeans and a man's cowboy shirt and they just assumed I wanted greasy hash-browns with my inedibly peppery scrambled eggs. The coffee was actually *gritty*, I think they just boil the grounds in a pot and pour it. I'm *sorry* you've been besieged by this retired general from across the courtyard but glad you decisively repelled him, even at the price of being rude. He sounds odious. As well as pathetic. Write me your health news as the A does its wonderful work. For now I think the address on this stationery (isn't the logo a riot?) will be best, in case I have to beat a hasty retreat. Say a prayer for me if you still do such things.

Love and hugs,
Sare

April 24

Gentlemen:

Enclosed please find endorsed checks totalling, by my own calculations, $174,963.02, for deposit in my account, #0002743-911. Kindly send my receipt and subsequent account statements to me c/o Babbling Brook Motor Lodge, Forrest, AZ 85077, marked PLEASE HOLD.

Thank you sincerely,
Sarah P. Worth

April 24

Dear Dr. Epstein—

I will not be in next Monday or any Mondays as far as I can foresee. I have taken a step—not *the* step, since over the years we have discussed so many steps I might take, but *a* step—out of my psychological impasse, away from the resentful dependency you and I have often agreed was so unhealthy. I feel fragile and naked but free. Thank you for giving me, in all our many talks—*my* talks, I should say, coupled with your wise listening—the ego-definition and strength to attempt this. Perhaps now the task next before me is ego-transcendence.

If Charles calls with some ridiculous proprietorial tantrum, you will know how to handle him.

With gratitude and esteem,
Sarah (Worth)

[*tape*]

Dear Midge. Hi. It's me. Sarah. I think it's May fifth, but there aren't many calendars around here. Oh, Midge, what a time I've been having! Just let me check and see if this damn thing is working, the little spools going around. They seem to be. Well, I got here. Tell Irving. We see the Arhat in person go by in a limousine every day, sometimes twice a day. It's bliss, tell him. Actually that's only half the truth of it, but there's no point in telling him the worst, he's such a gentle hopeful soul, Irving, and I'm sure he'll never make it here to see for himself. The fact is that along with its being really quite as heavenly and spiritual and freeing as we used to imagine there's also a strong element, everything being so loosely structured, of dog-eat-dog.

Where shall I begin? I left Charles, of course. He went off to work Monday morning as usual and instead of puttering about as usual I packed my more practical summer things and some raspberry-colored jeans I had found in some Army-Navy store up along where Boylston Street gets grungy, across from the Pru—purple is not an easy shade to find, I tell you—and my running shoes and an old denim jacket of Pearl's and two sweatshirts that really were more pink than mauve but I didn't know how strict the ashram's color code was going to be—I'm being boring about the clothes, I know—and off I set, in my one prim and proper suit, the black-and-white check with the boxy jacket and pleated skirt, and with enormous butterflies in my stomach. I mean, this is my life, and I'm throwing it away!

I landed in Los Angeles, to make it harder for Charles to trace me through the airlines, and, coming in to land, I couldn't help thinking of how planes keep colliding in the air there and how absurd if my big pilgrimage were to end that way, instant nirvana. But actually the landing was perfect, once we came down through the chop. Then I stayed in this motel near the airport in a dreary area called Hawthorne—I'd always had these glamorous illusions about Los Angeles and Hollywood but what I saw looked like just one big Neponset Circle—and after a bad night, where these Japanese kept knocking on the door, I rented a car and drove what seemed forever on Route, I think, Ten and didn't see anything of Palm Springs with all those celebrities and golf courses and arrived really bleary from the shimmer on the highway and the mirages. But once I got to this little sad town in Arizona called Forrest, just the air, Midge, was so good to breathe, so spicy and quiet and energizing—tell Irving all his lessons in pranayama came back to me and my sinuses felt absolutely cleansed, though the cold I had when I left has actually come back worse than ever, you can probably tell from my voice. Well, they work you like dogs here, at least at first, and there aren't near enough blankets for these cold clear nights, and it's a *real* dogfight at dinnertime for food, some people are just too tired to stand in the endless lines, and at noon they bring you these soggy vegetarian box lunches out in the fields or wherever they have you working, and sleeping six to a trailer everybody's germs travel all around—but I'm getting way ahead of myself, and don't mean to complain. Down deep in my atman, beneath all these sniffles and this hysterical physical fatigue, I am absolutely at peace. Tell Irving I'm tasting at last that samarasa he used to talk about, that I could never quite get to just by holding my breath or stopping all thought as he used to try to make us, which just sent us into giggles, didn't it?—how can you stop thought, since even in dreams it goes on, I mean. The electricity in your brain just crackles and crackles until you're dead.

Midge, I know I'm rambling hideously. I'm actually shaking, I'm so cold and probably feverish and achy all over. Those summer clothes I brought aren't really the right thing, and my raspberry-colored jeans get incredibly filthy and heavy and soggy. The worship crew—that's what they call a work crew—I'm attached to is pouring cement for the foundation of this building called the Hall of a Millionfold Joys, though they told the county commissioners it's just going to be an agricultural greenhouse and tractor garage, and all day long I shovel this gray goop so it goes into the corners of the forms without pockets of air under it and then smooth it with these big flat wooden things like huge rakes without any teeth. It's more fun than hoeing artichokes and setting out hybrid heat-resistant tomato plants, which I was doing the first two weeks in this absolutely merciless sun, but, my goodness, your shoulders do ache from pushing the goop around—I'm not sure a woman's muscles are put together exactly like a man's. And these aluminum trailers really aren't very well insulated, though from the outside they have that quilted look. The only heat they have are electric heaters, but between midnight and six electricity is cut off for every place but the guardhouses along the border and the section where the Arhat and his close advisers live and the Kali Club, a kind of disco or dance hall where the sannyasins express their joy and gratitude to Shiva for the eternal cycle of creation and destruction. Everybody in my trailer is hoping eventually to get into one of the new A-frames they're putting up, where only three or four sannyasins have to share the space and a family, if there is one, can get some privacy. You don't see many children here, the Arhat thinks birth control is the number-one global issue on a materialistic level, but there are a few, cute as can be in their little purple bib overalls and round-toed sneakers and whatnot. The color code asks we dress in the shades of the sunset, symbolizing the end of mundane concerns, and that gives us quite a latitude, when you think about it. You see people in red and orange and everything, really, but blue and green, though at sunset in this air there often *is* a tinge of green. Also the Arhat calls these the love colors—he has the cutest way of saying "love."

Midge, you should *see* me. I'm huddling in all my clothes except for my cement-covered running shoes in my grape-colored sleeping bag on the thin carpet over the cold aluminum floor a foot or two above the desert sands, which are crawling with scorpions and snakes and things like leggy pale rats—I always thought deserts were supposed to be dead but this one is just *hop*-ping with life, especially after the sun goes down—and talking into this gadget, a Seiko mini–cassette player I bought at this electronics boutique they have over at the ashram mall. They sell a lot of gadgety stuff here, I was surprised, even mugs and T-shirts with the Arhat's picture on them, and for what I'd call wild prices, since there's nowhere else to buy anything for forty miles around and anyway all the profits go into the Treasury of Enlightenment and represent the love we feel for the Arhat.

He *is* beautiful, tell Irving, and Liz and Ann and Gloria and whoever else shows up for yoga these days. So beautiful. The posters we had don't really do justice to the *glow* he has in person—the aura, I suppose it is—this incredible olive smoothness of his skin, which isn't half as dark as you think of Indians' as being, and a surprisingly substantial nose the opposite of re-troussé, and thick black eyebrows in two perfect arches, and these rich chocolaty eyes there seems no bottom to, just *pools* of knowingness, and this amazingly gentle smile that isn't exactly mocking but on the verge of it, and these delicate graceful hands with all their rings flashing when he waves through the limousine window. I see him drive by every day, now that I'm no longer stuck out in the artichoke fields—I got terribly sun-burned those first days, all across my shoulders and the back of my neck, since I had my hair pinned up, and you *know* what a good tan I usually take—and you wouldn't believe the *peace* he generates, even at thirty miles an hour. We all hold hands and chant for him and the feelings of positivity and centeredness are fantastic. Tears come not just to *my* eyes but everybody's, even people like Fritz who have been with the Arhat for years, even back in India, when the ashram began. Fritz is my group leader. My lover, too, I guess I can tell *you*. You, Midge, but not Irving or anybody else. Actually, Fritz'd kill me if he heard me calling him Fritz instead of his ashram name. The Arhat gives us all names, when he gets around to it, he hasn't given me mine yet and the others say it takes months often before he notices you. Fritz's is hard to remember if you aren't at home in Sanskrit yet. Something like Victor or Vic Scepter—that isn't quite it. Oh well. I'm tired. I say he'd kill me and that's not true, but actually he does have a funny little temper. He's German by birth and likes things to be *just so*. *Ach ja*.

The others who live here in the trailer are all over at the Kali Club right now. How they do it after work-ing—worshipping—twelve or fourteen hours a day I

have no idea, but they're all younger than I and tell me
if you love the Arhat enough you don't need sleep. Let
me go back to the beginning, I know this is confusing.
I stayed in this motel in this tiny town called Forrest,
with two "r"s, I don't know who he was, some rancher
or explorer or vicious Indian-killer I suppose, with all
ticky-tacky newish houses and nothing in the way of
trees except for a few straggly cottonwoods down by
the creek they call Babbling Brook but that to me
seemed dull as ditchwater and utterly silent, even
though April here is supposed to be the great run-off
time from the snowmelt in the mountains. The mountains are very far off and look transparent except for
their snowy tips. The rocks are reddish and have a soft
look as if a child just got done kneading them. That's
k-n-e-a-d. To finish up about the trees—there *was* a
lovely tamarisk in pink bloom outside the stucco post
office, and in the motel courtyard a strange kind of huge
tree with tiny oval leaves and long pods at least a foot
long hanging down rustling and clattering in the wind.
There's always a certain amount of wind out West. The
town seemed to be mostly cowpoke types and retirees
from the insurance business in Phoenix, and when I
asked about the Arhat's ashram you should have seen
how their faces hardened up. They *hate* him, Midge—
this is old Goldwater country and they still call people
hippies and say he's brought in all these hippies to have
drugs and orgies and furthermore the city he's putting
in illegally is playing havoc with the local water table.
They told me how he'd gouge all my money out of me
and work me to death and pump me full of drugs. The

man at the post office said, "That devil fella they call a rat sure earns his name." I can't do the Western accent very well yet. One man, I think he was an Indian, American Indian I mean, even though he wore one of those little plastic truck-driver hats, you know, with a visor and the name of a beer on them, spat at my shoes when I tried to explain how the Arhat's message was simply love and freedom and furthermore he was making the desert bloom. On top of all this, the motel gave me a breakfast with hash-browns that made me queasy all morning.

The roads down here are *endless*, and mostly dirt packed into ruts and ripples. It seemed to take forever to drive that forty miles, bumpety-bump-bump, trailing this enormous cloud of dust. I don't see how people in Arizona can have any secrets, because anywhere you go you leave this giant clue of dust in the air for hours. Not that there were any houses or people that I could see— not a sign of life except a few sorry-looking cattle and a lot of black-faced sheep who leave their wool snaggled all over the barbed wire. All the time, you are gradually rising, and the sagebrush, or maybe it's mesquite, getting sparser around you, and the ground rockier, and then suddenly you're overlooking this valley with tidy long fields of different shades of green, and yellow bulldozers and school buses crawling around on a system of roads below, and this big flat-roofed mall and rows of aluminum trailers, and on a shelf above them rows of A-frames being constructed on red earth scraped into shelves, and in the center of everything a sort of blue-paved space with an actual fountain, a fountain surrounded by rainbows and spray. The people in Forrest even mentioned the fountain to me as a waste of water, but I found out later it's perfectly ecological, just the same ten thousand gallons being recycled over and over as a symbol of the circulation of karma. Midge, I was stunned. I was stunned breathless. This *had* to be the place I was meant to bring my life to. My poor bedraggled silly life, to be recycled. Even though Irving had shown us a few photographs you have to see it in context, to be in the *space*—all that gentle gray-green desert and then this unexpected valley with slanting walls of tumbled orange rock in their weird, soft-looking shapes the wind has carved, and this mild blue washed-out Western sky over everything like a face of Brahma. Inside I just felt this glorious *relief*.

There was a gate across the dirt road, and a guard dressed in lavender uniform but with a real enough gun, one of those Japanese machine guns that look like toys; but he saluted me, "Namaste," just like Irving sometimes does, and was really only a boy, an ordinary curly-haired boy about Pearl's age, rather cute and deferential, really, once I got over the shock of being accosted. I explained how I wanted to join and he asked me if I had been in correspondence with the Master and I had to say no, it hadn't occurred to me he would answer a letter and I had come pretty much on impulse. I heard myself saying this and realized that up to that moment it had been like I was doing everything in a dream and with one-half of my brain expecting Charles to wake me up and take me home. But then I took courage from the way Irving had made us see that all life is like that—lived on the skin of the void and without real substance, just motions we go through by constructing these hallucinatory goals and short-term strategies.

The boy frisked me for weapons or drugs—I had to laugh, but then felt I was undercutting some little performance he must do, like when you betray children who are being very serious about reciting a poem or shaking hands the way they've been taught to—and he gave me a card to put on my windshield, and from a checkpoint down in the ashram they took me to a place where several trailers had been put together to make offices. They call this hodgepodge the Uma Room, I know now. After a rudely long wait I was finally taken into this windowless place where a striking but not very pleasant red-haired woman with a black pearl in one nostril put me through an inquisition. So I wanted to become a sannyasin, she said. How come? I explained with what dignity I could muster how I'd fallen in love with the Arhat through listening to his tapes and meditating on his photograph in a yoga class I'd been taking. Oh really? she said. Did I have any venereal disease and how much money was I bringing to the Treasury of Enlightenment? I explained to her I had left my successful doctor husband on a more or less sudden inspiration and all I could bring away was eleven thousand dollars. I had thought of saying ten, but eleven sounded more like it really *was* all I had. She said—her name, I should be explaining, is Durga, and she is sort of the Arhat's right-hand person, he's of course above the day-to-day details, and she has one of these quite red-headed complexions, with a face pale as ice, that opaque ice that builds up in the refrigerator, and furious green eyes and a cleft chin, which I think are generally handsomer on men—she said that didn't seem like very much and was there any way I could get any more? Did I have credit cards? Access to jointly held securities? To make a long story short, I got *very* dignified and said I had brought my body and mind and atman and what more could the Arhat in his transcendent wisdom desire? She got uppity on her own side and said the Arhat desires nothing, his name and the concept of desire should not even be put in the same sentence, but that his work was great, as I no doubt must have noticed while driving in as an uninvited trespasser. I said I *had* noticed and marvelled and firmly intended to put myself at the service of this work. She asked me what my skills were, and I said those of a homemaker and helpmeet who had completed only two years of college intending to major in French philosophy, and she said it would certainly take some ingenuity to put those skills at the service of the Arhat. She spoke in this stilted way, like the high priestess in the old Cecil B. DeMille extravaganzas, but with this lovely Irish lilt that kept coming through. I wondered if she were exactly sane, but now that I've learned she had been an artiste of some sort in Dublin once, I suppose that explains it.

Really, it wasn't all that intimidating, because outside the little windows of the trailer I could see these other sannyasins going by laughing and looking so happy and peaceful and hugging and kissing each other whenever they felt like it. She gave me a speech about how work here was worship, and the harder the work the more fervent the worship, and she doubted I could do hard labor. I said I had been an active gardener in my old life—my old life, Midge! as if I already had a new one—and played tennis twice a week all summer, and would she like to arm-wrestle? It just popped out, a little like the things Irving sometimes says to us at the beginning of a session, to cleanse our minds and shock us into satori. I would never have been so fresh and aggressive in my normal life. Already I was *liberated*. The Arhat's love was in the air here and giving me courage. You could see Durga was stunned for a second, her eyes narrowed and this chin of hers, like Cary Grant's only of course on a woman not so effective, this chin of hers lifted a little inch, and all she said was I should save my internalized violence and hostility for the dynamic-meditation session. So that implied I was accepted, but, Midge, if I'd known what a dynamic-meditation session was I might have gotten back into my car, but they had taken my keys and driven it away, like valet parking, and in fact I never *have* been able to find out what happened to it, so tell Charles, if by any chance you see him, that I can't help whatever notices from Hertz he keeps getting—they're not my fault. The rest of that day was spent filling out forms indemnifying them against all sorts of damage and taking Rorschach and personality tests to see if I was mentally healthy enough, for my own protection as well as theirs they explained, and having a really very thorough examination for venereal diseases—*very* disagreeably done—though when I asked for a Contac for my cold they said it was just maya and to ignore it.

Oh God, I am *tired*. And now I hear people outside coming from the disco and I don't want them to hear me talking to you on this thing—people *steal* here, there's nothing really against it in the Arhat's philosophy, and they say Durga has spies everywhere and is really paranoid about betraying our secrets to the outside world—so I'll say good night and tuck you into my sweater. You and the other girls would hardly know me. I sleep in my clothes and pretty much stink of sweat and cement, but after a while you don't mind it, in fact you rather like it, your own smell. Here they all come, high as kites.

Next day. Just a few minutes before I go and face the hideous dinner brawl. I really shouldn't say that; they do a wonderful job here organizing things, but the Arhat's spiritual magnetism has just overwhelmed the facilities—a setup designed for four hundred is being asked to house and feed nearly a thousand, with a lot of day trippers and curiosity seekers on the weekends. It's what Charles used to say of the hospital—no matter how many beds you put in, there's always one sick person left over. I've found a place to be by myself a few minutes, though some of our group leaders tell us a wish for privacy is very pro-ego and anti-ashram. I don't know—Buddha was always doing it, and the Arhat never tells us to go everywhere in a noisy smelly bunch like some of these sannyasins seem to want to.

Obviously, you need to be by yourself just for spiritual sanitation now and then. When I think of all those days rattling around in my old house, going from room to room picking up, waiting for Pearl to get back from school or Charles from work or for somebody just to *call* or the mailman to come up the drive with his Laura Ashley catalogue—fourteen rooms and four baths and two and a half acres of lawn all for me—it seems obscene in a way and yet a kind of paradise. Isn't it funny how paradise always lies in the past or the future, never exactly in the present? Just last night in his darshan, the Arhat said there can be no happiness in the present as long as there is ego. He pronounces it "iggo." *As lonk as sere iss iggo, the happinesss*—I really can't do his accent, he has the strangest, longest "s"s, different from any sound we make—*suh happinesss fliesss avay. Like suh pet birt and suh pet catt, zey cannot exists in ze same room. Ven suh Master doess nut preside, suh vun eatss se utter.* I make it sound ridiculous, but in fact I could listen for hours, it's like a fist inside me relaxing, like a lens that keeps opening and opening to let in more and more light. Even when I don't understand the words—literally, from the way they're pronounced—something very beautiful is going on inside me, by orderly stages, the way something grows, a few more cells every day.

For instance, Midge, I'm sitting out in the rocks about a half-mile from the Chakra—you know, where the Fountain of Karma plays—and there's a kind of natural bench—out here where I am, I mean—under what they call an Arizona cypress, with these drooping gray-blue limbs and little brown berries seamed like tiny soccer balls, and I wish I had words to say how *charged* it all feels, how *pregnant* just the rockiness of the rocks seems—the little silvery veins of some mineral, the little loose heaps of rosy dust, the parallel ridges showing all the millions of years of sedimentation—and then too the breeze and the cypress with its resiny essence and the distant mountains like wrinkled tissue paper—how *sacred*, really, and the whole matter of whether God exists or not, which I always thought rather boring, is just plain tran*scend*ed, it seems so obvious that *some*thing exists, something incredibly and tirelessly good, an outpouring of which the rocks and I and the perfect blue sky with its little dry horsetails are a kind of *foam*, the foam on the crest of all these crashing waves, these outpourings all through the aeons of time, and yet terribly *still*, too—I know I'm not expressing it very well. There is something in *every*thing, its *is*ness, that is unutterably grand and consoling. I just feel terribly *full*. I feel—how can I put this?—like I'm carved out of one big piece of crystal and exactly fitted into a mold of the same crystal. Tell Irving I feel *motionless*. Ask him if this is samarasa. My happiness is deeper than I've ever felt happiness before. It's as if there is a level the sun has never reached before. *He* makes it possible, the Arhat, he per*mits* it—his voice, his glow. God, I love him, even though he makes me suffer. Love—*luff*, he says—is agony. *A-go-ny*, Midge.

A cute little lizard has just showed up. He's quite bright green. As I'm talking he stares at me with one eye. He *really* knows how to be motionless.

I began to tell you about my dynamic-meditation session. It must have been a week ago, though it feels a lot longer. I wasn't nearly so secure here then, so plugged into the energy sources. About ten people, most of them younger than I, plus Fritz, whose name here, I must remember, is Vikshipta. A bit like "stick shift." Durga was there too, queening around with all her orange hair and a ton of bogus-gold bangles on her wrists and a big loose violet robe that didn't quite conceal how overweight her hips are. I bet she put him up to it: the boy who after we'd all settled into the lotus position in a circle shouted I reminded him of his loathsome mother, even though she didn't have a big black pussy like I did, and tried to hit me. I shouldn't say "tried," the little shit *did* hit me, right across the jaw so my back teeth on that side ached for days, and then tried to grab my arm to twist me down—you could see he was excited, if you know what I mean. We are all naked, I should have explained, except for the leaders, who keep their robes on. I was dumbfounded and numb, I initially went into what Dr. Epstein used to call my masochistic-recessive mode, of, you know, the good girl who retreats into the knowledge that *she's* not doing anything and somebody *else* is to blame. The few occasions when Daddy and Mother would get violent, over his drinking usually, I'd go into that mode, and in a way also when they bulldozed me out of Myron Stern, the boyfriend I had in college I know I've told you about, out of him and into Charles, who was just graduating from Harvard. Having all your clothes off in front of a lot of strangers makes you feel oddly detached. The meditation leaders in their robes weren't doing anything to help, just swirling around shouting "Who *are* you?" at people, or "Ko veda?," which means "Who knows?," and the other sannyasins were making a kind of moaning hullabaloo that wasn't any help either, and I looked up past this brat's shaved head—you don't *have* to shave your head here, but he was going all the way—and I saw this very Irish sort of Peg o' My Heart smirk on Durga's big white chalky face and I just got *mad*, Midge: you wouldn't have known me. He, the aroused boy, had me pretty much on my back by then, and I kneed him right where he was most interested, let's say, and then got a grip on his ears, since he didn't have any hair, and pulled his head this way and that, and wound up pounding it on the floor while Durga and Fritz, I mean Vikshipta, were trying to separate us, which they hadn't been doing while *he* was on top. Somehow that boy, who you could tell from the few words he pronounced and the supercilious way he tipped his head back and tucked up his upper lip had had all the advantages, was that particular kind of boy I've always taken an irrational dislike to. You see them all the time, the sons of people you know and the kind of country-club kid who used to be hot after Pearl. They act so—what's the word?—*entitled*, screwed up or not, flunking out of Andover or not, and if they don't rack their Porsches up against a tree or overload their little heads with cocaine will end up being a professional something-or-other just like their smug chauvinistic absolutely insensitive old-fart daddies. The *language* I used against this poor boy you wouldn't believe, Midge. It just vomited out of

me, with all this suppressed rage. Tell Irving that meditation with him was never like *this*.

I don't know what it was set me off, really. Nobody
likes somebody trying to rape them, especially after
insulting their pussy, but in a strange way it had to do
with forces beyond that, with this boy's—Yajna, his
name is, we've made up a little since, he even tried
apologizing, he said his head was in a bad space that
day, and I had to tell him it was all all right, I felt very
motherly toward him, and his mother, wherever she is,
no doubt loves him and is worried to death about his
being here with what she imagines are terrible creepy
people—as I was saying, with this boy's being a *man*
and *not* being a man quite either, my brain waves or
whatever they are oscillated between these two poles—
his being and his not being, his maleness and his imma-
turity, his bully-power (I was terrified, remember) and
yet his pimply shaved-headed *cal*lowness—and I just
got more and more indignant. If I had had the strength,
I would have torn him to bits and ground the pieces
into the mat, the way you do a wasp that's been annoy-
ing you all afternoon, you know how in the fall they
come out of the windows on the sills somehow on
sunny afternoons and bumble around on the bedspread
and the kitchen table so stupidly and into your half-
empty coffee cup—I just *hate* it!

Of course, we can't all go around all the time getting
hit on the jaw and trying to tear somebody's ears off,
but I must say it did wake me up. That's a phrase the
group leaders and encounter therapists around here use

all the time—"waking up." "Getting rid of the garbage" is another thing they say. That oscillation I felt inside my head got me to thinking about men in general, my feelings about them. It must all go back to Daddy, who just basically on weekends and bank holidays if he didn't go off to play golf at Brookline hid in the library reading Thornton Wilder or those dreary Metaphysicals. Maybe I'm angry, deep down, because, though I loved him and knew he loved me, he wouldn't *come out*. But then this rapist-boy *did* in a manner of speaking come out, and I don't seem to like that either. And then, even more confusingly, Fritz looked me over afterwards to see if I had been damaged and should go to the ashram infirmary, and on the way walking back to my trailer to get my jeans and sun hat and work shoes—this was all around nine in the morning, just beginning to get hot—we went to his A-frame and I slept with him.

It was nice, Midge. Nice. Though with Germans there's a distance, they have difficulty showing their feelings. His eyes are so pale they seem transparent, you can look right through them into nothing. He told me what his name means: it's a modality of consciousness halfway between total confusion and total concentration. I *love* that part of it here, learning all these new things, and not just with your brain but your body, with your spirit and whole self—with your atman. You should have seen me, though, that afternoon: big blue swollen jaw and one eye half shut and a lot of stiffness around the neck and shoulders from when all the rage came out. I looked so dreadful they left me off from the artichokes two hours early—I think they *do* treat me with kid gloves a little, compared to some of the younger, more trampy women—and next day I was told I had been transferred from fieldwork to construction assistant at the Hall of a Millionfold Joys—people call it Joy-Six-Oh, the Arhat likes jokes and encourages everybody to make them. The work is right at the Chakra, which makes it handier for me and Fritz to steal the odd half-hour. He's so efficient. I hadn't slept with a man except Charles for so many years—that thing with Ducky Bradford you were all so curious about never got past a few stilted luncheons downstairs at the Ritz, there was something missing, I'm not sure he isn't a bit gay, it would help explain why Gloria always seems so skittish when the girl-talk gets gutsy— for so many years, I felt a bit shaky at first, but so far, if I do say so myself, it seems to go just fine. I was afraid of seeming too old, but he's very complimentary about my figure and the ojas shakti expressed by my glossy hair—it's the supplements, Midge, vitamins A and E-complex and the zinc and that evening-primrose oil!— and says he's bored silly with these twenty-year-old guru groupies, as he calls them. He says they have perfect bodies but no real spirit, and maithuna is above all a spiritual act. He himself is older than he looks, thirty-seven. He was with the Arhat in India, at the first ashram, in Ellora. He says he was really one of the founders—it was his idea to combine encounter therapy with tantric yoga. He shares this A-frame with only one other man, Savitri, who's out on the road a lot of the time, giving interviews and selling the Arhat's books and tapes and meditation aids, and there's a whirlpool bath, one of those you can sit in up to your neck, instead of just a trailer shower the size of a mailing tube where you keep bumping your elbows on the soap rack and treading in everybody else's germy wet towels that they just leave where they dropped them. Disgusting!

I know you won't, but you *must*n't tell Charles about Fritz—my hunch is he's going to start suing me. Charles, I mean. About Vikshipta: a lot of the people here, actually, are well into their thirties and forties, with Ph.D.s and jobs they left in city planning or architectural offices or legal firms—they're not crazies, the place really runs, we really *are* accomplishing things. Joy-Six-Oh will be up by the end of the summer, with air-conditioning throughout and all the electricity solar-generated from panels on the roof. Is that what they call a zero-sum situation? Today, for the first time, they let me drive a backhoe. It's such a darling machine. It lifts this big obliging hydraulic arm with its elbow up in the air and instead of a hand it has a scoop or bucket they call it, with these four pointy fingers shiny from gouging at the ground—they're replaceable, I never realized that—and you sit there in this shaking cab scared to pick the wrong lever because this huge mechanical animal under you, that feels so gentle and plodding and patient, has so much blind power it could crush somebody just as easily as it picks up a boulder. I adored it, being allowed to run it. Its controls are all sticks, so it's almost more natural than a car. Everybody, including the foreman, who used to be a Mormon, said I was very good—I really have the touch. It's like I become the backhoe's spirit, its jiva.

Forgive me, Midge, the way my mind is flipping around, but everything here is so energizing I said to Fritz I don't see how the Arhat does it, all of us feeding off him this intensely spiritual way. He said—Vikshipta, I must learn to use his real name—that's why he must conserve himself and needs all these women to hide behind, living so withdrawn you hardly ever see him except at darshan and when he drives by in his limo. We drink his silence the way he drinks Brahman's, Vikshipta said.

How can I describe to you how I feel here? Tender and open as if I've shed an old skin, Midge. Everything makes such an im*pres*sion—the rocks I'm sitting among, and the sunset in its love colors like some great slanted fragmentary walkway we're seeing from underneath, and a breeze that stirs up the resiny smell in the cypress and reminds me of a smell from my childhood, some deep secret kitcheny scent out of a grandmother's drawer, and this little lizard who's been keeping me company. He's like a perfect little living jewel. He's been absolutely frozen as my voice rattles on and on. I'm getting hoarse. And just *then*, when I cleared my throat, up he stood and raced away on his two hind legs like a tiny man with a long green tail! He had a collar around his neck and for all I know a bow tie! He was— how can I say?—*one* with me, as the buzzards overhead riding the air currents home are one with me, and my birth and death, and you are one with me, dear Midge, and my lover is one with me when we can find a half-hour. Vikshipta's hair is nearly as long as mine and utterly bleached on top from being out in the sun. When he isn't leading therapy sessions he helps on the crew that's building a ring road to keep cars out of the Chakra, looking ahead to the time when this will be a real city of many thousands, a thriving alternative to the atrocious way people live now.

Can you hear the supper blast? It's an old foghorn that used to be on a boat in San Francisco. They use it to call us to dinner, or in case there's nuclear war. You can hear it for miles, way out in the artichokes, and it reminds me of the only thing of my old life I, miss, besides you and the girls and Irving—the sea, the triangular piece of it I could see from our front windows. It was never the same. Every day, every hour, it was a slightly different color, responding to the wind, and the sky, and my mood. Do you think I was going stir-crazy?

It's still me, Midge, a few days older and wiser. Happy Mother's Day. I *must* finish this tape and get it off to you. There's just so much *hap*pening. I know your image of us, and mine too used to be, is of people in lavender robes sitting around in a trance, but what we are trying to do here isn't escape the world but revolutionize it—offer up a model of creative activity without ego and competitive antagonisms, so that from our central crystal here in the desert human society will spontaneously restructure itself, like certain chemicals when you put in just a pinch of the right precipitant. Vikshipta explains it better than I can; he used to be a chemist. He gets quite lovely when he talks about the new world we'll concoct here. He worked in West Germany for some huge I. G. Farben spin-off until it seemed to him everything they were making—fertilizers, industrial additives, pesticides, even medicines and drugs—was poison, that the whole human species was a kind of poison, worse even than rats and cockroaches and viruses, and he left his wife and little child and went into the world to search for purity. This was in the Seventies sometime, when you and I were being suburban. He went to Nepal and the Himalayas but it was too cold there, no matter how pure, and he kept getting parasites, and then, drifting south to visit the great carved caves at Ellora, he came across this little ashram run by the Arhat in this pale-green farmhouse on the edge of town. It was like, he says, a carnival—absolute freedom and a lot of abuse of the freedom, of course, but in the still center of it all this utterly calm and rather humorous man who just *ra*diated vidya, and prakhya. Not that he ever said so much, he still doesn't and, when he does, afterwards it's almost impossible to remember what was said, you just have this wonderful feeling of being washed clean inside, of everything klishta, everything impure and painful, having been gently purged. What Vikshipta liked about the Arhat was that unlike a lot of gurus he didn't demand quiescence, he invited dynamism, and instead of just being a slave word by word to what Patanjali wrote about yoga over two thousand years ago he had heard of Freud and modern psychotherapeutic techniques and in this cosmically good-humored way of his was willing to give anything a shot. There weren't these usual repulsive little anatomical stunts like sucking things back up through your anus and cleaning out your sinuses with a silk string, but a lot of group encounter, and hydrotherapy, and some primal scream, and strange things like food fights and blue movies—anything to wake people up, was the Arhat's approach. He embodies or localizes, that is, purusha to such an extent that it leaches away all the prakriti in the people around him. What *I* find sweet, in all this, and not so chauvinistic as it sounds, is that purusha, motionless inactive spirit, is male, and prakriti—active nature, you could say—is female, so that in the ideal maithuna, that's what they call fucking in Sanskrit, the woman does all the work! The men always sit and she is always on top, the way Shiva and Shakti do it! I was shy at first but now I like it, its being up to me, so to speak, even when there's all these men in one of these groups. They sit in a circle called the shri chakra and what you do is called chakra puja, or purnabhisheka, the complete consecration. You have to see them all as motionless purusha and your yoni as a purifying fire. Midge, it does work! It gets very impersonal, and that's not such a great loss, it turns out. You become all yoni and your spirit gets delightfully unattached.

Enough of my lecturing. For God's sake don't tell any of this to Charles or even to Irving. What other news do I have? I still haven't figured out where my rental car went to, and I know Hertz must be bugging Charles, but what can I do? That cold I had when I came is still hanging on. I must say there's a lot of minor illness around here, colds and fevers and aches and pains. I think people get groggy, the twelve hours of work as worship is too much physically, though wonderful spiritually. Even the girls who come to make the beds and tidy the trailers in the morning with the most radiant look on their faces have these awful coughs and sniffles. I've changed jobs again, just when I was getting so good at the backhoe some of the guys would let me scratch their backs with it as a joke. I guess it's a promotion, though I miss the healthy mindless outdoors—you get hardened to it, and there's always a satisfaction when your body responds to a challenge. It settles the mind into silence, physical labor. But Durga came to me and asked if I could type. She didn't like me from the start and I believe she hates me now because of Vikshipta, though I don't know what their relationship was before me. She *is* beautiful in a way, with those pale-red eyebrows and that black pearl above her nostril, and wears those flowing robes to make the best of her figure, but she doesn't give off really man-pleasing vibes—she seems too angry at something, and it could be is too close to being a man herself. Wimpy types like Yajna are terrified of her and whine all the time about how she's abusing the Master's trust, the way she runs the place along these kind of paranoid lines. But for some reason I'm not scared of her. I said I wrote a mean letter but never had typed professionally. She said they needed another typist in the Uma Room pool to answer the Arhat's mail. It pours in from everywhere—Europe, Australia, Africa, even the South Sea Islands. Our run-ins with the local ranchers and the state land-

use freaks have gotten us some national publicity, you
may even have seen some of it on the seven-o'clock
news, after Natalie Jacobson. People send checks, just
for what seeing the Arhat on "Sixty Minutes" has done
for them. They fall in love just like I did. He really *is*
a master of the interview—so funny and relaxed and
sweet and respectful and solemn and sly, like the baby
of the family that's always been made much of. Actually, his early life was very hard and cruel. A person's
moksha is supposed to erase his past, but the story you
hear is that his father wanted to mutilate him as an
infant to make him a more effective beggar but—this
was all in Bombay, where as everybody knows the poverty is terrible—but his mother hid him under a heap
of rags or cow dung and smuggled him to her sister in
the countryside near Ellora, and that's where he grew
up. He's enchanting to me on TV because the camera
gets so close to him; otherwise he's whizzing past in a
limousine, and even onstage he seems very far away,
and dwarfed by this huge silvery-polyester armchair he
likes to sit in, and on weekends, when the day trippers
and who knows what crazies are there—if they shot
John Lennon they'll shoot anybody that appeals to
them—he's behind a curved Plexiglas shield that makes
him even harder to focus on. But on TV you can see
exactly the way his slightly chubby cheeks kind of tense
up when he's speaking on an allegorical level, and the
beautiful way his mouth moves in his beard, especially
that amazing "s" he makes, his front teeth not quite
together like he's holding something between the back
ones, and his really incredible eyes—they seem abso-

lutely to have no reflected highlights, just this smooth
dark bulgy inky brown that goes in and in. I love his
lids, too—they're so *sculp*tural somehow, and how the
lower ones get this funny bunchy extra wrinkle when
he's said something sly, that you can take two ways.
And his hair, the kinky energetic grayish bits you can
see at the edge of the turban. It's hard to know how old
he is. He might be our age. Or ten years older or
younger. There's a new videotape, made since the one
on ego-negation and prapatti we used to watch together—on sachchidananda and moksha, it's really
wonderful, for $39.90, and if you order it direct from us
never mind about the five-percent Arizona-state sales
tax, nobody pays it around here because we're a religious organization. *Do* let me know if you don't adore
it as much as I do.

Anyway, Durga comes up with this same icy face she
had the day I pretended to have no credit card, and told
me to join the typing pool. I said to her I had the
impression she hated my guts—you learn to say such
things here, everybody does it, it gets the garbage out
and clears the air—and she said her feelings and mine
were of no consequence, all that mattered here was our
service to the Arhat, though she *had* observed that
women of my social class tended to play at enlightenment for a few weeks and then go on to some other style
of vacation, and once we were out tended to be very
cozy with both the press and the law-enforcement authorities—she has these phobias about the FBI, the IRS,
the CIA, and the Immigration Service, not to mention
the local sheriff. She said the Master had become aware

of my presence, and the executive committee had concluded I had the requisite energy and karmic potential to serve at a higher level than skimming concrete or even operating a backhoe. My heart sank. I loved that big sweet sleepy yellow thing, a brand-new diesel John Deere. But, softhearted me, I said O.K. and have been working in the Uma Room for three days now. It's all little cubicles. They give you these form responses and after a while you can elaborate on them to suit your own style, within limits, but even so it's not really en*larg*ing labor like the other was, the outdoor work. One advantage, it brings you quite close to the Arhat, though I haven't seen him yet—he lives in the original ranch hacienda, which has been remodelled and connected to these fitted-together trailers by a kind of breezeway. They say Durga is always slipping in to consult with him, and some of the others. The executive committee is mostly all women—the Arhat has this theory that women are stronger in selflessness than men, which may be a nice way of saying they're subservient. I couldn't wear my ratty muddy work clothes to the Uma Room, and the other typists wear saris, so I've gone and bought myself a couple at the Varuna Emporium and spend about a half-hour every morning trying to fold it so it doesn't fall off or get all sloppy whenever you lift your arm. They offer quite a line actually of clothes in these sunset shades of purple and violet and dusky lavender and even burgundy and magenta and a very attractive rosy brown. The Emporium puts out a catalogue I'd be happy to send you, along with the order form for the moksha videotape if you and the girls want to get it.

I keep waiting for *this* tape to run out, since my Puritan conscience, it must be, won't let me send it off to you until I've filled every inch. You and Irving and Ann and Liz and Gloria too and Donna, if they're around Wednesday, do the same and send it back—I'm not so far gone into prapatti and all that as not to miss a lot of the good things I've left behind. The ocean must be full of sails by now on the weekends, and the tulips up everywhere. I've missed the daffodils, the apple blossoms, and the hawthorns. Above all, Midge, I miss your friendship. The women here try to be nice and friendly but they tend, frankly, to be from different social circles from what you and I are used to. A lot of them of course are very young, for one thing—just teen-age runaways or dropouts still acting out their adolescent crises. The Arhat is what they're doing instead of bulimia or drugs or turning tricks on Sunset Boulevard. They're young but not very often glamorous—rather the opposite, dumpy in fact, though how they get fat on the diet of rice balls and artichoke paste they serve in the mess hall I have no idea. I've lost seven pounds, myself. Then the ones that are older were hippies, many of them, fifteen years ago, or beach bums, and the drugs left some short circuits in their heads—little gaps they just smile through as if what they said made perfect sense. I'm not speaking of the psychotics and addicts, though we have a few of those too. But they don't push themselves on you, they tend to stick to themselves and are rather shy.

It's the women of some quality and education who are so disappointing. They have this—I don't want to be unkind, but—this Midwestern blandness, even when they come from the West Coast. There's no history really where they're from except old Spanish missions or Russian fishing settlements or Mickey Mouse back when he was Steamboat Willie—that's as far back as the collective memory goes. They've been to college, a lot of them, and some have advanced degrees evidently, they're not exactly dimwits, but really they don't speak my language—everything has only one dimension for them, there's no *double entendre* and the *double voir* that goes with it—it's just impossible to have with them the kind of *silly* fun we used to have. There is one, I should say—from Iowa, of all unlikely areas—called Alinga, with *some* refinement and subtlety. That reminds me, a fascinating thing Alinga *did* tell me this morning about the

[*end of tape*]

May 12, 1986

Dear Ms. Grumbach:

It filled me with limitless happiness to receive your precious letter and to hear of your perfect love. Selfless and loyal love such as you profess is one of the greatest weapons Man and Woman can have in their ceaseless struggle to escape the cruel cycles of karma and enter into everlasting moksha and sachchidananda. I accept your love, my dear pilgrim, and would welcome you at Ashram Arhat if certain technical requirements can be met.

Millennia of yogic experience have determined that the individual spirit cannot return to the Atman if encumbered by worldly possessions. I ask merely that for the duration of your life here under my protection and guidance—may it be eternal!—your financial savings be placed in the care of the vigilant and efficient custodians of our Treasury of Enlightenment. Their infallible wisdom and the irresistible success of our communal enterprise will ensure that your assets shall be returned to you greatly enhanced if you ever were, most regrettably, to decide to leave our company.

Demand for places amid our limited facilities is such that we must ask a minimum deposit of ten thousand dollars (U.S.). In addition there are fees totalling eight hundred dollars monthly to cover a modest portion of the unavoidable expenses of your food, housing, health and accident insurance, lecture and darshan fees, and supervised meditation. Sannyasins are of course expected to practice worship in the form of constructive labor for twelve hours a day and either to bring with them sturdy boots, a sleeping bag, a sun hat, and appropriately colored garb or else to purchase such supplies at the Varuna Emporium located to the right of the ashram Chakra, with its famous fountain. A mala of beads of sacred sandalwood ending in a beautiful hand-carved pendant containing a color photograph of myself plus a hair from my head or beard will be provided free, as a benison of Buddha, and should be worn at all times, save when bathing or (at the wearer's discretion) engaged in sexual intercourse. A full range of contraceptive preparations and devices may be obtained at the Karuna Pharmacy; and various iconographic aids to life at Ashram Arhat, including incense and other purifying inhalants, can be purchased at our shops, as described in the enclosed catalogue.

These aids, and my inspired and unexpurgated books, videotapes, and audio cassettes, not to mention posters depicting my present (and final) physical incarnation, selected Hindu deities, tantric visualizations, and ritually constructed mandalas can of course be ordered and utilized by those who do not yet feel able to cut their sordid earthly ties and surrender to the new order of existence established here at Ashram Arhat, amid the immemorial peace of the healthful semi-arid Sonoran Plateau.

Dear Gladys Grumbach, I return your love a million-fold and with tranquil exultation await your reply. Come and join me! You and none other ignite my heart's flame. As the Lord Buddha asked, "Who shall find the Dhammapada, the clear Path of Perfection, even as a man who seeks flowers finds the most beautiful flower?"

> Shanti,
> Shri Arhat Mindadali, M.A., Ph.D.
> Supreme Meditator, Ashram Arhat

/spw

May 13, 1986

Sir:

Your recent editorial in the Forrest *Weekly Sentinel* condemnatory of the Ashram Arhat as a "glorified summer camp" for "bored yuppies" and "pathetic societal strays" would be beneath our notice were we not sincerely anxious to cultivate good relations with our fellow-citizens of Dorado County and to have our substantial contributions to the regional economy recognized. A barren tract of exhausted range has been transformed into productive agricultural land at no cost to the water table. Our extensive irrigation and sanitation draw solely upon an aquifer confined to the valley of Gritty Creek, now happily renamed the Sachchidananda River and not to be confused with the miserable alkaline trickle the good "citizens" of Forrest have amusingly dubbed Babbling Brook.

To correct a few other misapprehensions or deliberate misstatements: (1) Our facilities for meditation, therapy (both physio- and psycho-), non-soil-depleting agriculture, and hand manufacture have never claimed tax-exempt status; via real-estate tax and other levies the ashram has contributed $46,742.07 to Dorado County coffers in the fiscal year ended this March, in return for which we have received precisely *no* public services—neither police protection nor trash pickup nor highway maintenance nor water nor sewer mains nor anything but the forced enrollment of sixteen of our children in public schools where, after sickeningly long bus rides, they are bullied and tormented by their teachers and fellow-students alike and subjected to a bowdlerized, anti-evolutionist, right-wing curriculum that would insult the intelligence of a chuckwalla. (2) Our armed security forces exist solely to defend our property and personnel against the attacks of trigger-happy rednecks and beered-up adolescents who have repeatedly damaged and fired upon our water tanks, our outlying pumphouses and tool sheds, our faithful watchdogs, and our signs of welcome in many languages. (3) Our so-called "orgies" are in fact exercises in the ancient art of tantric yoga, wherein the participants worship one another as Shiva and Shakti, the fundamental forces of the cosmos; sexuality and spirituality are forms of one energy, proclaims our Arhat, whose love unites us all and in ecstatic love of whom we are all made new.

With united voice, therefore, we remind you that this is supposedly a free country. Accredited lawyers among us stand ready to defend our constitutional rights. Defamatory and false information infringes these rights. Ashram Arhat holds out the hand of peace to its neighbors in Dorado County and the "city" of Forrest. Let us live side by side and strive to make our hitherto sadly neglected region the paradise it can become. The world is weary of the old agendas; let us welcome in the new agendas. Vindictive and mendacious editorials such as yours feed the atmosphere of hate that has grown up needlessly, and in his ineffable sorrow our

Master has empowered me to compose this letter of friendly correction.

> Yours most sincerely,
> Ma Prem Durga
> Executive Director, Ashram Arhat

/spw

May 23

My dear Charles,

I was sorry to receive your letter. I am *so* sorry that Midge gave you my address, after I begged her not to. She is still, as I must not forget, very much of your world, very much attached. Even Irving, I fear, is just playing at dvandvanabhighata—the cessation of trouble from pairs of opposites. You and I, my dear, I see now, were such a pair of troublesome opposites.

You speak of our bank accounts and stocks. You even write the slanderous word "theft." Were not those assets joint? Did I not labor for you twenty-two years without wages, serving as concubine, party doll, housekeeper, cook, bedwarmer, masseuse, sympathetic adviser, and walking advertisement—in my clothes and accessories and demeanor and accent and even in my body type and muscle tone—of your status and prosperity? How can you be so mired in prakriti as to care what numbers are printed on the bank statements that you never used to read anyway? Those numbers flowed effortlessly and inevitably from your work—you did not work to produce those numbers. I always did the accounts and the budgeting. For you as well as for us here at the ashram, work is worship—but you worship a stupid god, a stodgy pudgy god of respectability and outward appearance, a tin snob god of the "right" cars and shoes and country clubs, of acceptable street addresses and of acquisitions that dissolve downwards into démodé junk rather than, as for those who take the path of yoga and non-ego, dissolve upwards, into samadhi and the blissful void of Mahabindu. I pity you, darling. Your anger is like that of an infant who with his weak little rubbery arms beats his mother's breast and produces no effect but her loving, understanding laugh.

You dare drag in our daughter. You say Pearl is appalled. You threaten me with the loss of not only her love but all communication with her. You say she will renounce me. How absurd. One cannot renounce a parent. A parent can renounce a child, for purposes of future inheritance, but a parent is unrenounceable—a parent, however inconvenient, is a fact. Facts cannot be renounced, though they can be not known, through avidya, or, through vidya, transcended. A parent can be, if not transcended, survived—you have survived your own father but carry him with you like one of those fetuses that in some unfortunate women turn to stone—every time you cleared your throat with one of those prissy little "ahem"s it was your father clearing his, fat old poker-faced Freddy Worth—you even had his supercilious rapid eyeblink when you were trying to put something over on one of us—me or some gullible misdiagnosed patient or one of those poor doctor-crazy nurses you persuaded to spread her legs in their grotesque white stockings—a parent *should* be transcended, I'm trying to say, as a snake sheds its skin. Pearl and I are women and on the same continuum, and, having contributed your microscopic ridiculous sperm with its bullet head and wriggling tail, you can stand there all you wish, clucking and wringing your hands and telling her to hate me. She won't. I am her mother. I am she as she was once I. At the age at which I very immaturely married she is trying to become a free intelligent woman among her boyfriends and girlfriends and the scenery and ancient glories of England and shouldn't be bothered with our old spites and injuries and your impotent rage. Don't you see, dear muddlehead, we were a *wave*, a certain momentary density within the maya-veil of karma-events that produced Pearl, but now she is moving on and we must too. Let go of her and me. You have the houses and the New Hampshire land and all the silver that didn't come from either the Prices or the Peabodys—the Worth stuff is clunky but sterling and you could sell it on consignment through Shreve's if you're feeling so desperately poor. You have your profession and society's approbation. I have nothing but my love of the Arhat, and he promises me nothing. Nothing is *exactly* what he promises—that my ego will become nothing, will dissolve upwards.

I do hope you aren't letting the lawn boys scalp that humpy section out by the roses with that extra-wide Bunton. They should be spraying for aphids now. The peonies should be staked—the wire support hoops are in the garden shed, behind and above the rakes, on nails, in the same tangle that last year's boys left them in. I *do* hate missing the azaleas—that deep pink is so stunning against the ocean this time of year, all steely-blue and sparkly and bitter cold and dotted with whitecaps and the first brave sailboats.

The cold I left home with is at last getting better. Since you have the address there's no harm in telling you that the days are so hot and bright your lips and elbows keep cracking, but the nights can be quite chilly still. I didn't bring enough warm clothes and sleep sometimes in a parka and longjohns and have become quite deft at draping myself in a sari. At first I was assigned to a trailer—the others with me were more Pearl's age than mine and always wanted to go dancing—but now I'm in an A-frame I share with only two sannyasins, and these suitably mature. The word "sannyasin" originally meant someone who's become a holy beggar wandering from place to place. Our guru says that we travel most when standing still. We wear purple and pink because those are sunset colors and the world, he thinks, is in terrible decline. Also these are at the "love end" of the spectrum. I've become quite brown and my hair quite unruly. You would hardly know your smooth old coefficient in that baby-making wave we together formed twenty years ago. We seem quite sweet in our Brighton apartment as I look back on it—for all of your ugly present noises.

Fondly,
S.

P.S.: If by any dreadful misestimation of your rights and powers you carry out your threat to show up here, please understand that you will be taken into custody by our ashram security forces, a team of zealous young men I don't think you will find as cute as I do. They wear lavender uniforms and carry real guns and all graduated in the top third of their classes at the Arizona Police Academy. You will be held in a little detention room filled with pictures of the Arhat while tapes of his discourses play continuously through a loudspeaker. You will be released only when (a) a sannyasin vouches for you as a visitor (b) you find yourself on fire with love of the Arhat and humbly request to join the ashram (c) you make a generous contribution to our manifold good works and promise to go away. Since (a) will not forthcome from me, nor, most likely, (b) from you (though your expertise would be very useful here—the medical services are overstrained and the head of the clinic, a woman called Ma Prapti, seems to be in a gloomy trance most of the time), you should save yourself the ignominy of (c) and stay where you are and take care of our joint property. I assume you will be renting the Cape place this summer. Be sure to send me half the proceeds.

May 26, 1986

Dear Mrs. Blithedale

It filled me with limitless sorrow to receive the letter of your lawyers inquiring after the whereabouts of the principal amount so graciously made available to the work of the ashram some few years ago. Our accounts fail to show that any fixed term was set for the return of these most precious and cherished funds, nor that any rate of interest was determined. Had interest been your aim, perhaps you should have entrusted these funds to a federally insured bank, with its glass windows and fashionably attired tellers and total lack of spiritual benefits.

But no, at such time by no means were you interested in the banks: you were interested in the peace that Brahman brings when reunited with your atman; you were interested in samadhi and casting off the sordid claims of our illusory material life. Your legal servants write that you now regret your months as a sannyasin with us and have re-embraced your forefathers' creed of Presbyterianism—a Calvinist sect which presents earthly prosperity as a sign of divine election. We rejoice if you have thus purchased inner peace. Vishnu has many avatars.

However: we have been carefully consulting your records and conclude that your ascent to samadhi was regrettably arrested at the third, or Manipura, chakra.

As you will doubtless remember, this is the "gem center," whose presiding deity is Rudra, whose lotus displays ten blue petals with an inverted red triangle, and whose subtle-body site is the solar plexus. We now believe that the burning you felt there, which we joyously took as a sign of ascent toward the fourth chakra, Anahata, located at the level of the heart, may have been merely psychic resistance or simple indigestion. Your practice (abhyasana) of the asanas and mudras was ever desultory, Madame Blithedale, and your attachment to the five counterproductive vrittis of the psychomental stream (ignorance, individuality, passion, disgust, will to live) was never—we now sorrowfully feel—disengaged. The cleansing fire of asceticism (tapas) encountered in you an ego (aham) sheathed, as it were, in asbestos. Your vasanas—your subconscious sensations and urges—have stubbornly retained phalatrishna: the egoistic "thirst for fruits."

Yet we cannot find it in our hearts to condemn you, to cast you out. Such is the lavish scale of our generosity that we would welcome you back. You would rejoice to behold the many practical improvements at Ashram Arhat made possible by the ocean of generosity of which your own constituted but a single small, though infinitely treasured, drop. Our work does not cease, that ocean must flow on! Even as I dictate this affectionate missive, the steel girders of our splendid mandir, our Hall of a Millionfold Joys, are rising and being thunderously riveted together! There is not time nor strength for the backward glance! Come and rejoin us and all accountings will be made anew! Your Presbyterian legal advisers merely cast doleful shadows upon your atman, which longs to be free. As the immortal Utterly Enlightened proclaimed in the blessed Dhammapada, "Sorrow cannot touch the man [or woman, the scribes assuredly meant to add] who is not in the bondage of anything, who owns nothing."

> Your eternal servant,
> Shri Arhat Mindadali, M.A., Ph.D.
> Supreme Meditator, Ashram Arhat

/spw

May 26, 1986

Dear Mr. Rogers:

It filled me with sincere regret to hear of the loss of your two heads of prize cattle. However, your accusation of theft against the Ashram Arhat because the fence between us had its barbed wires snipped falls upon barren ground, for we are vegetarians at this place and have no need of rustling protein from you. So kindly look for your cattle elsewhere, among your other ranching friends, who are rumored to relish liquor and gambling to the extent of unhinging their better judgment.

And no, we will not join you in the costs of repairing the fence and reinforcing the same. The fence is your affair, as all who are in our ashram wish to stay in and, unlike underfed steers living under sentence of death, they have no need of barbed wires.

> With neighborly affection and esteem,
> Shri Arhat Mindadali, M.A., Ph.D.
> Supreme Meditator, Ashram Arhat

/spw

May 26, 1986

Gentlemen:

The large unpaid bill for six Lincoln limousines must be a deplorable clerical error. I have referred it to our chief accountant, Ma Prem Nitya Kalpana, who is unfortunately enjoying two weeks of uninterrupted meditation.

> With my generous blessings,
> Shri Arhat Mindadali, M.A., Ph.D.
> Supreme Meditator, Ashram Arhat

/spw

June 2

Dear Irving—

Just a quick Monday-morning note on my trusty office Selectric with its lovely augmented memory and magical erasure features. I often think of you and assume that Midge has shared at least the gist of the tape I sent her it must have been three weeks ago. Time flies! Things hum along here, though the noon sun is getting so hot now the Master has decreed a siesta time from eleven-thirty to three. People were fainting in the fields, especially some of the girls who have been up half the night absorbing energy at the Kali Club.

Your lessons have really stood me in good stead—a lot of the younger people have complimented me on how flexible I am. They run the Salutations to the Sun at a somewhat slower pace than yours, but then you were trying to fight flab on middle-aged matrons where here the Master is getting us in training for Sahasrara. The adept who supervises our group—Bhava, his ashram name is—*cruelly* emphasizes heels flat on the floor on the forward stretch and not only the throat bent way back but the tongue out just as far and hard as you can do. It hurts at first and feels embarrassing but is the very best thing for the thyroid and even the viscera apparently. Then, on the standard asanas, he likes you to do the Fish out of the lotus position, and the strain on the insides of the thighs is *agony*, plus the ache on the top of your head after a while. And on the Pashchimottanasana I really can't come near touching my forehead to the floor no matter how wide I spread my legs. But Bhava *loves* my Plough, he says, and I must say it's always been my favorite: with my knees pressed against my ears and my bottom straight up in the air I always feel so *cozy*, like I used to as a little girl hiding behind the sofa, so cozy and safe and absolutely *me*—I hold it to the point that when I close my eyes I get these things that I don't know if they're what they call visualizations but I do feel I'm in another world, or *just* on the verge of it. They like us to hold the asanas, except of course the Locust and the Bow, for fifteen deep breaths instead of the five you let us off with, you old softie. But some of the people, like this crybaby Yajna who's in my group, just stop when they feel like it. There's a lot of that kind of freedom here; nobody is "uptight." Whatever we do is within the Master's love, and that gives a great feeling of ease and suppleness. You should see me go into my headstand now—I absolutely *uncoil* and am up in about two big breaths, and using my elbows at the two other points, too, instead of the hands, which I could never bear to lift up before. Such a scaredy-cat! You were right—once you've found the zero point the trick is to *completely* relax your shoulders and you can go on upside-down forever. One tip, though—here they always follow the Cobra with the Locust and not the other way around the way you taught us. The Half-Locust (the Ardha-Shalabhasana) makes a very nice transition and the stretching in the abdomen doesn't feel so violent then when you go into the Bow.

But the main thing I want to scold you about, dear Irving, is—you never told us about Kundalini! I mean, not really. Just hints, and asking at the end of a session if we felt anything at the base of our spines. As if a bunch of middle-aged women full of coffee and bran muffins would be feeling anything much except plain relief at having stopped. The reason I'm so "into" Kundalini suddenly is—do tell Midge—it's my name! My ashram name. At last I met the Arhat and he gave me my proper subtle-body name.

Actually, for a week or more now I've been taking dictation from him instead of just typing out variations on form letters. Alinga, the least creepy of Durga's assistants, came in and asked me if I could take dictation. I told her I knew nothing of shorthand but she said that didn't matter since you're basically there to inspire him. He loves women, not in the way most men do or say they do but as *energy entities*, as vrittis in the ocean of prakriti. I of course was very nervous going into the presence of *The Master* but in fact he has this marvellous gift of taking you in with these enormous sad bulging bottomless eyes, of seeming to be letting you in on some huge unspoken deeply philosophical secret.

This first time, Alinga, who is very blond and slender and serene and efficient, led me back through the cubicles of the Uma Room—it's not really a room, it's a rather higgledy-piggledy arrangement of trailers with doors and walls cut through and welded back together to make a lot of office space—out through a breezeway across a kind of courtyard I've never seen before, with these old tan rustling trees that from the size of them were planted years and years ago. They had big bumpy pods hanging down, and smelled of something like cloves. This was the old adobe ranch house, the hacienda before the Arhat came and bought all these acres. There were cats on the veranda and pegs bits of rotten rope and harness were still hanging from. Inside, the air-conditioning began again. The furniture was what we New Englanders might call vulgar but may be the best you can buy around here—heavy squarish matching pieces with a silvery shiny look to the fabric, and plastic sleeves on the chair arms, and a lot of milk-glass and painted porcelain doodads displayed on open shelves, and just the hugest television set I've ever seen, the kind that projects onto a curved screen like you usually see only in bars.

The furniture didn't really give the impression that anybody lived here, if you know what I mean—it was more like the window of a furniture store. But I suppose if you're moksha you don't leave the dents on things more sthula bodies do. He wasn't in this living room but in one beyond, which he uses as an office, with a lot of off-white padded contour furniture on swivels and casters and a long desk of bleached wood, the kind that looks as though powdered sugar has been rubbed into the grain. Alinga left us and I sat down on the opposite side of the desk and tried to take dictation, my hands all jumpy and the pad trying to slide off the knee of my slippery silk sari. Some rich patron of the ashram was trying to get her money back and that was what the letter was about. It got rather technical about Kundalini and he had to keep spelling things. Several times he stopped and asked me if I thought a certain sentence was funny enough. I hadn't known any of it was supposed to be funny so I didn't know how to react at first. But we got through the letter and he seemed pleased. "We will buffalo that old bitch," he said, and then asked me if that was a correct American expression, "to buffalo." I said it was and he smiled his beautiful warm sly smile, so detached and sweet. He has this darling little gap between his two front teeth. His purple turban is just as it is in the posters, only woolier, somehow, with a nap that takes the light differently as the strips of it twist. His robe I think was a very pale peach, so shimmery it looked white, and on his hands he had all these rings that I'm sure were very expensive and authentic jewels but reminded me of those paste things people at fairs used to fish for by operating a little bucket crane, after putting in a dime.

I shouldn't be putting all this into a letter—Vikshipta and Alinga say that Durga and her henchpeople have the mail read, coming in and out—but I know how much you love the Arhat; it was your love that inspired mine. He is a beautiful presence in three dimensions, Irving. He is *real*. Not too tall and with a little gray in his beard but not too old either. He is paler than I expected but then of course Indians come in all shades; those invading people who brought the Vedas were just like Vikings. His cheeks and forehead are so free of wrinkles the gray in his beard and his eyebrows almost looks frosted on. His office had the air-conditioning turned way up, which went with the frosted look—I thought to myself I should wear a sweater next time.

Anyway, after the letter and a few other, shorter ones—
he has so many people *after* him, everybody wanting a
piece—he asked me in that thrilling funny accent of his
what my name was. I said Sarah Worth and that I
hadn't been given my ashram name yet. He looked at
me the longest time, with this little smile, and these
bottomless eyes, and said, "You are Kundalini." *I am?*
I said, blushing—I just went *hot* all over. "Veritably,"
he said. "You are she at last. You have come to burn
away everything klishta, everything duhshama. You
shall save us from our sorrowful impurity."

This seemed flirtatious and almost aggressive, so I
just stood there blushing. He admired my healthy tan
complexion. He said I was darker than he was. I was all
flustered and said it was just genes from my father, plus
vitamin E and PABA and oil baths twice a week when
I was at home in Massachusetts, but of course baths
were more difficult here and the desert air was very
drying to the epidermis. Then he said something like
"You are smooth and electrical" and settled back into
his silver armchair—like a Barcalounger with high
squarish arms and a padded rest for the head as on a
dental chair—and I decided the time had come for me
to go. I've taken dictation a number of times since then
and am hardly nervous now at all. Irving, he really is
all we imagined he is, and more. I mean, as well as being
divine he's *nice*, and shy, even.

Some years ago, while still at the Ellora ashram, he
cut a tape on Kundalini, and I enclose one, free, though
they go for $14.90 in our catalogue. Play it for yourself
and the gang some Wednesday when you can all take an

extra half-hour. Hope everything goes well with you and you're not too busy in the framing shop—you must be absolutely *buried* in diplomas this time of year. And graduation pictures. Soon, June weddings! Or do people just put those in albums? Or in those little store-bought frames that sit on the piano and look chintzy and somehow *scary*?

> Your grateful former student,
> Kundalini!

[*tape*]

We will talk today of Kundalini. She is the female energy in things. Not just women we are speaking of; she is in all things. She sleeps coiled at the base of the spine, in the root chakra, which is called Muladhara. The lotus of this chakra has four red petals. On them are inscribed the Sanskrit letters va, śa, sa, and sa. These letters are contained within a yellow square; this represents the earth element. An inverted triangle within the square holds Kundalini coiled three and one half times around the linga. The linga is the male organ, and also it represents the subtle space in which the universe undergoes the repeated process of formation and dissolution. Also in this chakra is Brahma, the creator-god of the gross material world. He has four arms and three eyes and four faces and holds, the sages say, a trident, a jar, a rosary, and with his remaining hand makes the mudra that dispels fear, the abhayamudra. His energy is called Dakini and is shining pink and also holds many things, such as a sword and a drinking vessel. Also in this chakra is a large elephant with a black strip around its neck. He forms the symbol of physical resistance. The principle of smell is associated with this chakra. That is all we know of Muladhara, at the base of the spine.

You ask, how does Kundalini awaken? How does she leave off her sleeping coiled around the linga? Pranayama, proper breathing, and pratyahara, the shutting down of the senses, send willpower down the two great nadis, ida the lunar channel and pingala the solar one. You ask, what is this, these nadis? They are the nerves and veins of the subtle body, which coexists with the material body. Subtle is sukshma, the other is sthula. When enough willpower goes down these nadis, Kundalini stirs. She hearkens to the vibrations of the mind meditating upon the syllable Ram, and then alternatively upon the syllable Yam. Also the great metaphysical syllable Om is frequently pronounced, and the sphincter muscles are contracted, sucking upwards. All these things waken Kundalini. Like a woman who is restless under the bright moon, she can no longer sleep. When she leaves Muladhara, there is the sound of a chirping cricket.

Kundalini uncoils and goes upward then to the chakra of Svadhisthana, which is located in the spine just above the genitals. Now there is the sound of the tinkling of an anklet. A sexy sound. She looks around. What is here, in Svadhisthana? Vishnu is here, dark blue, with four arms holding a conch, a mace, a wheel, and a lotus. His energy is Rakini and holds a trident, a lotus, a drum, and a chisel. Do not ask me what Rakini chisels [*laughter, tentative*]. Perhaps he is a chiseller [*laughter, less tentative*]. Perhaps with one of his arms Rakini is an illegal card-sharp dealer going to cheat Vishnu [*less laughter, uneasy*]. The lotus here is red and has six petals, bearing the letters ba, bha, ma, ya, ra, and la. The chakra's animal is the makara, a great monster like a giant crocodile. He is to water as the elephant is to earth. The principle associated with this chakra is taste. Kundalini tastes many things now, many sweet things from her childhood and spicy things from her girlhood and sour things from time as a mature woman. The dominating element is water. She feels clean, so very clean, and hears everywhere this rushing sound. The breath of life, Prana, is here and her lungs are full; they expand like clouds. This is a happy chakra, but Kundalini leaves it and goes next to Manipura, at the level of the solar plexus.

Ooh now, what is here? Now there is the deep sound of a bell. The god of this chakra is Rudra, who is red and sits upon a bull. He holds in one hand a fire and his energy is called Lakini and is dark blue. Everywhere in this chakra there is fire. There is a great inverted triangle, radiant like the sun, which represents fire. Kundalini swims in this fire. As she ascends it is very common for the person to feel very hot, to feel hot flashes. The head feels giddy. The body tingles. There may be, the sages tell us, constipation or diarrhea. The anus contracts and draws up. The chin sinks down. The eyeballs roll up. There are convulsions and visions. There is an experience of being a witness within the body. Sometimes the body feels as if it is being lifted into the air, and at others as if it is being pressed into the earth. It may feel very large or very small. It may tremble and ache and the tongue may protrude from the mouth. There may be a feeling of having no head. There may be the feeling of seeing things all around even though the eyes are closed. The sexual organ may become very erect and hard and painful. All this agony and embarrassment while Kundalini ascends. The lotus of Manipura has ten blue petals and on them are written ḍa, ḍha, ṅa, ta, tha, da, dha, na, pa, and pha. Its principle is that of sight.

Kundalini must travel on. She must continue her ascent. She is merciless upon herself. She wishes to become perfection. She travels upward to Anahata, located at the level of our hearts. Now there is the music of a flute. The music of a single flute. Now there is a golden triangle, as bright as ten million flashes of lightning. Now there is a lotus of vermilion and of twelve petals bearing ka, kha, ga, gha, ṅa, cha, chha, ja, jha, ña, ṭa, and ṭha. Now there is the god Isha, who is brick-red, dressed in shining white. He represents the whole world system. Space and time now are revealed; they are interlocked. Two triangles represent male and female; they are united. Now purusha for the first time is glimpsed, the unmoving essence beyond phenomena. The principle of this chakra is air, which is invisible. Its name, Anahata, means "unstruck," which means "without sound," which is silence. The animal here is the black gazelle, symbolizing lightness, symbolizing Vayu, the god of winds. Air, wind, brightness are all around. Brightness! It is frightening, it is immensity. Kundalini dashes from side to side, she desires to ascend in a straight line but must each time untie the knot of the chakra. Kundalini burns, she makes the yogi to feel very heavy and dizzy and hungry. The saliva pours from his mouth. His jaws, they stick together. His throat feels very dry, as dry as a dead prickly-pear cactus. Isha makes the gestures granting boons and dispelling fear. Isha's energy is called Kakini, who is bright yellow and holds a noose and a skull. These are not such pleasant things.

Kundalini is now halfway through her voyage, in the material body up through the spine, but in the subtle body the sushumna, the central channel around which twine the pingala and the ida in that basic pattern of life called the double helix. Kundalini's voyage is half done and has reached the throat chakra, which is called Vishuddha, which means "pure," but resistance remains; the next step is very difficult for it means the dissolving of the apparent union of matter and psyche, the recognition that external facts have nothing to do with internal facts. The yogi, the sannyasin, feels dreadful heat and the flashing of many little lights. Also deep numbness. Also the feeling of poison having been inserted in the body: this is energy, which must burn until the channels have been cleansed and can carry the terrible energy, the terrible shakti. There are many undoubted accounts of these feelings in the writings of the sages.

The fifth chakra is located at the base of the skull and is very complicated. The lotus here is a smoky purple, like perhaps the fuzz of grapes, and has sixteen petals, holding the sixteen vowels a, ā, i, ī, u, ū, r̥, r̥̄, l̥, l̥, e, ai, o, au, am, and ah. There is a white triangle and the sound is nothing but Om, Om, the sound of the cosmos. The god here is of two halves, Shiva and Shakti, the two gods male and female combining into Ardhanarishvara, the right half Shiva and glorious white, the left half Shakti and lovely golden. A god of both sexes. No man is just man. No woman is just woman. Men hold the seeds of womanhood within themselves and women hold the seeds of manhood within themselves. Ardhanarishvara represents this. He—let us say he-she— he-she has five faces and three eyes and ten arms. In his-her ten hands he-she holds nine things: a trident, an axe, a sword, a thunderbolt called in Sanskrit "vajra," an endless serpent with uncountable heads called Ananta and upon whom sleeps the great god Vishnu, a bell, a pointed stick with which to urge on a beast, fire (ouch! that must be hot to hold!), and a noose. With the tenth hand Ardhanarishvara makes abhayamudra, the gesture dispelling fear, which our dear friend Kundalini surely needs when she looks at those other terrible things being held up [*polite laughter*]. Ardhanarishvara has his-her hands most full [*again, the polite response muted by a certain impatience in the audience, a desire to get on with the ascent*]. The element of this chakra is ether, the element that is to the subtle body as air is to the material body. Its animal is Airavata, the white elephant with six trunks. He is a funny-looking fellow. The heavy, heavy earthy elephant of Muladhara has become etherealized. And that is Vishuddha.

The sixth chakra is located between the eyebrows. It is called Ajna. It has only two petals. They say ha and ksa. They are white. Everything is moon-white. There is an inverted triangle and it is moon-white. Inside there is the linga. Linga means "phallus" and also the subtle space, the ether. "Li" means to dissolve and "gam" to go out. There is the mantra Om. *Om*. OM. OM. It is the vibration from which all things emerge and into which all things are absorbed at the end of the cosmic cycle. There is a bindu—that is a very tiny point where everything is concentrated. The god is Paramashiva, which means Shiva and Shakti come together in a wonderful fucking. That makes the Mahabindu. Also the energy now is Hakini; he is moon-white and holds a book, a skull, a drum, and other such stuff. Here at Ajna the ida and pingala nadis meet the sushumna nadi and then separate again, running into the right and left nostrils. It tickles the yogi's nose. He has to sneeze: a*choo!* Ajna is a very high-up chakra. Kundalini must be very tired when she gets there. She is tired of bells ringing. She is tired of burning sensation. She is tired of sound of waterfall, of being lost in an ocean of light. But she must go on, go on ascending.

The seventh chakra is Sahasrara. It is located four finger-breadths above the top of the head. To get to it

Kundalini must jump [*laughter, as if at a sudden gesture*]. Now, where is she? All colors are merged into one. All sounds into one. All senses into one. The lotus is now of a thousand petals holding the fifty letters of the Sanskrit alphabet many times. Little Kundalini, she is now Shakti. She is now also Shiva. She knows everything and that everything is nothing. She is very happy and yet feels nothing. There is nothing but Brahman. From the inverted lotus cosmic radiations fall upon the subtle body. Kundalini is possessed with glorious insights into the indefinable depth-dimension of existence. She becomes Kula, the all-transcending light of consciousness. She inhabits Mahabindu, the metacosmic Void.

Then she must descend. She comes down. Like an elevator, she comes down. She goes back between the eyes. Sixth floor, wisdom center. Next floor, throat chakra. Then still lower to the heart chakra, and to Manipura, that is called the power center. As she slithers down she sheds wisdom, speech, love, and power. She sheds them one by one. She arrives at the level of the genitals, where libido lives, and sheds that too, coiling around Muladhara again, three and one half times. Muladhara is earth, it is childhood. We all come from earth, from childhood. So does Kundalini.

She is the female energy in things. In some biological women she is very weak. In some biological men she is very strong. The burning sensation we feel as she ascends, the blinking lights and roaring like a waterfall which many sages have seen and heard, this is the male garbage being burned from the system. It is obstruction. This obstruction comes at knots, called "gran-this." It is especially thick at the Muladhara chakra, and Anahata, and Ajna, called the Brahma, Vishnu, and Rudra knots. These places are clogged with ego and conscious thought and obstruct Kundalini from finding realization of oneness with totality, of transcending samsara and entering samadhi. She burns them through. She burns away garbage. We all come burdened with much garbage and it must be burned away. Our minds must become pure like fine ash, or like the sand of the seashore in the dawn when the tide has erased all the footprints and carried away all the Coca-Cola cans, all the candy wrappers. Kundalini herself, she is a candy wrapper. Did you believe the story of her journey? [*Sounds of assent.*] If you believe her journey, you will believe any foolishness. Modern science shows her journey cannot exist; Einstein showed there is no ether, medicine shows there are no nadis. All a lie. [*Silence.*] The story of her journey is a very detailed lie, like the horrible cosmology of the Jains or the Heaven and Hell of Dante, but so many endless details do not make such stories true. The more details they hold, the more lies they hold. They are like old newspapers. They are garbage. They are like organized religion, like the Holy Bible and Talmud and Koran. They are old newspapers. They are like the bound collected works of Sigismund Fried and Carlos Marx; they are garbage, full of details that are lies. Details obstruct us from enlightenment, from samadhi, from surrender of ego. We must forget. We must drive out foolishness from our systems. We must use foolishness to drive out foolishness. If you were not foolish, you would not have come across the sea to India. You would be in Germany drinking beer [*startled laughter*]. You would be in America eating steak and whiskey [*more of same; an undertone of relief*]. That is why I have told you the fairy story of Kundalini, the little snake that lives at the bottom of our spine. While you were hearing it, no other garbage was in your hearts or heads or stomachs; little Kundalini burned it all away.

[*end of tape*]

June 7

Dearest Pearl—

How I *loved* receiving your letter!—though it *could* have been longer. The courses you are completing are still vague in my mind. What exactly *are* Deconstructional Dynamics, and how can they be applied to Paradise Lost and the Faerie Queene? As you remember, Granddaddy Price had *lovely* editions of both classics— much too expensive, though, to be deconstructed. And

you say the man teaching it is a Communist! I'm sure
it doesn't mean in England quite what it does here—
something much more woolly and amusing, like
George Bernard Shaw—but still I do wonder why Mrs.
Thatcher and the Queen would give such a man control
of young minds when there are so many honest and
intelligent loyal Britons out of work.

I am *pleased* you are not coming home for the summer. I think it's a very mature decision. You would find
the house very gloomy with just your father in it showing up now and then to change his shirt, and of course
Europe has *so* many delights and you are *so* close to it,
just a Channel away! And you *are* a bit old to go beach
bumming and wind-surfing all day the way you could
with perfect propriety when you were seventeen (not
to mention the hideous damage you can do your lovely
fair skin) and, though it makes me sad to think it, I do
agree that your old job as lifeguard at the club pool
(such a *vision* you were in that high chair, in your bikini
and sombrero, with that cord of braided gimp holding
the whistle around your neck) should go to someone
younger. So Europe is fine, darling. But—*Holland?* Isn't
it just the dullest country on the Continent? Or at least
the flattest. Surely once you've seen one little genre
painting and one windmill you've seen them all. Your
friend promises all this boating in the canals but it
sounds very buggy to me, like bumping about in the
Ipswich marshes. And I can't believe the beaches there
aren't just *coated* with oil from all the tankers going by
in the Channel. And when I try to picture these lumpy
Dutch women in bathing suits I *shudder*.

Your friend sounds charming, perhaps *too* charming.
Charm is what European men are famous for, but there
are qualities our ungainly native boys have that are
worth treasuring—trustworthiness, for one, and the
willingness to work to support a family. If Jan's father
is a count, why are they in the brewery business? And
why was Jan at Oxford studying economics when the
London School is the one you always hear about, where
the Arabs and everybody go? I know you're finding my
motherly concern tiresome but one does read stories
here of the goings-on in Amsterdam, right out in that
big main square—it's the drug capital of Europe, evidently, and still has boys with hair down to their shoulders and wearing buckskin and all that that went out
here when Nixon finally resigned. *Do* be careful, dearest. You were sweet to reassure me that Jan is not a
homosexual, but in a way it would be a relief if he were.
You are all of twenty and very much feeling your womanhood. The strange thing about womanhood is that it
goes on and on—the same daily burden of constant
vague expectation and of everything being just *slightly*
disappointing compared with what one knows one has
inside oneself waiting to be touched off. It's rather like
being a set of pretty little logs that won't quite catch
fire, isn't it? Though every day when the sun shines in
the branches outside the window or the fruit in the
bowl matches the color of the tablecloth or your favorite Mozart concerto pours out of WGBH at the very
moment when you pour yourself a cup of coffee, you

feel as if you *are* catching or *have* caught, after all—somebody held the match in the right place at last. Really I shouldn't be putting being a woman down—it has its duhkha but I wouldn't be a man for anything, they really are *numb*, relatively, wrapped in a uniform or plate armor even when their clothes are off—or so it has seemed to me in my limited experience. And I sometimes wonder if my limited experience, limited really to your father for twenty-odd years and a bit of hand-holding and snuggling before that, wasn't enough after all, and if for your generation more wasn't less. I mean, we all only have so much romantic energy with which to rise to the occasion, whether one man or two dozen makes up the occasion. Of course your Jan seems to you to be a fully feeling and responsive human being now, just as Fritz did to me a month ago. But afterwards, if you can bear to talk to them—these meaningful men—it turns out that their minds even at the *height* of the involvement were totally elsewhere—were not really in the relationship at all! They were only and entirely what we in our poor fevers made of them.

From my tone you might gather that I have moved out of Vikshipta's and Savitri's A-frame. I am living instead in a nicer, newer one, with two of the women I work with in the ashram offices—Alinga, a tall blonde from Iowa (tall, but without your beautiful generous figure with its long swimmer's muscles and your lovely *push*) and Nitya, who is the head accountant here. Nitya is rather small and dark and nervous and has been quite sickly lately. I can't quite tell if she and Alinga are lovers or just like sisters, but they spend a lot of time

in the tiny kitchen, with the curtain that separates it
from the room where I'm sitting drawn, murmuring
and even arguing about this other woman called Durga
and drinking jasmine tea. Vikshipta was furious when
I told him I was leaving and—don't be alarmed, my
sweet—became a bit violent. It turns out that far from
being Durga's lover as I once imagined, he *hates* her for
having (he imagines) corrupted the Arhat and shifted
the emphasis away from hard-core psychotherapy to
large-scale utopianism. He was always going on about
the good old days in Ellora before the Arhat became so
soft, when they were really making breakthroughs in
consciousness-smashing, using Jung and tantra and
human potential and "cathartic physicality," which
seems to mean people got beaten up. Besotted as I was
with love—a woman's drug—I slowly realized that he
was really sounding very compulsive and fanatic about
it. I said to myself, *This man is a Hun. He can't tell tantra
from a tantrum.* He had a lot of unresolved anger and,
looking back at that first encounter (did I tell you about
it, or was that Midge?), I wonder if Yajna wasn't acting
out Vikshipta's desires, in trying to break my jaw and
the rest of it. (If this is news to you, don't worry about
it, darling, I feel fine now, never better in fact, though
I was afraid for a while my molars were shaken loose
and I'd have to fly back to dear fussy Dr. Podhoretz.)
I've gotten to know Yajna a lot better now and he's
extremely suggestible—just a boy, though he's something like twenty-three or -four, perfect for you, in a
way—his family is nice old railroad money from Saint
Louis and I think if his head weren't shaved his ears

wouldn't seem to stick out so much, and in a seersucker coat or a quiet tweed he would be quite presentable.

But, my darling, you are on the other side of the world and have your own life to lead and I mustn't be matchmaking even in my silly head. I *do* wish I had more positive associations with the Dutch, instead of clumsy wooden shoes and leaky dikes and Dutch treats and that awful way they treated the natives in Java when they had a chance, and still do in South Africa. You say Jan is lean and speaks English perfectly and plays the keyboard (is that really a musical instrument now or still just part of one?) beautifully, and if he pleases and amuses my Pearl I will find it in my heart to love him. I mustn't love any of your gentlemen friends too much, for I expect there will be many.

The young men here are rather realer to me than the beaux who with sneaky sheepish looks on their faces would appear at the door to carry you off in their convertibles and pickup trucks. Isolated as the ashram is, and united as we all are by our love of the Arhat, the generational barriers that at home (but this *is* my home now, I must remember!—they have a droll way here of talking about the United States, the country we after all live in, as "the Outer States") prevent us from seeing one another except as the stereotypes that television and advertising wish upon us melt away here, the barriers, and a not-at-all-uncommon sight is to see a young sannyasin in his violet robes and running shoes walking hand in hand with a gray-haired woman in her fifties. The other combination, the one we all know about in the outer world, the young chick and the old guy, is oddly rarer—their superior shakti perhaps gives the women here the upper hand that money gives men outside. At any rate, the boys would not by and large do for my Pearl. The gay ones have that gay way of walking so there's no up and down to their heads, just this even floating even when they're moving along very briskly, and their voices have that just perceptible fine-toothed homosexual edge that used to get my hackles up when I'd hear it in Boston (though of course I knew it shouldn't) but that here I've become quite happily used to. They're basically so *playful*, at least in regard to someone like me who is not quite ready to stand in for their all-powerful mothers but getting there, and good-hearted actually (they've suffered, after all, much as women do) and so *devoted* in their love of the Arhat, not to mention clever, truly handy at making the place run, in regard to things like electricity and irrigation and drainage and security and surveillance and counter-propaganda, which we have to put out or be *crushed*. They tend, incidentally, to be pro-Durga—she appeals to their sense of camp. Then the other type of young men, and they probably overlap but I'm never sure how much, are the thoroughly habituated—the outside world says brainwashed—adepts at yoga and detach-ment and biospirituality and holism, young men who when they wait on you in the Varuna Emporium or the drugstore have this ghostly sweet hollowness in their voices as though *nothing* you did would break their tran-quillity or alter their karuna for you. It makes me want sometimes to throw a fit or spit in their faces to get their reaction, but I fear that's the old devil in me—the prakriti in me, the impure transitory nature that hasn't yet been burned away in self-realization. I sometimes feel as if I have traded being mother to one beautiful long-legged heartbreakingly intelligent and emotionally sound daughter for a tribe of shadowy, defective sons. As I write that, I sense your father's homophobe prejudices—he sees them as all *diseased*—speaking through me, and that *is* the old me, from the Outer States, terribly unworthy of all the love and trust showered upon me in this divine place by both the sexes.

I *wish* you could meet Alinga and get to know her. Like you, she has blond hair, but with less body and radiance than yours. How I used to love, when you were little, to give you a shampoo in the tub, just for the tingly way your clean hair smelled afterwards and the angelic way it fluffed out about your head as it dried!— we assume little girls play with dolls in anticipation of motherhood but it could almost be we become mothers just so we can play with dolls again. Up to about the age of eight you *did* resist it so, screaming about the soap in your eyes. Children feel everything so much more keenly than adults—a bad taste is *mountainous*, and a single particle of soap in your eyes was the horrid blinding end of the world. I bought something for you called baby shampoo (No More Tears, the label said) but I could never make it lather *near* as well. Alinga's hair lies flat to her elegantly narrow little skull and falls utterly without a curl away from a central parting so bone-

white it's like a chalk line drawn in a diagram. I love
that innocent prim straightness, it reminds me of how
we girls used to look in the morning at Miss Grandison's Day School before the day mussed us up. She—
Alinga, of course—is I believe thirty-one and has been
around the world several times since leaving Cedar
Rapids and arriving here, and I *know* you and she could
share so much—through her, my dear elf-child, I often
feel drawn closer to you. She can be very funny and
irreverent, even about the Arhat, and you would enjoy
that, with your wicked sense of humor that you inherited from my sly father. From almost the time you
could toddle and babble you used to poke fun at me a
bit, mimicking my expressions, I was such a *serious*
mother, so earnestly playing with my doll, my poor
paperback copy of Spock consulted absolutely to tatters
the way people's Bibles used to be.

Of course I was amazed and chagrined to hear that
your father is flying to England to see you. In all the
years of our marriage I could never persuade him to
take the time off to go to Europe with me, except that
disastrous trip to Florence, when he couldn't find the
Uffizi or *any* place to park the car we had rented and
clung to the strange idea that The Last Supper should
be somewhere nearby and complained he couldn't sleep
because of all the motor scooters echoing off all those
stone walls—it became *my* fault because I *could* fall
asleep—I was so tired after all day of trailing around
behind him getting lost every minute and assuring him
that the Italians weren't cheating him as much as he

thought, I could have slept in an auto-body shop. Even with the Cape house that you and your friends enjoyed so much (remember all those potato chips!) his idea seemed to be to park me in it among all those gloomy pines whose needles everybody's bare feet kept tracking into the house while he stayed up in Boston ministering to the sick and, I'm afraid, to the healthy too. He is of course your father and you must love him. Love him if you must, but *don't show him my letters.* I very absurdly keep feeling guilty about this rented car of mine that disappeared when I arrived here and I know is costing our charge card forty-five dollars a day at least. His ability to instill guilt in me was always tremendous, *don't* let him do it to you. His very courtship began in the odor of guilt I was supposed to feel over a few dates with this sweet shy boy Myron Stern and, looking back at it, I see that Charles took up right where my parents left off, as enforcers of the stale old order. I *do* hope we never struck you as such ogres as *our* parents appeared to us. They *had* to, I suppose, since they had all these imaginary ogres leaning over them—not just the Russians but outsiders of any sort who might push or tempt them and their children into falling off the creaky old bandwagon of respectability. Well, your mother has done gone and fallen.

But I'm letting my "wiggles" run away with me. I am so *happy*, darling. This A-frame looks directly across the flat rooftop of the Chakra mall at the scrubby rocky hills that separate us from the territory on the north, where a lot of our legal trouble comes from. The rocks have this strange soft globby look and the Saguaro cactuses instead of being green and formidable as I pictured are weathered and blackened and battered like rather pathetic old giants. You rarely see one in good condition. A hummingbird comes to visit the little cactus flowers in the rock garden Alinga and Nitya made in the shade of this hairy old box elder. It's lovely to sit out here in the evening cool before dinner, feeling serene and changeless purusha underneath and at the beginning of all things and thinking of you in wet green England with its meadows and mossy spires and iron fences and layer upon layer of the human presence—generations, each doing their busy little bit to cover purusha up. You can talk to your father when he comes about the expenses of your jaunt to Holland—he has *total* charge of the family finances now, when he never so much as balanced a checkbook before in his life. I did all that for him, without pay and without thanks. He has all the worldly possessions we once supposedly shared, and I live here as free and as poor as the gray-throated flycatchers that dip about in the lengthening lavender shadows—poorer, since I'm not quick enough to catch flies in my bill. In *my* day, of course, a young man would either pay for such an excursion as the one Jan proposes or else not invite the young lady to come on it. I must leave it to your judgment, to what extent it is still true that a young woman compromises and cheapens herself by openly lending herself to the companionship of young men, with all that that implies. Boys pretend to scoff at such things but I don't think they do really—they like us to be pure and at their mercy or else whores who needn't trouble their consciences. But whores at least get *paid*. To me you are a pearl of great price whose value will never diminish, but, then, I am your intensely loving

Mother

June 8

Vikshipta—

Your conduct toward me during meditation today was unforgivable. It is one thing to "let the garbage out of your system" and another to spew it all over another person. Our relationship was always somewhat primitive and tinged with your acculturated hysteria and sadism but your remarks spoken before the entire appalled group were beyond all bounds. I am no doubt the humblest of fledgling sannyasins; the other person, however, whom you named in your grotesque fit of jealousy and abuse is close enough to the Arhat, I believe, to see you removed from your present pseudo-psychiatric position of petty tyranny and stationed instead for your own therapy in the farthest, hottest artichoke field, where the Sachchidananda can just barely be coaxed to insert its trickles. I will *not* mention this degrading incident to her. In return for my tact I ask—*demand*—respect, restraint, and relinquishment from you.

> Sincerely,
> Kundalini

June 15

Dear Mother—

Please don't send me any more trashy clippings from the Miami and Fort Lauderdale papers. It is sensationalist untruth based on third-hand rumors, by reporters who wouldn't know a spiritual value if it came and bit them on the ankle. If Charles hadn't somehow found out where I was and told you and you hadn't told all your neighbors they wouldn't be upsetting you by showing you all these stupid clippings. There are no orgies here. There is just love in its many forms. The only hot tubs are for religious purposes, to give sensory-deprivation drills and to encourage people already inclined that way to have out-of-body experiences. If you knew anything about yoga or Buddhism you would know the idea is to get out of the body for good, not to achieve physical pleasure. The state we all strive for here is perfect indifference. As to the Arhat's legal troubles back in India, which these so-called "investigative reporters" keep digging up, any government now has so many rules and regulations that if the officials get it in for you they can hound you into jail or out of the country if they want, as happened in his case. It's the same sad story here. The immigration people and the land-use technocrats and the local ranchers' hired legal guns are doing everything to crush our beautiful experiment in non-competitive living. The Arhat preaches peace and serenity in a world whose economy is based on war and agitation. The commercials on all those shows you poison your mind watching all the time (did you get the packet of the Arhat's pamphlets I sent you?—try for starters *Transcending Abhinivesha: Beyond the Will to Live*, or maybe the one on the three gunas and the fifteen sub-modalities, to give you a necessary frame of reference)—what are they all *doing* (the commercials) but agitating you to want something you don't have? Not you personally—you should have all the things you want and need, thanks to Daddy and both my grandfathers, not to mention all the ancestors before them, piling up earthly goods to signify divine election—but people in general, the American people. No other people in the world is expected to get as whipped up over wanting as we are. The consumer society needs people in a constant state of material agitation but not so much so that the agitated people violate others' property rights—if you can't hold on to a thing you have less motive to acquire it, and that's what drugs and all the crime with them are doing, de-materializing America to an extent. That's why every city keeps a police force the size of an army, to keep the wanting and buying feasible. *Our* police force does nothing but guard our fences and screen visitors. People at peace within themselves and non-attached from material things don't steal and don't need laws. We do what we want, but under the Arhat's gorgeous influence we all want the same thing—his love and approval. One of your articles, I forget which—I got so mad I threw the whole batch into the shredder the office has here at the back, in case the federal authorities ever descend—called us brainwashed yuppie slaves but the fact is work is worship for us, and when you are in the right space spiritually the more you give the more you have. It's even in the Bible but no Christian believes it any more.

What made me absolutely the *most* indignant and heartsick, though, was that snide piece about the Arhat's limousines and wristwatches with diamond-studded bands and his shoes ordered by the dozen from a London bootmaker and the rest of it. The fact is the Arhat is absolutely penniless—everything goes into the Treasury of Enlightenment and is incorporated or set up as a trust and he has no idea of what comes in and goes out. He is so truly beyond material things that he just innocently assumes whatever he needs or desires will materialize. He really *does* live like the lilies and the birds of the air. Furthermore, his diamonds are meant to symbolize for his followers the jewel trees of the Buddha Realm, the incredible Land of Bliss that we meditate upon to break down the logical mind so nirvana can enter in. As it happens, I see the Arhat fairly often now in connection with my work—not just taking dictation as I was but giving advice sometimes (something Charles incidentally never asked for, my advice) and other times just sitting and sharing his silence—and there has never been a sweeter, gentler, wiser, saner man. One half of me wants to get the entire world to love him as I do, and the other half selfishly wants to keep him all to myself. Not that that's possible: he is surrounded by love, he gives off so much love-energy himself. "Luff-enerchee" is the way he says it. He even says that I—*I*, Mother, whom you raised to be such a proper little Bostonian female prick—have this luff-enerchee. One of the things he likes about me (you will die) is my skin, which you always said was so disgustingly dark and oily, so I looked dirty even after I'd had a bath—you wanted me to have your own rice-paper complexion, with a few tasteful freckles across the shoulders and on the back of the hands just to let us know you were real, and you *did* use to look stunning, like some powdery woman from Marie Antoinette days, going out to a formal do in a low-cut dress, leaving me all lumpy and plump and adolescent and miserable and dirty-looking behind in the house. I *do* hope, on this subject, you've given up your absurd attempt to get a tan and are using a Number 15 sunblock even if you're just going outdoors to get into the car and go shopping. With PABA—not only does it prevent further damage but it helps mend the DNA damage that has occurred, along with the zinc and A and E you should be taking as I think I wrote you before.

Charles, as you may know—I have no idea how much you two are communicating behind my back, I can't bear to think of it, it's too klishta, too duhshama as we say—has gone to England to press his side of the story on Pearl, who seems infatuated with a very unsuitable-sounding boy from the Lowlands. I've always hated the Dutch ever since that sadistic Mrs. Van Liew you used to stick us with while you and Daddy went off on one of your cruises or precious New York or Tanglewood weekends. She had these really delusional things about germs and God and kept making us wash our hands before even having a graham cracker and would go into these religious raptures at bedtime that got me so upset I would wet the bed. Jeremy I don't think ever did recover, that's why he went to South America—so he could have a graham cracker without washing his hands. Only down there they call them tortillas.

I'm *glad* you rolled over the CDs as I suggested. The stock market really isn't for people advanced in age with short-range goals; don't forget that, buy or sell, the broker takes a commission, and that's all he cares about. If you're *frantic* to get rid of some of all that old IBM and AT&T Daddy bought for a dollar a share, the head accountant here, a very clever woman called Nitya Kalpana, with as it happens some nervous problems at the moment, has developed a really advantageous method of giving whereby you sign over shares and take a tax deduction for the full market value somehow twice, without paying for any of the capital gains—strange as it sounds I think you'd show a better profit giving it to us than by selling it. And besides which, you'd make your little daughter *very proud*.

Isn't that a *crime* that that admiral is so shameless and

obtuse? Isn't there a rules committee or some such body you could complain to? It seems a pity to call the Boca police but he *does* sound unbalanced and not merely senile and though I know most crimes of passion are committed by Hispanics there's always the exception that makes the papers. Keeping your hurricane shutters down on the side where he comes knocking is all very well but as you say it cuts out the cross-draft and the view of the courtyard. Could you move to a second-floor condo? If he's as infirm as you describe him I don't see how he could climb the stairs. Really, aren't most men just terrible? Charles has got this new tough lawyer called Gilman who keeps writing me these rather comically officious letters about a Hertz car I mislaid and some other financial details that you can bet if a man had done them wouldn't strike him as nearly so high-handed. But the head cold I came with is quite gone at last and I feel quite *aklishta* (undisturbed, empty of impurities, only like every Sanskrit word there's more to it than that, there's a whole *lotus* of meanings). Without even trying I've lost five pounds (I think it's the not drinking that does it, and the no meat with its fat) and got my hair cut rather short—a friend of mine says I feel now like a nylon teddy bear. Don't forget to take calcium, and A not only for your skin but thyroid and eyes too—the best pills are the ones made from fish-liver oil—and to keep especially the Perkins silver out of the Florida air, in the *bottom* of the breakfront.

Many hugs,
Sare

P.S.: I was just joking about you and Mrs. Van Liew being responsible for Jerry's going off to South America. Don't brood about anything I write. I'm absolutely *hyper* with happiness these days, in spite of Charles and his clammy shadow, and have to let off steam.

June 18

Dearest, dearest A.—

It's so horrifying out here I have to drop you a note, on this motel stationery that amuses me so much I keep stealing it. *What* Babbling Brook? And who is this child dabbling in it? And these dark ominous trees? The real world hit me like a big hot fist. Traffic jams! Men in suits! Filthy sidewalks! Ugly unloving looks on all sides! The girl at the Hertz counter in Phoenix looked utterly bored to have the car back—*thank you* once more for finding it for me, and the keys—it was on my old-fashioned Puritan conscience and now I'm finally cleansed of my last, last iota of guilt toward Charles—and they will be billing the poor man thousands of dollars. She told me I should have gotten the long-term rate, I said I thought I would have it only a day or two. Now I'm terrified of taking the bus back to Forrest. I can't deal

with outside people any more. The terminal is sheer
hell—plastic bucket seats bolted to the floor, a whole
row with individual television sets screwed into the
arms so we can all keep up being cretinized while waiting, hideous non-music blaring, greasy people eating
greasy tacos and cheese-and-onion subs—the pathetic
stench of unenlightenment, of avidya. Obese morons in
cowboy boots and profoundly drunken Indians stare at
me as I sit scribbling this, trying not to tremble—I don't
look to the right or left, everybody looks so rough and
savage and *purposeless*, while this huge rude incompre-
hensible male voice keeps announcing bus departures—
it's as if I'm inside something horrible, churning and
stinking and grinding, it's as if I'm being *digested*, or will
be if I don't hold fast to the peace of the ashram. And
of you. I can't stop wanting to be with you. The quiet
of it. The non-speaking. The lightness of the speaking
when there is some. I keep touching my hair, that I cut
to please you, and the bristle and tingle of it startles me,
as if I'm not touching my own body, and I think of your
hair, its severely straight parting and the shimmer of it
brushed flat against your perfect skull, and the startling
darkness of it at the nape of your neck—like some animal glimpsed asleep in the dark of his burrow—when
your head nestles at the bottom of my abdomen, my
tummy you call it, your nape hair at its roots the same
raven-blond shade as that where there is, so beautifully
and refreshingly, no linga. Was he thinking of that
when he named you? He knows so much, even into the
future. I wish I could have sometime that tape of his you

mentioned, on Woman as the Portal to Moksha. Now I think my bus is being growled over the loudspeakers, people are milling at the gate already, crowding around as if to gobble up the carbon monoxide. What a trashy death pit the world truly is!

I won't send this in case D. *does* read our mail, but I so much wanted to reach out and touch you *now*. I'll slip it to you when you and Yajna pick me up in Forrest. I can't wait but *must*. I am, indeed, your devoted nayika,

K.

June 18, 1986

Gentlemen:

Enclosed find an endorsed check for eighteen thousand dollars ($18,000) for deposit to my account, #0002743-911. Your earlier receipts and statements are hereby acknowledged. My address continues as you have it.

Yours sincerely,
Sarah P. Worth

June 18

Dear Dr. Podhoretz—

Thank you for your cordial response. No, a July appointment will not do either, as I am staying in Arizona for a while longer. I am not living at this motel, by the way, but at an agricultural community about forty miles away. The drugstore there does have unwaxed dental tape and I have been fairly diligent, though sometimes at night I am so tired I can't make myself believe flossing matters as much as you say. Do Africans and Afghans always floss? They seem to have lovely teeth and gums, in photographs.

I bit down hard on a betel nut the other day and ever since then there has been not an ache exactly but a sort of apprehensive tenderness—not exactly tenderness, more of a vague *punky* feeling—in the lower right quadrant, where you said there tended to be tissue inflammation in any case. I do hope I don't have to go through another root canal! If worse comes to worst, I'll have the endodontist out here send you an X-ray for your records. The dental facilities are surprisingly adequate in this agri-commune, though I believe they use an outside lab for their gold and porcelain crown work.

Warm regards,
Sarah Worth

June 18

Dear Dr. Epstein—

I enclose a check for $180 to cover our last two appointments as billed by you. I trust that this clears up our accounts. I feel *I* should render an accounting of what I've been up to—as if the pseudo-daughterly guilty feelings that you led me to override in regard to Charles remain undischarged in regard to *you*. Looking back at my years of therapy, I confess that it all now seems much more patriarchal and Judeo-Christian than it did at the time. Far from being my ally against Charles as I fantasized, you were *his* ally against my liberation. Not that I blame you: I, too, was resisting my liberation, since I had no confidence of my finding a place in any world but the atrophied Puritan theocracy in which I had been raised, by parents whose sense of their own worth was inordinately tied to ancestral achievement, to being "our sort" of New Englanders. My father took, I think, real and dimly perverse pleasure in doing the absolutely predictable thing, in doing his piddling trust-officer thing in Boston and going to his clubs and dressing like a Harvard undergraduate to the day of his death, in striped tie and gray flannels and oxblood cordovans with little waxed laces.

Even at the time when I was most enchanted with our process it *did* cross my mind that Freud's notion of what went on inside Viennese women was somewhat absurd. I was once a little girl, for example, and until I was four, when my brother was born, I had no idea that little boys had penises, let alone that I should envy them for it. His looked like quite a comical little button, as I remember. My father always dressed in his room and once forbade me to go with him and Mother to a nudist beach on Martha's Vineyard, as I more than once told you. You never commented on whether or not this had been repressive of them.

I wonder now if the precious classic therapeutic silence isn't just another version of the Victorian father's silence, his awe-inspiring absence except at dinnertime, with the same disciplinary implications, at least as regards women. My knowledge of Hindu and Buddhist psychological thought is very imperfect but the notion of the subconscious as a pool of eddies (*vasanas*) that originate in memory and feed the conscious eddies (*chittavrittis*) and which certain exercises can eventually erase in a blissful motionless (*nirvana* = without wind) state of *samadhi* has—this way of putting things—a certain intimate, non-terroristic simplicity that appeals to me. Western psychology interfaces—to use a fashionable term—with society and morality, and Eastern with the body, with physiology—which rather better fits with the way, most days, I feel. I mean, should the game be to referee the war between superego, ego, and id, or to relax the whole system, by letting the ego and its harassing entanglements just fade away?

At any rate, you did your best by your lights and that

is all any of us can do. I don't want to harass *you* with a long letter—though your bill gave me a shock, arriving out of a world of petty finance I had rather forgotten and showing by its resubmission that Charles has abandoned his responsibilities toward his wife's medical care. In fact, I *can't* write a long letter, since this motel where I am waiting for some friends to pick me up isn't very generous with its stationery to those who are not staying here as guests. I obtained my present supply by sauntering around outside and then nipping into a room that the Mexican maid had left open and stealing from the desk. Our old Sarah wouldn't have done that, would she? But once you perceive that all material and intellectual phenomena are just threads in a great weave of illusion (*maya, samsara*) it becomes oddly easy to act on your impulses. Property is not only theft, it's nonsense.

My best to Mrs. Epstein. All those years of Mondays I used to wonder and wonder what she was like and what *it* was like being married to such a marvellous understanding man. I suppose I was madly jealous of her—I know that's the kind of thing you people like to hear, it's all grist to your "transference" mill. But now she can be Bianca Jagger for all I care, and good luck to you both.

> With warm regards,
> Sarah Worth

June 18

Dear Martin—

Your mother in a nice letter to me thought it would help if I sent you a card. I'm sorry you're in jail but I have recently learned that all the material world is a jail. Develop inner *peace*.

Your well-wisher,
Sarah P. Worth

June 18

Dear Eldridge—

This is a mesa, which is Spanish for "table." There are a lot of them here, and you've probably seen some in television commercials—the one with the Nissan truck.

Your friend,
Sarah P. Worth

[*tape*]

"Sarvasam eva mayanam, strimayaiva vishishyate."
This is from an ancient Mahayana text and says, "Of all
the forms of illusion, woman is the most important."
For Buddha and his followers, woman is the portal of
release. She is that within the world which takes us out
of the world. She is that being through whom is made
manifest the karuna, the compassion, of nirvana, of
non-being. She is the living wonder of the world. The
mounds of her body are like temple-mounds; they symbolize nirvana. The lotus of her body is the lotus of
Sahasrara, of final illumination. "Buddhatvam yoshidyonisamsritam." That is a very important saying.
Repeat, please. "Buddhatvam yoshidyonisamsritam."
[*Responsive mumble.*] It means, "Buddhahood is in the
female organ." The yoni. The cunt. Buddhahood is in
the cunt. OM mani padme HUM. The jewel is in the
lotus. The jewel is the mind. The lotus is nirvana.
The mind dissolves in nirvana. But also the jewel is the
linga, the cock. The lotus is the cunt. The cock in the
cunt. This is bliss, rasa. This is samarasa, the bliss of
unity. This is Mahasukha, the Great Bliss. This is
Mahabindu, the great point, the Transcendental Void.
This is maithuna—fucking. This is Shiva and Shakti
united, purusha and prakriti united to make bliss; this
is sahaja. Sahaja is the state of non-conditioned existence, of the pure spontaneity. We must learn to acquire
the pure spontaneity. When Kundalini unites with

Atman, this is also sahaja. That is why we learn our mantras, learn our mudras. That is why we learn pranayama. That is why we strive to cleanse ourselves inside and out. To be nonconditioned, to have the pure spontaneity. Ommmm!

Buddha was not a nice boy. He was not a nice quiet boy with fat cheeks always sitting with his hands folded in his lap. He conquered Mara by the technique of maithuna, of fucking. Mara means "death." First Mara came to Buddha in the form of Kama, desire. When Buddha was not deterred from enlightenment by seductive desire, Mara got rough. Mara assailed Buddha with visions of many horrors, demons, animals, monsters with very bad-smelling breaths and armpits, shrieking ghosts. Among these horrors danced a little naked black woman bearing in her hand a skull and wearing a necklace of many little tiny skulls. This was Kali. She is death. Also she is desire and delight. She is the goddess of time. Death and desire are the children of time.

But our Lord Buddha had done his maithuna, his fucking. He had fucked his wife, Yashodhara, and made Rahula, his poor abandoned son. A prince in those days had many other ladies also. His father, Shuddhodana Gotama, had built for his son, called then Siddhartha Gotama, a pavilion of much luxury and equipped it with many ladies skilled in the ways of music and dance and love. So Mara could not shake Buddha. He who has known love has passed through the center of the world and cannot be shaken. Krishna among the Gopis knew endless love. Radha, his favorite mistress, became a goddess, bruised as she was by love, scratched and bloody with love, her clothes torn by love, her hair tangled, her body wet with the sweat of love, which is sweet. Again and again Radha faints. Again and again the touch of Krishna restores her to vigor and to love. Then he multiplies himself nine hundred thousand times and copulates with nine hundred thousand Gopi women. The gods and the goddesses and the sages in the heavens watch with dumbfoundment. The goddesses faint many times while watching but in the desire to learn maithuna ask to be born all over India in the form of little princesses in the palaces of kings. They are born then. This is the fact. This is what happened in the glades of Vrindavan, as reported faithfully in the Brahmavaivarta Purana. OM mani padme HUM.

Once a Brahmin sage comes to Buddha very indignant. "What is all this fucking?" he says. "It is not in the Vedas!" Buddha says to him, "Women are the gods. Women are life. Be ever among women in thought!" This is a true historical saying. There is this evil thought in religion: Women are impure. Women distract men away from God. They are like dirt on the lens. Their rajas are impure. This is evil superstition. The rajas of women are no more impure than the sukra of men. Sukra is bindu, the point from which all comes. All life comes from sukra and rajas. They are joy. The lotus has its seed deep in the muck of the pond, and then its flower blooms on the surface, in air. That is why the lotus is the symbol of wisdom as well as the symbol of woman. The lotus is the symbol of Lakshmi, the wife of Vishnu. She is the Mother Goddess. Now, what does a mother do? She sends the children out to play, then she calls them back in, back home. She calls them home to earth, to death. The lotus is nothingness. You in the West fear nothingness. "Save me from nothingness, great bearded Jehovah!" you cry and imagine He says from the cross, "Today thou shalt be with Me in paradise," when in fact He says only, "I thirst." You in the West fear nothingness and the beauty of the lotus. You must learn to worship the lotus. Men and women alike must learn to worship what a woman has at her root. There is this phrase, "lotus-eaters." It means someone who is asleep. But in fact the lotus-eater is not asleep, he is wide awake, his consciousness has ascended to its limits, his consciousness is no longer captive to his ego. What is ego? It is ahamkara. "Aham" is the sound "I," ego is making the sound "I." As soon as in evolution prakriti learned to say "I," it first felt fear, and then desire. That is ahamkara.

He who learns to worship the lotus, to dissolve his chittavrittis in consciousness of the lotus, that man—or woman, it might be, for woman is in the man and man is in woman—that man or woman says "thou," knowing that "thou" is the same as "I." Tat tvam asi: that thou art. Thou art atman, thou art brahman, thou art adipurusha, the Universal Man. He or she who knows that is wide awake. He or she eats the lotus. He or she drinks the rajas, which means not just blood but all female secretions. The rajas are nectar. The rajas are angel food. The rajas are rasa, which means "bliss." Rasa also means "sap." The divine sap rising in the woman, that is rajas. A man who is not enlightened has this fear of nothingness that comes from saying "I." When a man has this fear, he turns to woman. She is mother. She is common sense. She has no fear. She is prakriti before it thought "I." He turns to her. He makes love to her. He inhales her aroma. He looks into her black eyes and sees the redness of her mouth when she laughs. There is a poem that says, "Put away the idea of two and be of one body." The fear that he has goes away. She is maya, she is nothingness. Who knows the name of the mother of Buddha, whose father was called Shuddhodana? [*Distant shout.*] Yes. It was Maya. Buddha was born of Maya.

You in the West fear nothingness because you think God is a big bearded fellow in the sky who will crush you. You think, "How can I make that Big Guy like me better?" You think, "I will hate myself, then He will like me. I will hate all cunts, because they give me bliss. Then God will like me very much." In India too, they torture themselves, to burn away the ego and its fear. They sit naked on burning rocks. They stare at the sun until the eyeballs are all white and quite blind. They make fists until their fingernails grow out the other side. You ask, "Is it hurting?" They say, "No, it feels fine. I am enjoying samadhi." That is one way. That is the way of "neti neti"—"not this, not that." Not anything, and then what is left will be good. That is the way of yoga. There is another way, the way of bhoga. Bhoga means "pleasure." The way of bhoga says "iti iti"—"it is here, it is here." Buddha and Brahman are in everything. In kama, pleasure. In rasa, sap. Say no to nothing. Brahman, Buddha are in you also. You are the same mystery. When ego dissolves, purusha is there. Eat the lotus. No Big Guy will crush you. You are Brahman. [*Loudly*] OM. Buddha is yours. You carry him about like a little fetus curled in the shadow of your mind, and in this same way he carries you. [*Louder still*] OMMM.

[*end of tape*]

June 26, 1986

Gentlemen:

To follow up our letter of May 24: our former chief accountant, Ma Prem Nitya Kalpana, has due to the mental stress of her responsibilities taken a permanent leave of absence, and the matter of your unpaid bills for six Lincoln limousines is being investigated by her successors. The disorder of the accounts is formidable, but we hope to be getting back to you soon.

With every good wish,

Shri Arhat Mindadali, M.A., Ph.D.

Supreme Meditator, Ashram Arhat

/k

July 2

Dear Jerry—

What a pleasant surprise to hear from you! Yes, I am well, and trust you are the same. Caracas must be lovely this time of year—but, then, it's lovely all the time of the year, isn't it, being on the equator and a plateau and near the sea all at once? Here it is *hot*, 110° is not uncommon, but as I work in an air-conditioned office I don't really mind it, except that in changing from the chilly indoors to sizzling outdoors I've caught one of my wretched colds. When we were growing up I used to blame the germs you brought home from the boys' gym or locker room—I can't do that now, can I?

I don't know what alarming stuff Mother has been feeding you but your implied chastisements are really rather amusing. And old-hat! This is a spiritual place but also a hard-working place, and my colleagues are not outmoded flower-children and drug-dazed losers as you sweetly put it but well-educated and highly integrated men and women trying to create here an alternative life-style for so-called *Homo sapiens*, based on our higher instead of our baser attributes. We are not the first and won't be the last to beat against the tide of consumeristic materialistic capitalistic garbage, but the effort is at least as worth making as your life which as far as I can tell is spent sucking up to the Venezuelans who are getting rich sucking the oil out of poor helpless

Lake Maracaibo. I don't judge *you*, and when you made the South American move it was I, at that time Mommy's good little girl, the typical doctor's wife tending the garden of her typical lovely North Shore home, who stuck up for Kid Brother and suggested, albeit timidly since Mother was still in her fearsome prime, that approaching thirty maybe you had a right to your own life. You're welcome, though I don't recall getting any thanks.

The person you *should* be writing sly advisements to is our dear *madre*. Never, really, the most acute manageress of her affairs, family or otherwise, she is flipping her lid down there, in my opinion—acting and dressing like a seventy-year-old beach bimbo (she watches with inane delight something called "Golden Girls" on television), going out on disgusting dinner "dates" (I think at that age the thrill is mostly in just the eating, but God knows) with some octogenarian former admiral she's lured into her sun porch, and doing unspeakable things with what little of Daddy's money she hasn't already wasted. She's fallen in with some smooth young broker who's got her to believe she's the Hetty Green of South Florida—by the time the two of them get done "adjusting" her portfolio there won't be so much as a treasury bond left. There is a whole tribe of people in Florida— brokers, podiatrists, chiropractors, faith healers, home helpers, seductive practical nurses—who prey on the old and senile, and one of my fears as Mother gets battier is she'll give all the silver away as a tip to the boy who trims the palm trees in her patio.

To Jerry

You're just a little blue water away from her, and all of your fancy hidalgo friends have fail-safe apartments in Miami in case the Sandinistas take over—couldn't you go visit her and see what's going on? My intuition is she's being taken terrible advantage of by *men*. She always was man-crazy, let's face it—all those nights dragging poor Daddy off to some party or other so she could flirt and flash her boobs while all he wanted was to sit home marinating in his old books and having yet another whiskey, leaving us in the care of some evangelical monster like Mrs. Van Liew or that girl from Needham whose boyfriends tried to keep us quiet with tokes of pot. Think of it if she gets married again—Daddy's ashes whirling in their grave, and all those lovely Perkins and Price and Peabody antiques distributed among our step-siblings, of whom I'm sure the admiral will supply a greedy passel. I'd go myself but I'm very tied up here—I've become rather important in running the place, funnily enough.

Happy Independence Day, if you remember what that is, and *devoción mucho* to Esmeralda and the six little ones from their loving *tía* and *hermana política*. The Latin element you see in the Southwest isn't as classy as your set in Monte Avila. Actually, Jere, you'd like it here—lots of after-hours action, and more opportunities for wheeling and dealing than you might imagine.

Fondly in spite of all wrongs past and present,

Sis

To Midge

[tape]

Oh my goodness, dear Midge, what a time we've been having! *Loved* hearing all your news, it brought me back to the real world. How awful that Irving's framing shop was robbed! Well, as you say, it should strengthen his non-attachment. Thank God he never has any *real* works of art in there. And how sad about Donna's husband! They really had no warning? It's hard to believe we're all getting to that age, when the wheel of karma takes us for another spin. Of course, he *was* ten years older than she, and Donna a bit elderly herself. I used to worry about her noisy breathing during the Sun Salutations—it was rather distracting, to be frank. As to Ducky Bradford, I'm not surprised. There was always something not quite *right* there, even when he and I were closest and I suppose you could say I was in love with him. I wouldn't have admitted that four months ago, but needless to say I've shed some inhibitions. Tell Gloria being left for a gay is no worse than being left for another woman, in fact it's better, since it shows you were fighting a losing game all along. Foolish is what she must feel, mostly—men *do* make you feel foolish, unless you watch your step with them *every inch*. What a woman has to realize is that as far as she's concerned *she's* number one, too, just like a man. I don't mean number one-two, I mean number one also. You know— we're conditioned to think of ourselves as number two, like Eve and Avis.

Where was I when we left off? I can't believe I was still in love with Vikshipta and bumping around on a backhoe. I'm living now with two other women—one other woman, really, since the third woman, Nitya, has had a kind of nervous breakdown or overdose of something and is in the infirmary here. She was the head accountant and juggled all the finances—you have no idea, Midge; they have investments everywhere, and Kali Club discos in places like West Germany and Israel, and meditation-and-massage centers, and of course bookstores and video outlets in a lot of malls and downtowns now across the entire U.S., around the world in fact—there's a very important bookstore in the Bahamas, on one of the outer islands where you wouldn't think people would read much, but apparently they must, or maybe it's mostly mail-order business. The way it seems to function, the publishing end of it, including all the tapes of the Arhat like the one I sent to Irving—evidently free of charge since I haven't received any check from you yet—and the therapy and yoga lessons you can take from video cassettes, all this end of it does its accounts through this one store because banking in the Bahamas is somehow easier, I guess because, being so tiny, it doesn't have all the usual oppressive regulations and wants to encourage dollars. As a businessman, the Arhat is wonderfully open and permissive—whenever a group of sannyasins start up a car-wash business or a restaurant or an escort service, he lets them use his name and picture and the sunset colors. I guess anybody could put on a purple jumpsuit and a mala and perform the same services, but people

like to see the Arhat's name on the front door or up in
lights or wherever, because it signifies that the people—
the people operating the businesses—are always so serene and cheerful and don't drink or do street drugs,
and of course, because work for us is worship instead
of slave-wage labor, we can charge a little less. It's a
beautiful philosophy, as you can see from the fact that
it *works*. I mean, it works in the world as well as here.

Anyway, poor dear little Nitya, who used to be a
stock analyst in Seattle before she saw the Arhat being
interviewed on "Donahue," has been under the
weather mentally, and the various medications that Ma
Prapti—she's the head of the clinic here, and a *very*
impressive woman, absolutely dedicated and the direct
opposite of all Charles's money-hungry pretentious colleagues at MGH—the different pills and injections she
was giving Nitya to keep her on an even keel began to
work at cross-purposes, and my friend Alinga, I think
I mentioned her briefly before, is training *me* to take
over. You know I used to be good at numbers, I used to
do all of Charles's billings and insurance-claim forms,
before he got a secretary to take over, that slut Marcelene Rabinowitz as it turned out. Well, I'm all over that
now, and beyond anger, really, of any sort, or any emotion except love and acceptance. Charles now just seems
impossibly small, like one of those bugs you see crawling across a piece of paper or a bathroom tile and
though it looks like a mere dot you know if it was
magnified enough would show fangs and hairy legs and
long pokey things, but who wants to bother? He's been
rather quiet since he went to spy on Pearl—I bet she

told him off. Do tell me if he approaches you again, and don't not be rude to him for *my* sake. You can be as rude as you want.

I'm sitting here in my office, it used to be Alinga's but she's moved up to Nitya's, which is next to where Durga, when she's here and not on the road doing talk shows and promotion, has a kind of anteroom to the Arhat's ranch house, which I think I told you about last time, with all this silvery fat cheap furniture in it, and the bleached-wood desk. Everybody else is off for their siesta but, you know me, I never could take a nap in the middle of the day, I'm too hyper—Irving used to say my subtle body was tuned up too high for my sthula one. Also there's a lot of sludge to work through in Nitya's account books and records—*heaps* of papers and figures, and nothing quite matching up, as far as I can see—it's really too much for anyone to make total sense of. I shouldn't talk, I guess, even to you, about the finances, but, in a nutshell, on the one hand there really *are* substantial assets and income and some very generous donors, mostly these women and widows who either live in Beverly Hills or in Canada, oddly enough, which you don't think of as much of a place normally either for money or for Buddhism, and then on the other side of the ledger a lot of leakages that aren't just the Arhat's limousines and diamond wristwatch bands. Even though everybody works free as a form of worship, the ashram still didn't come out of thin air; there were millions spent on the A-frames and the trailers and the mall and now the Hall of a Millionfold Joys—the steel is all in place but they're waiting now for the sunset-colored vinyl panels—and all the kinds of construction—just one backhoe costs sixty thousand dollars, did you know that!—and the irrigation and septic systems, even though both could be better, let me tell you, especially the latter. Now that the really hot months are here, there's a stink comes up from where they buried the septic tanks, and the creek is so low they've turned off the Fountain of Karma except for half-hours at sunset and dawn, and the fields are baking hard as clay even though Hanuman, our agricultural supervisor, who used to teach plant synergy at Michigan State, bought miles and miles of gauze and had the artichokes and hybrid tomatoes and experimental poppies covered with it to make shade. Also all the fencing and armaments and surveillance equipment our security forces need costs more than a penny, believe me, Midge. Their chief, this nice young man Agni, is very close to Durga and in her office all the time, murmuring and shouting and laughing, and I suppose there can be no arguing that we do need all this security, there is so much hatred in the world against simple love and peace. The lawsuits are another expense—these various pompous self-important authorities are pretending we've infringed water rights, zoning laws, land-use regulations, even immigration laws—they want to send Fritz back to Germany and the Arhat back to India! Really, this is what you get nowadays for making the desert bloom and offering our poor poisoned world an example of life-style a notch or two above the rat race. I'm telling you all just so you'll have an idea of the tangle I'm trying to deal with in my new capacity.

You ask about the Arhat. What can I say you don't already know from his publicity?—except that, up close, he seems a little sad, and I have this ridiculous instinct to mother him. I see him quite often now, usually along with Alinga or Durga or Satya, who's in charge of PR, and it seems often they have to put the words in his mouth, since he does nothing when they describe this or that emergency to him but smile and look as if he wishes he were elsewhere. Of course, he *is* a jivan-mukta, which means he's really in nirvana and is staying on earth only to be polite, in a way—about the only thing that perks him up is getting more publicity for the ashram, even publicity that seems adverse to the rest of us. For instance, he insists on being driven every afternoon way over to Forrest to get a Diet Coke from the machine in the bus station there—not actually a station, just a cement shelter next to the motel—and every time he does it there are more picketing people there, local rednecks and Pentecostal Chicanos angry about one thing or another and most of all about the Arhat's being so simply *beautiful*, and so now Agni has to send a vanful of security personnel along in case there's an attack, which in turn brings out more rednecks, with shotguns and clubs and ropes—it's not as if we don't have Diet Coke right here at the ashram, but when Durga pointed out all this to him he just smiled and said—I *wish* I could do his accent—"We must rup the bastards' noshes in it. It amushes me and it amushes Buddha."

[*Leaving off attempted accent and becoming conspiratorial.*] Midge. I just had the most ex*cit*ing idea. It's *scary*, it's so exciting. If the next time I go in to see him I could carry this little tape recorder in my bra under my sari, so the little grid that picks up sound sticks up so only the one layer of silk is in the way, maybe I can get something of his actual casual conversation for you and Irving and the girls to hear! It would be strictly private, of course—you mustn't make or sell duplicates or anything—but I *do* so want to share with you his precious presence while I still can. It would also be for history— I don't really think, *entre* just *nous*, the ashram is going to last forever. I think it's too big a step up for the way the world is now. The outside pressure—all these lawyers and reporters and visiting firemen and county officials in suits, they've become so common around the Chakra we don't even chant and shake tambourines at them any more—all this outside pressure is beginning to tell, everybody acts antsy and spooked—Ma Prapti says she has no more beds for bad drug trips, and Durga goes around with this icy-white face and staring green eyes looking like the Gorgon, and my dear friend Alinga spaces out more and more—sometimes, honestly, I feel I'm the only sane one left. The heat, no kidding, is terrific! A hundred twenty, twenty-five every day from eleven to four. That place I used to go out by the red rocks to be by myself is like an oven now, even after the sun goes down. I don't know how the lizards keep from getting fried. Be grateful for your sea breeze and all those leafy oaks and maples. To think, we used to sleep under a puff even this time of year! If I sound homesick, maybe I am. I miss the sea and also frankly I could do sometimes with a pop of Jack Daniel's, the way we used to do after yóga, to settle the shakti and stirred-up vrittis, after Irving had left. Oops. I shouldn't have put that on tape, in case you play it for him. And I've never figured out how to erase. Well, anyway, I've said plenty for now, let's leave some tape for later, for what I said.

[*Breathlessly*] O.K., Midge, here we go. [*Noise. Amplified cloth and finger friction. Underlying rustling that may be heartbeat. Much ensuing silence and some unintelligibility. Female voices, difficult to distinguish. One male voice, indicated below by italics.*] Shanti, guru.

Namaste, Master.

Namaste, my nayikas.

Come on, let's get the shit rolling.

Durga, don't be so rude. Just because you're uptight—

Oh listen to her now. Listen to the corn-fed princess. Easy for you to say don't do this or that. For you this is all one more space shot. I wouldn't be uptight either if I were you. When it all goes down the drain you'll go back to Cedar Rapids and have Daddy finance six weeks in Guadeloupe at an all-girl Club Med.

Oh dear, one of those days. Darling Durga. That's quite unfair. I'm as committed as you are.

Why would it all go down the drain? How could it, when it's so basically splendid?

Committed to your own artha is what you are. Committed to your own kama and your little roommate's padma. Could you ask her possibly to keep her mouth shut where she doesn't know a bloody thing? She just got here, for sweet Jesus' sake.

She is not little. She is stately.

She knows plenty. She's been facing up to the mess Nitya left in the books, while you've been off with your great gift of gab telling that talk show in Phoenix what a shit every official in the state is.

I didn't say the state, I just said Dorado County. And I restrained myself from saying a blessed word about all the shits in the FBI and the INS.

I thought it was truly delicious. The lady hostess, the talk-show lady with her enamelled face and little microphone in her lapel, quite forgot her smooth talk. She suffered the shock of enlightenment before the eyes of her million viewers.

And while you've been off playing Ma Barker to those freckle-faced security kids up in the canyon, Satya and Prapti and I have been trying to cope with all these old wheezy guys from the county that keep showing up.

The building inspector says the whole septic system is illegal and must be dug up before it bubbles up. He says we're sitting on a volcano, so to speak, and obviously can't have outdoor plumbing on the A-frames, and that on the original application they were called "winterized tents." This other man, from the medical licensing board, says our so-called clinic is simply a drug distribution center.

That must be libel. That must be legal slander. I have my licenses, everything is licensed and they know it.

It's the bloody nuisance value, that's all they care

about. That's all any of them care about. They're shits. They're ignoramus cowboy fascist shits.

Well, you can see how it must all look to them. They're under pressure—

Shut up, you. Alinga, can't you shut your sweetheart up? Just because she's twice as old as you—

Why should Sarah shut up? She's been digging into facts while you just keep dealing in fantasies.

Let Kundalini speak.

I was just going to say, the county is under pressure from the state officials, who are under pressure from the ecology lobby and the newspapers and the nationwide media. The way they see it, we've made Arizona into a laughingstock. If we could just have fewer stories for a while, and be less confrontational with the other people in the county, who after all were here first—

You know nothing about these rotten shits. They carry shotguns. They're fanatic ruthless Protestants. You come here from some prettified Eastern suburb and you think making a Buddha Realm in the teeth of all this fascism is like throwing a tea party for the fucking hired help.

Maybe if we didn't keep calling them fascists. They're just Americans—

I can't listen to her any longer. Master, I can't. I can't stand her voice, that simpering Lady Bountiful voice. Look at the way she keeps patting herself on the chest, as if to say, "Oh, dearie me." I abhorred her emanations the day she showed up here—I knew she didn't understand us and never would, how we're trying to make something *new* here, and the new always has to destroy the old. The old ego has to be destroyed. She doesn't understand that. She hasn't listened to your wisdom. She's full of phalatrishna, full to her blooming eyeballs. I dare say she doesn't even know what phalatrishna is. It hurts me to listen to her, and that's God's honest fact. Physically *hurts*. Her smug voice goes on and on in my head like a buggering dentist's drill.

Honestly, Durga. You're the one who's going on and on. Maybe you should take a rest in the clinic along with Nitya.

There are no beds. We are almost out of tranquillizers.

It means "thirst for fruits." Phalatrishna means the thirst for results satisfying to the ego. I am not that. I thirst only for the greater glory of the Arhat, that the peace we enjoy within his love may be extended to everybody.

Begob, listen to her! Like a bloody parrot!

I have said, Let Kundalini speak. What does she find in Nitya's books of accounting?

There are assets, still. But not what there should be, in view of the tremendous expenditures here. And not what they were. The sale of books, tapes, posters, and T-shirts are all off. The perfumed soaps and bath oils and incense cones are holding up, but I'm afraid they were always a minor item. The worst thing is that a lot of the regional meditation-and-massage centers have simply gone out of business rather than conform with the centralization policies that have been handed down.

Those little centers were pits. They were cesspools.

Some hadn't the foggiest idea what massage therapy was, or bioenergetics. They were plain and simple whorehouses.

Durga dear, you've become such a prude. You used to be fun.

Aye, your kind of fun.

Still, the staff were donating their services and shared their profits with the Treasury of Enlightenment, in exchange for using the Arhat's image.

And his inspi*r*ation, Polly. Don't forget to parrot that. The ex*a*mple of his *love.*

Quite so. Work was their worship and they were happy, as we all are. Why turn them off? You went around terrifying everybody, demanding more and more, a bigger and bigger cut, saying they should rob their parents, pretend to illnesses they didn't have, smuggle dope—

I never told them to smuggle dope.

You told them to gather sweets where they could. The two sannyasins who were caught with cocaine down in Nogales said it was on divine orders and they had been brainwashed.

Of course the little twats would say that. Anything to save their little skins.

I am disturbed about the T-shirts.

Durga, I've *heard* you tell the sannyasins at darshan that on their visits home if they steal their mother's jewelry it would be doing her a favor.

We perhaps need another scandal to increase the sale of T-shirts. Always in America there is the danger of being forgotten. Fashion moves with a shameless speed.

I said it would help their parents spiritually, and in God's truth it would. What's happened to you, Alinga? This person has reinfected you with bourgeois values. This whole squabble is bourgeois. Am I the only man, woman, or creature here still trying to create the future?

That sounds like rather a bourgeois thing to be doing, if I may say so.

You looked as smug and sassy as *she* does, saying that. That same little cock of the head, the little complacent tucks in the corners of the mouth. Maybe *you're* the parrot.

Dear Durga, if you'd ever listen to our Master, instead of trying to become Master yourself—

Oh! That's too vile. That's too easy. That's shit and you know it.

I don't know it. How would I know it? Everybody in the ashram, everybody down to the flakiest sannyasin, knows you're trying to take over but don't have the touch. The touch has to be light, my dear. Light. You're heavy-handed. *You're* the fascist, not those poor cowboys and Indians and plumbing inspectors out there.

Ma Prapti. You heard this butch bitch. You heard what these harridans are saying to me. Say something.

What can I say? The spirit of our enterprise is changing. You might say it has been poisoned. Many of those who come to the clinic are unhappy. Formerly they were happy, even when they were very disturbed.

Order must be allowed to emerge from disorder. To impose order is to create another layer of disorder.

You. Don't *you* start in on me now. Your foolish

limousines. All those ostentatious jewels. No honest
jivan-mukta needs tons of useless jewels.

*Amitabha goes drenched in jewels through the Buddha
Realms in the West. Millions of jewel flowers tremble wherever
he walks, through the towering jewel forests.*

Oh sweet Christ. Come off it, Art.

Art?

That's what she calls him.

She does?

Look, all of you. There's a conspiracy to destroy us
out there. The state is suing us, the county, the Keep
Arizona Clean crazies, the parents of that sannyasin
who died of hypothermia coming back from the Kali
Club—

And *why* are they suing, dear Durga? Because you're
constantly provocative. Because you've turned this
charming dream of a Buddha Field into Gestapo head-
quarters.

To maintain order. To maintain our privacy. So female leeches like you can go around with your wide
smirk of a mouth and suck hold of the next new body.

*Perhaps, were it to be announced that I have attained yet
another level of enlightenment—*

The press is bored with your enlightenment. They
never believed it anyway. They want dirt now. Dirt
and blood. That's what they always want, actually.

They want rajas. They want action. Ha.

Uh, not to be compulsive about detail, but there were
some practical things I noticed, going over the account
books. There's a great deal of long-distance telephoning
from the Uma Room and the hacienda. Australia, Thai-

land, Scandinavia. It adds up terribly, even with direct
dialling.

What's Polly saying now? We should all take vows of
silence? We should give up being international and con-
fine ourselves to converting the fascist shits of Dorado
County?

And the travel expenses—

I have to make appearances. I have to solicit support.
I have to contact these filthy regional centers you're so
enamored of.

But the hotels you stay in, and the number of people
you take with you on these jaunts—

They're not jaunts. They're raids into enemy territory. I need every soldier. Vikshipta makes a spellbind-
ing presentation, and if people don't hear about the
Way from a man they think it's just hysterical meno-
pausal voodoo. Satya has a cunning head for details and
contacts everywhere—without her, I'd have no visibil-
ity. Nagga is learning the ropes and enchants people;
everybody adores her, even the most cynical. And who
are *you* that I have to justify myself? Alinga, Ma Prapti:
why am I being challenged by this, this novice, this
interloper? Were *you* with the Master in Ellora? Did *you*
have to suffer three years of dysentery and sixteen grill-
ings by the Indian police? They'd never seen a redhead
before, they couldn't get enough of me.

I'm sure they couldn't.

It's just that the sannyasins in the fields and the
kitchen, the young people making the beds and building the ring road, doing all the dirty work, are well
aware—

Let them *be* aware! The snivelling shits. We're giving them the ride of their lives. No responsibilities. No guilt. Just fucking and dancing and saying Om and watching God go by in a stretch limo. And what do *they* contribute? Hardly enough labor to make it worth feeding them. It *isn't* worth feeding them, in fact—the kitchen runs at a terrible loss, that's why I have to go around begging and making an impression all the time, to raise the contributions to keep these parasites in the bliss of living here. Spoiled Americans, they eat like pigs. They should be eating less. The meals are *much* too extravagant—sannyasins in India get by with a spoonful of rice and a raw locust or two. In Ireland they got by generation after generation on a potato a day and still wrote the greatest poetry in the world. Don't ask *me* to pity these greedy fat Yanks, they'd eat the world if the Russians weren't around. They're supposed to come here giving us all their worldly goods as the most basic spiritual exercise, the very bloody least they can do, and as sure as Harry's hat they've all got millions tucked away in bank accounts. Gob, right in this very room—

—are well a*ware*, is all I was going to say, of the dreadful inequalities here. Of course they want the Master to have all the jewels he wants, as an outward sign of—

Say it! His inward grace! See! Sari and all, the bitch still thinks like a Christian! Like a stinking little Anglican!

This is too wild. I can't go on.

Good. Your humble servant neither. I've been

humiliated and heckled enough for one day. I've absorbed enough shit from this person—this little Miss Priscilla Pilgrim here.

But Durga darling, what shall we all do? About everything.

Not only tranquillizers and antidepressants. We're out of antibiotics for venereal disease, the ones we can still treat, and lithium for the bipolars. . . .

The chairman of the County Commission and the sheriff have both written threatening to get warrants issued. . . .

[Silence. Rustling. Heartbeat?]

You ladies are all looking toward me.

Not me. I've given fucking up on you, to be frank.

You are looking toward me because you have not learned your lessons well enough. You have not practiced your asanas. You have not destroyed your egos. Therefore you feel fear and you feel uncertainty. You are still full of garbage. I cannot release you from garbage. You must release yourselves. When you are klishta, when you experience vairagya, answers will arrive. Money will arrive, or money will not arrive. People will come, or people will go. The county commissioners will screw us, or will be screwed. It is all one. It is all of indifference. It is all of less matter than a blink of Buddha's eye.

Lord Jesus. And they call this a man.

Two great notions come to me. One, I wish to be on this John Carson show, as an amusing guest. I think he reaches many people of the night and thus he will re-energize our field. Also, he is amusing. This Ed McMahon. This supposed feud with Joan Rivers, and all this Hollywood wise talk. Ha. Two, let Kundalini stay with me, as you others go. We must discuss my jewels. Perhaps I must sacrifice them to her merciless account-ings.

You do that, Art.

Shanti, Master.

You two be good now.

[*Unintelligible voices, fading. Silence. Heartbeat.*]

It is not so, when ugly Durga calls you little. You are tall.

Five eight. Five eight and a half, actually.

You are not young, but your skin is smooth. Your hair is dark and abundant. Your posture is excellent. That is why I called you Kundalini. For her to make the ascent up Sushumna, the spine must be held very straight.

My mother was a stickler for posture. Posture and what fork to pick up and how to leave your knife so the waiter will know to clear.

This mother. Where is she now?

Florida.

She must be very rich.

Not really, Master. In truth I believe she is squander-ing in foolish investments the small amount that my late father did leave her.

She would perhaps think our ashram a foolish investment.

It would be, for her. Not for me. I love it here.

You have a good friend in Alinga, perhaps. She is also tall, but not so stately and upright as Kundalini.

She is very beautiful.

In an imperilled way. The way of a flower. She has imbibed too much indifference, not the holy vairagya of the yogas but that of this country, of its flatness and muchness that drives its people to sarcasm and mass murder. I am thinking of your West. Your East is more like my India. It teems—is that the expression? One big appetite, with the energy of appetite. You have this appetite, this energy. Alinga does not. Already, she slouches. She slumps. Her hair goes unwashed. She begins to wilt. She is like a cut flower.

She's been very kind.

She has shown you new asanas, I think. But once you had a husband?

I believe I still do. He was—is—a doctor. Rather handsome. Very efficient and work-oriented. An internist with an office at Massachusetts General Hospital.

Yet after some years with this technological marvel, you became bored. You took up yoga. You had flings.

Not very many. I've always been a good girl.

And you are a good girl here. Your letters are excellent. You can balance the books. You do not yet seem to have the madness.

The madness?

As you notice, with Ma Prem Durga. After much valuable service to Buddha and to Vishnu, she becomes irritable. She becomes erratic and overflowing with grievance. She loses spiritual touch. It is this stress of maintaining a religious ideal, of bucking the trend. In the larger world, responsibility is remote. In our smaller world, responsibility is intimate. There is no Big Guy to which the buck passes. We are the Big Guy. It is heavy.

For even you, Master?

Very heavy, I think, in my vasanas. All these operations— the agricultural workings, these therapies, the publishing houses that make my image over and over, the bookstores selling these images and my darshans with many typographical errors, the boutiques selling all clothes in the sunset colors that are also the colors of love, the natural-food stores and the massage parlors in these many places here and abroad that Durga must visit with such great expense—all these things run from my spiritual energy. You smile, why is that?

They *stem* from your spiritual energy, they run *on* it—either would be correct.

So. These things run on me, as you say. English is strange in its little words. In German there is the same thing, the strange floating little words only the natives can dispose properly. I have often considered that language is stranger than it seems. It conveys meaning, we perceive that, yes, but also it makes a tribal code, a way to keep out others. It is of that intricacy which in paper currency is meant to defeat counterfeiters. The religion of the Hindus and even more of the Jains has this repellent intricacy, which to be ideal must be endless, which piles upon the mind until the mind goes blank and may receive enlightenment. I forgive you for smiling at your Master.

Also, I love the way you say "love." Lufff.

Kundalini is a cruel tease of her poor overworked Master. Even she runs on me. The beelike sannyasins in their long lines come in from their ten or twelve sunny hours of work as worship and imagine they are now saints entitled to dance all night at the Kali Club and sneak their drugs and have their highs, but why are they permitted to do this, how have all these structures to ease their chittavrittis arisen? They are running on me, my spiritual energy, my lack of ego. It is false to say all things have a material explanation. All things material have a spiritual explanation. What do you think, Kundalini, is the essence of the world, of prakriti?

Its essence is illusion.

No. That would be too jolly. The essence of the world is pain. Is duhkha. Duhkha, and fear.

Oh dear.

Truly. "Oh dear" is the truth. You do not feel dubkha and bhaya because I am with you. But the pain and fear that is suppressed in you pushes over onto me, I have sucked it out of you, it comes into me as if into a vacuum. Dreadful terror. Only men and gods can hold such terror. With animals, death is over in an instant. With men, too, in actual misfortune, it is over in an instant—the animal numbness mercifully comes. But a man in repose, he can hang forever over this abyss of bhaya, this steep invisible terror that being alive brings. It is the clamoring of the million demons of death unleashed by Mara on the night of our Lord Buddha's enlightenment.

You mean—there is no release? There is no salvation?

There is for the disciple. Not for the Master. There is for the bees, but not for the queen bee. For by consenting to be a guru, I am permitting prakriti to contaminate my purusha, to make it heavy. I am trading on my atman. For this sin I have this horrible heaviness. Perhaps my energy is no longer fuelling our enterprise. Perhaps my oil filter is dirty. Can you smell it, my fear, my dirtiness? Come closer.

[*Rustle.*]

And you, do you not ever feel this dirty?

Oh yes. My mother—

Your sari fits you very pleasantly. You look Indian. You need only the pearl above the nostril, and the tikka, the third eye, between your brows. You have the eyes of an Indian woman. The beautiful dark eyes of ressentiment. *In India women are worshipped and degraded. It is a good combination.*

I would not think a jivan-mukta could feel fear. In achieving samadhi he has put away kama and krodha, lobha and bhaya.

He is mukta, yes, saved, but also he is jivan, living. That is his tension. That is his duplicity.

Could you not withdraw deeper into purusha, to lighten and cleanse yourself?

Ah, Kundalini, I cannot. I am always, as they say, in play. I must inspirit the ashram. I thought to hide behind a screen of women, but as you see they quarrel, they make very bad vibes.

Women feel fear, too.

No. When they do, it is the man within them who is fearful. There is no fear in the woman herself. She is a goddess. To touch her is to feel fear vanish. Your hips are solid. Your husband, did he admire your hips? Did he seize them in the night, for comfort?

He—

Your feet look comely in sandals. Such long straight toes. So many American women, I thought when upon arriving in this continent, have ugly toes, from being squeezed inside the pointed shoes.

My mother believed in sensible shoes for children. We went barefoot all summer, especially in Maine, and when we used to rent a cottage on Martha's Vineyard.

A woman is flame. A woman is smoke. A woman is Radha, sweaty with love. Sweaty with rasa. Your breasts—

[*Rustling. Louder heartbeat.*] No. Not my breasts. Not today.

[*Laughs.*] *Neti neti? Is there something wrong with your breasts?*

No, people—I mean Charles—

Ah, this Charles. He is in my path. I think you have not yet burned him away.

I'm sorry. I'm not inwardly prepared for—for this step up. I must go and think. I must meditate.

Meditate well, Kundalini. You can help me.

How? Never mind. I suppose I see how.

Perhaps you do not see all. My desire, my kama, is to turn your body into spirit. I have this power. The adept man has this power. I promise what is called Paramahasukha—instant purusha.

It sounds like just the thing. Master, I must go.

Go, then. May you rise to Sahasrara. May your Shakti merge with Shiva. OM mani padme HUM.

Oh Midge, I can hardly think, I can hardly talk, I never dreamed—I was so terrified he'd touch it, between my boobs. Now what do I do? I shouldn't even send the tape to you, but I can't have it around here—suppose Durga got ahold of it, or Vikshipta, they both hate me so much anyway. But it seems a blasphemy to erase it—I mean, when all is said and done, he *is* a kind of god, at least the closest we're apt to come to it. He didn't really strong-arm me, he seemed sort of fumbling, even, and rather pleased when I turned him down. It was sad. And the worst thing was—oh God, I could cry, I feel like crying suddenly, just to be away from them all, the relief—the worst thing was, I'm not attracted to him, I don't think, not in that way. I mean, I *love* him, the way you and Irving do—I adore him more than ever, now that I've seen him up close instead of on some fuzzy videotape or out-of-date poster and actually seen him *breathe* and felt his personal energy-field. I've never felt anything like it, all other men by comparison are brutes or wimps. Though he's not especially handsome, not as handsome as the posters. He's really quite short—he keeps talking about my tallness when as you know I'm not especially tall for an American woman—Gloria's taller, and so for that matter are you—and he has a potbelly, and his front teeth have this cute space between—maybe it's something they do to Indian children when they're little, you know there's this story about his having been maimed to make him a beggar child—and I have the feeling beneath that twisted-wool turban he wears he's probably pretty bald, men with hair of that wiry type—you can see it beside his ears, where the turban doesn't cover, and his beard of course—tend to have that happen. But, my God, the gentleness of the *force* that comes off of him, it's like an oil bath, it's like the shot of whiskey we used to take working its way into our blood, all churned up, those first few minutes. And once he slipped out of—what can I call it?—his Masterhood, his cosmic distance, and perched forward on that big silver-threaded armchair he uses as a sort of throne to grab my ass, I had this incredible wave of pity, of wanting to open myself the way I used to to little Pearl, to become this brainless fountain of life. I mean, the vibe I got was not so much that he needed to fuck me as *feed* on me, the way he says we all feed on him. With Vikshipta there really *was* this sensation of his wanting to sock it to the whole world and I was there under him as a kind of delegate, and the joy of it all for me was my ability to "take it," to absorb the fury and make it into something positive—but with the Arhat there was just an utterly unaggressive *needi-*

ness, when I thought the whole idea of being a jivan-
mukta was that you needed nothing.

And though this will shock you—you mustn't let Irving or any of the others except maybe Donna, if it will
distract her from her mourning, listen to this—I don't
want him to come between me and Alinga. Between her
and me there has been giving and taking both, and what
he said about her being a wilted flower wasn't exactly
the way I would have put it, though there is a way in
which I, though I'm older, am younger in spirit—all
that bourgeois repression and watered-down Puritanism has kept me fresh, you could say, in a way a lot of
the very charming and gifted and committed people
here aren't, quite—they give the impression even when
they're just in their thirties of having run everything
through already once and knowing that nothing is
going to work, really, that all these therapies, the Rolf-
ing and massage and dynamic meditation and rasaman-
dalis and Primal Scream—though here they don't
scream, they just say "Hoo!" over and over until they
feel empty—are just a way of turning a sick person over
in bed, of changing position, of having a "trip" though
you're going to have to have another in a few hours, just
like a meal or a nap or a crap (my language! I know) and
the beauty of what the Arhat says he wants is to take
us beyond all that, out of the cycles, and with Alinga,
I guess is the point of what I'm trying to say—my heart
is still racing, my thoughts are tumbling all over themselves, and they're doing something noisy with the
vinyl panels out at Joy-Six-Oh so I can hardly hear
myself think—I had *peace*, I felt complete, comple*ted*,

just watching her move around the A-frame lazily with the sunlight slanting in on her long hair and making the top of her brushed head shine and then, the way the A-frame is built, with not too many windows, just the few thin skylights high up, the next moment vanishing, Alinga this still is, all but swallowed in the shadows like some lanky drifting plant that grows in utter quiet under the water. A peace like no man can give. Men stir you up. They give you a poke. They always come on too strong or not strong enough, and emphasize the wrong things. They're always trying to find *out*, they don't just take things in. Maybe that's why I loved our group so much, nobody had to say anything except silly things and giggle when Irving tried to bend us all into pretzels.

Tell Irving you can't share this tape with him but it's nothing against him personally and I hope the insurance has covered all the losses in the shop. The good thing is he wasn't there, they might have killed him— just boys usually, stoned and scared out of their minds. It's the frightened people that do the damage in the world. In your next tape do let me know if you see Charles around town ever. I don't have the slightest emotional curiosity about him but I'm beginning to get these legal letters from his hired thug Gilman that make me, honestly, worry for his sanity. How can you share a man's bed for twenty-two years, picking his socks up every morning and trying to make them match when they come out of the dryer, and then find him so full of sheer malice and hatred? It's like these things in those newspapers you can buy in the supermarkets, *I Married a Monster* or *Hubby Reveals He Came From UFO*. And you *must* let me know how the August boat races went. I'll never forget the year Pearl came in second in the junior division, the Rhodes 19s, with all these brave puffed-out sails thick as snowflakes flecking the horizon out by the far nun, and the biggest darkest most terrifying thunderheads I've ever seen building up in the northeast, beyond the lighthouse on Ferry's Point, and my heart

[*end of tape*]

August 4

Dear Mr. Gilman:

I've been puzzling over your several letters for some days here in the desert. The ashram's spiritual routines make it difficult to focus upon the nasty worldliness that, evidently, still goes on. In my view, I removed from the accessible joint holdings of Dr. Worth and myself merely my proper wife's share—rather less, indeed, since most of our property could not be carried away or divided. I am confident that a divorce court, were we to come to it, would grant me no less and probably more. I would gladly consent to divorce proceedings whenever you can persuade your client to forgo such hurtful and inappropriate terms as "desertion," "adultery," and "theft," and to approach me not in a spirit of bitter adversary but one of sober, saddened mutuality as we lay to rest a partnership long shared, one to whose virtues and fatal defects we no doubt contributed equally.

Equal division of blame and assets does not seem to me a very radical principle. In fact, as of course all males know, and male lawyers doubly know, the division can never be truly equal, since the man retains the professional skills and status to whose acquisition and consolidation the subservient wife sacrificed her prime years; he can rapidly earn his way out of any momentary financial setback, whereas the wife is forever financially maimed, and unless she leaves the marriage with enough capital to support her—which is rare and growing rarer in this day and age of misogynistic judges and shameless lawyers—will be thrown back upon the job market like a load of old laundry, fit for nothing but the rags and odd buttons of employment.

It saddens me, Mr. Gilman, to receive your blustering missives, on such nice creamy stationery, engraved with all those names of younger partners no doubt looking to you for some sort of moral example, and to read, amid all these physical signs of pomp and prosperity—engraving, watermark, dear little etching of your office building on Devonshire Street—these squalid threats of "prosecution" and "extradition" and "deposition" and "restitution." I scarcely know what the words mean; I feel I am being sent back to Latin class.

And I sadly marvel that my former (for so he already

is in my mind, irrevocably) husband has the preposterous temerity to claim "damages to his mental health and professional reputation" due to my "desertion" (a tactful withdrawal, was how I felt it); and to sue for "alienation of affections" the utterly otherworldly man who passively allows his beautiful presence to shed divine light upon his disciples and who was known to me while living with Charles only as an image on a poster and a voice on a tape; and furthermore and most brazenly to list as "stolen property" flatware, a tea service, and candelabra which have been in a branch of my family since their initial purchase (and all, indisputably, monogrammed "P"; anything marked "W" Charles is welcome to) not to mention some precious old books that were the only luxuries my dear dead father allowed himself and that since my earliest girlhood I have often seen tenderly held in his hands. I cannot conceive of any judge who, however corrupt and woman-hating, would not dismiss these charges with the contempt they deserve. Honestly, Mr. Gilman, can you?

So, why are you, presumably hitherto a reputable man, consenting to play a part in Charles's psychopathetic farce? Do you have no wife or, as they say now with such cumbersome euphemism, "relationship"? Have you never had a daughter, or perhaps sisters? Surely you have had a mother, and were not discovered under a cabbage leaf like a slug. Consider even the poor female office-slave who takes your hesitant noises grunted and mumbled into the Dictaphone and turns them into the correctly spelled and grammatical letters which I keep receiving in all their impeccable masculine effrontery.

Think of the indispensable female presences in your life and ask yourself if you can continue to execute the commands of this crazed and vindictive client and to run, via registered mail (itself unutterably pompous), his demeaning errands. He at least has the excuse of wounded pride. He at least once shared my bed and still imagines, albeit falsely, that his abuse has some charm for me. But you have no such excuses. Come off it, Mr. Gilman. Go back to evicting the poor and defending rapists and leave good women alone.

Sincerely,
Sarah Price Worth

August 6, 1986

Dear County Commission Chairman Aldridge:

"He who does what should not be done and fails to do what should be done, who forgets the true aim of life and sinks into transient pleasures—he will one day envy the man who lives in high contemplation." Thus spoke our Lord Buddha, as recorded in the sacred Dhammapada. We are in receipt of your letters, documents, and diagrams. The nature of our offenses remains obscure. The wiring and plumbing arrangements that your inspectors discovered are inappropriate, you say, to "winterized tents," as the jargon on our initial permits had it. Then, let us call them "substantial dwellings," which more befits the condition they have grown into. When the sapling becomes a tree, or the bulb a flower, we do not cut it down because it is no longer what it was. You accuse that we applied for a permit for a "greenhouse" and that the greenhouse is now a two-acre assembly hall and an attractive vinyl-clad meditation center of fourteen soundproofed rooms. Is this not cause for rejoicing rather than official rebuke? Is this not the American way, to progress from the humble log cabin to the mighty skyscraper? And you say that our initial announced intent to form an "agricultural commune" of no more than twenty-five members has been played false by our present-day shopping mall, terraced A-frames, paved avenues, trailer parks, printing plant, fabrics factory, and population numbered in the hundreds. Our agricultural commune has prospered; shall it therefore be destroyed, as your Hebraic God destroyed with fire and brimstone cities too happy and serene to make bloody sacrifices to Him every day and twice on Sundays?

You assert that your statewide "land-use" laws were enacted by concerned environmentalists. It is our impression, instead, that such laws are the pliable tool of fat-cat ranchers owning tens of thousands of utterly idle acres, snobbish restriction-minded "snowbirds" from the teeming Northeastern states, and Los Angeles–based real-estate developers who have already transformed Phoenix into a smaller version of their nightmare metropolis. *We* are the concerned environmentalists, we of the ashram, who have taken an arid, abandoned environment and made it not only habitable but paradisaical. The technicalities you raise could be settled in an hour by men of true good will.

If our population exceeds that allowable without declaring the existence of a city, then let us declare it a city. We propose the lovely name Varunaville, in honor of Varuna, the heavenly encompasser. This celestial god placed fire in the waters and hung the golden pendulum, the sun, to swing above, regulating day and night. The rhythm of his order is the order of the world, called *rta*. In his mansion of a thousand doors Varuna sits observing all deeds; everywhere his spies survey the world and are undeceived. He is a glorious deity, appropriate to this sunny land and a county called Golden. But if you wish to give our city a more indigenous-sounding name such as Crusty Elbow or Flat Tire, please do. We will govern ourselves nicely, posting speed limits and route signs and all that. Already we have been constrained to create quite a large police force, due not to any derelictions within but to harassment from without. Perhaps once our legal status is clarified we can work with the law-enforcement officers of your estimable county to rid its territory of ruffians and rascals and rednecks and reactionaries. To quote once more the Dhammapada (which means "Truth-Path"): "Weeds harm the fields, passions harm human nature."

We future citizens of Varunaville look forward to hearing from you in a spirit of amiable cooperation in achieving our mutual goals.

Most hopefully,

Shri Arhat Mindadali, M.A., Ph.D.

Supreme Meditator, Ashram Arhat

/k

August 8, 1986

Dear Sheriff Yardley:

We of the Ashram Arhat are indeed sorrowful to hear of these two unfortunate young women, Rhoda Lou Pollitt and Phoebe Gellerman, who were apprehended in the act of intravaginally smuggling cocaine across the border at Nogales. A search through our records shows that two sannyasins named Bhanda and Gauri originally registered with us under these two state-imposed "Christian" names on November 19, 1985. They stayed here for three months, offering up to the Arhat, and to the aspects of Shiva made manifest through the Arhat's overwhelming presence, worship in the form of work as chambermaids, kitchen assistants, and messengers on ashram business to the outside world. They were absent, singly or together, for various periods and were last in residence seven months ago. Notations on their records credit both Bhanda and Gauri with above-average spiritual energy and egolessness.

We of course greatly grieve to learn that, according to you, both women in their confessions have implicated the ashram not only in their reprehensible drug-smuggling activities but in numerous acts of prostitution and petty theft committed in three states and Mexico. But what, really, is meant by their claim that "they did it all for the Arhat"? The Arhat, even if omniscient (as many believe), cannot be held responsible, surely, for illegal acts committed by his misguided devotees. These former sannyasins claimed to you that, after their modest living expenses were met, all the profits of their various sordid activities were forwarded to our ashram. Sheriff Yardley, we receive many donations every day from those literally uncountable grateful men and women who have been brought closer to lasting peace and unalterable enlightenment by the teachings and example of Shri Arhat Mindadali.

You ask whether our records show receipts from these poor young women whom you have so cleverly apprehended in the act of bringing a controlled (for obscure reasons, since it is relatively harmless, except to the nasal membranes and the attention span, and certainly less corrosive and lethal than tobacco and alcohol, those brother poisons that powerful vested interests keep pumping into our national bloodstream with scarcely a demur from legislators and law-enforcement officers) substance to those that peaceably desire it for recreational purposes. Our policy is to pay all receipts into the Treasury of Enlightenment without any numerical notation that might encourage an ethic of competition and invidious comparison among our benefactors. The widow's mite (to use a phrase perhaps familiar to you) and the millionaire's largesse dissolve one and all alike in our Treasury, which has been likened to a vast white-hot cauldron that accepts all earthly scrap, be it in the form of pistols or clockworks or bracelets or ploughshares, and resolves this dross to a molten formlessness then poured into pure ingots of the Arhat's deep and serene intent.

So we most regretfully cannot aid your investigation, only ask your mercy upon the two accused. Their "crimes" are so labelled by a Puritanical and patriarchal society that seeks to punish its own dark cravings. How much better it would be to legalize drugs and prostitution and out of surfeit discover, as did the Lord Buddha, the middle way that leads to non-attachment and nirvana. To quote the Bhagavad-Gita: "Action rightly renounced brings freedom, and action rightly performed brings freedom." As you doubtless know, there existed and perhaps still exists in India the "left-handed" path (Vamachara) of tantrism, in which unspeakable orgiastic excesses, even murder and necrophagy, were performed as acts of worship under the rubric that "perfection can be gained by satisfying all one's desires." Certainly temple prostitution held an honored place not only in Hindu but in Hellenic religion, and is dimly echoed in the numerous scandals in Protestant churches today involving church secretaries, choir sopranos, etc. While we at the ashram hardly dare hope

that these somewhat general considerations will deflect
you from the enforcement of laws however stupid and
unjust, I myself would feel remiss if I did not point out
to you how frequently these life-denying laws pertaining to "vice" are used to afflict not the men who serve
as both administrators and consumers of the prosecuted
activity but—as in this case—the women whose only
offense has been to satisfy the desire of others.

Sincerely yours,
Ma Prem Kundalini
Assistant to the Arhat

August 18, 1986

Gentlemen:

We are in receipt of your several inquiries as to our
tax-exempt status as a religious organization. But we
have never claimed to be such; in fact the Arhat and his
spokespersons have repeatedly placed on record, in nationwide press and television interviews, his marked
distrust of organized religion in any form—Buddhist,
Hindu, Moslem, Christian, Judaic, Shinto, Zoroastrian,
or shamanist. *Un*organized religion—the sort that each
human being harbors inchoately, often without knowing it—is more our métier.

Our tax-exempt status instead rests securely upon our amply justified claim to be an educational institution. We administer courses in hatha-yoga, zazen, shiatsu, acupuncture, bioenergetics, dynamic meditation, pranayama, dance and aerobics therapy, the sitar, Hindi, Sanskrit, Pali, the Upanishads and related classics, arid-area irrigational techniques, intuitive ecology, vegetarian food-styling, solar-panel engineering, zero-sum mechanistics, spiritual reprogramming, post-materialistic Marxism, subtle-body anatomy, and a host of other reformative subjects, not to mention tutorials in enlightened accounting and business techniques (as opposed to unenlightened, as practiced on Wall and Main Streets). Most of our instructors have advanced degrees from such bastions of conventional learning as Harvard, Yale, Duke, Kenyon, Utah State, and the University of Southern California. We ourselves award degrees ranging from the B.Med. (Bachelor of Meditation) to the D.Phil.Med. Our most recent catalogue is enclosed, along with completed or partly completed Forms 1023 and 990.

"Partly" because our extensive records have been left in some confusion by the sudden retirement of our former chief accountant, Ms. Nitya Kalpana; it has fallen to me, though bereft of any formal training in business mathematics or double-entry bookkeeping (in fact, I skipped math beyond plane geometry, being rather foolishly infatuated at Concord Academy with the French teacher, whose third-year class met at the same hour as trig and introductory calculus), to straighten matters out. If you have on file any previous

tax returns filed for Ashram Arhat I would be grateful
for them, to use as a guide. Rest assured of one thing,
however, gentlemen of the IRS: religious or educational, tax-exempt or not, our organization owes you
absolutely nothing for fiscal 1985, because we have been
running at a terrific loss.

Voluntary contributions, our main source of income,
have dropped catastrophically, due principally to basically uncomprehending reporting in the Arizona press,
beginning with the Forrest *Weekly Sentinel* and spread-
ing to the media nationwide, but also perhaps due to the
ripples or eddies (vrittis) that occur within the cosmic
spiritual currents. The fees paid for lodging and in-
struction by our sannyasins (permanent students) and
by enlistments in our many short-term (two- to eight-
week) courses or therapeutic programs are significantly
lower, as are receipts from sales of books, posters, fabric
and ceramic products, and agricultural produce. Mean-
while, the expenses of maintaining and expanding our
ashram facilities to a level commensurate with our ex-
alted aims have increased formidably. Our best estimate
is that between two and three million dollars has drifted
away within the present fiscal year.

Not, of course, that we expect the Reagan government to make up ou losses. But we don't expect to be
dunned for money we don't owe, either. During my
attempt to fill out your forms, a number of questions
arose; let me mention only the most nagging:

In Form 990, Part VII, yes-or-no Question 79 asks,
"Was there a liquidation, dissolution, termination, or
substantial contraction during the year (see instruc-

tions)?" As I say, there seems to have been a contraction, but how substantial relative to previous years I have no way of knowing with the incomplete information at hand. My sense is of a material contraction of some duration, amid a deceptive explosive spiritual growth. The instructions I am parenthetically instructed to "see" do not seem to be attached or included, or else I have not grasped what instructions (in your sense) are.

Re Schedule A of Form 990, Part II, "Compensation of Five Highest Persons for Professional Services (See specific instructions)": Does spiritual guidance delivered in platform lectures and darshans (informal teaching sessions, with questions and answers) and in the even less tangible form of physical proximity and meaningful silence and *abstention from* public appearance constitute a "professional service," and does compensation include limousines and bejewelled timepieces as well as cash? Again, *what* instructions?

Page 2029-8 of Form 1024 lists four columns of numbered types of Exempt Organizations and invites us to "select up to three codes which best describe or most accurately identify your purposes, activities, etc." Number 030—"School, college, trade school, etc."—of course is one. And even though we are not 001 ("church, synagogue, etc."), number 008—"Religious publishing activities"—is rather tempting, since our books are indeed—in the broad sense specified above—religious. But number 260 ("Fraternal beneficiary society, order, or association") also appeals to a number of us here, since fraternity (which I assume includes sorority) is our goal, not only for ourselves but for all mankind. Along the same lines, under "Advocacy," numbers 520 ("Pacifism and peace") and 529 ("Ecology or conservation") seem very much to the point, while others in the same "Advocacy" category, such as 522 ("Anti-communism") and 539 ("Prohibition of erotica"), do not. But no doubt just two or three code numbers are all you need, and I am being, as a novice tax accountant, much too conscientious.

Yours sincerely,
Ma Prem Kundalini
Temporary Accountant,
Ashram Arhat

August 24

Dearest Pearl—

I'm sorry to have been so slow to answer your letter. The truth is, darling, it hurt your mother's feelings a *teeny* bit. Of course I'm delighted that you and Jan had such a lovely summer in Europe—it was brutally hot here, and people, even the ones that didn't get heat stroke, began to act very testy—not Vikshipta, the vile-tempered German I mentioned before—he actually left in July and I've heard is trying to get a counselling job in Seattle or Portland or some other cool misty place, but my guess is he'll be back; there's even less of what he wants out there than in here—but the women I work with. The sannyasins call us the "godmothers," not entirely kindly I think. Perhaps women together all day and night are too much of a good thing—that female *attentiveness* begins to work on the nerves, one begins almost to long for a man, who doesn't notice *anything*—your own father certainly didn't have that among his faults, that tireless nervous susceptibility—I mean bursting into tears or storms of rage over each imagined slight or deviation from utter devotion. In the nature of my expanded duties here I've been spending more time with the Arhat himself, and one woman, called Durga, who still claims to be his chief executive assistant—though she does nothing these days but agitate and storm and sulk and consort with the security forces, young men full of guns—is jealous of me, and another, Alinga, my dear housemate, is jealous of *him*, our adored Master. I used to think women were so prone to jealousy because the patriarchal society denied them any power except that which they could extract from interpersonal relationships, but now I wonder if it isn't more biological than that—the women here have power enough: the Arhat in his total goodness and rather playful fatalism grants them *all* of it, really—and relates, at a wild guess, to the vigilance female mammals have to have in regard to their young when they're helpless, which continues even when no children are on the scene, except the infant we forever carry inside us, waiting to suck and be fondled. There are, as I know I already wrote somebody, a few children here, brought by single mothers or mated couples and even one or two born in the clinic since I've come, but by and large children are one area where the Arhat *isn't* totally accepting and benign. He calls them "human tadpoles" and speaks of the overpopulation in India and parts of Africa and the starvation as a horror worse than Hitler's extermination camps because nobody's able to invade and stop it, and indeed the Western nations' efforts, shipping in food and inventing new kinds of wheat and rice, just postpone the problem and make it eventually worse—I think his own experiences when very young whatever they were were so horrendous that just the sight of a child is painful to him. The ashram keeps a little school up through sixth grade but older than that the children are bussed to the Dorado Regional High School forty miles away and come back as you can imagine with a great many conflicted and angry feelings from their contact with the children of the "Outer States." They are encouraged to drop out as soon as they legally can, at sixteen, which is in a way sad, since their parents here tend to be if anything *over*educated.

All this as a prelude to speaking honestly with my own child, my lovely little priceless Pearl. I am glad as well as surprised that you found Jan's parents so delightful—their house in Amsterdam dating back to 1580 and on a lovely quiet canal, their country estate with its working windmill and squawking peacocks, their apartment in Paris, their twenty-meter yacht kept at a Turkish harbor, their fluent English, French, German, and Italian. I still don't understand why Jan's father is entitled to call himself a count if they come from this long line of innkeepers and beermakers, but I'm glad you found the brewery itself so thrilling—though *of course* everything is *clean*, dearest, otherwise their precious beer would taste of lint and cobwebs and cockroach feces. The whole dreary process has to do with bacteria—a rather hideous microscopic kind of farming. Frankly I have always found the idea of fermentation rather disgusting, and even in college when it was the thing to drink and I had no figure worries I hated that sour bitter burpy taste of beer. It has been really not the least of my blessings these last months to get away from your father's martinis and all those suburban cocktail parties and to be in an environment where the human vessel and its conduits are as much respected as those giant glass vats and shiny copper tubing you were so impressed by are. Think of where the beer goes then—into the ulcerated guts of drunken loud barflies and then vomited out into bathroom bowls and onto the sidewalks.

Most of your life stretches gloriously before you and of course part of it must be exposing your sweet and unspoiled self to all sorts of people, including these van Hertzogs, vulgar and yeasty as they sound. And it is no doubt beneficial to add new words like "flocculence" and "wort" to your vocabulary. But I am, frankly, offended at your report of their excessive curiosity as to my present situation and, more hurtful still, your own embarrassment in regard to it. Whatever can be embarrassing? Your mother is seeking truth, beauty, and freedom, and *finding* it—what is there to be ashamed of? Be ashamed, rather, of her previous twenty-two years of respectable bondage and socially sanctioned frivolity. Who are *they*, these brewers, living as they do off of human drunkenness and forced bacterial labor, to turn up their noses at a "cult" which is striving to offer the world a new model of human arrangements? With their alcohol they are anesthetizing sick Mankind; we are attempting a cure. These vain and vapid van Hertzogs' opinion concerns me less than that of a pair of their pet microbes—what saddens me beyond description is that my own daughter, the female child of my female womb, loved as much as any mother ever loved a daughter, appears to share the doubts of these square-headed Dutch folk. You ask me if I intend to stay at the ashram "till Kingdom Come," if I haven't already "got out of it" all I am going to "get." You speak of my renewal here as an "ego trip" when in fact the *flight from ego* is what I have undertaken, and you write the jeering words "group grope" when in truth the grope is all behind me, in that pathetic suburban squirming in the closets and backstairs of respectability. The relationships I enjoy in the ashram, those that wound as well as heal, all transpire in the bright sunlight of amaya, of non-deceit. I regret even so much as hinting at my friendships here, since you seem to discuss them promptly with Jan and thence they are relayed, in the language of prurient gossip, to your—I shudder to write it—possible in-laws.

Dear Pearl, I literally *did* shudder then, and had to steady myself by getting up from my bench beneath the dusty airy box elder in our little rock garden and walking out to the front of the A-frame to look toward the hills that shelter us from the north. Dawn light lies on their lavender tips like crinkled gold foil. I woke up in the dark this morning, writing this letter in my head. Alinga is still asleep. She and I had a long good talk last night, and like all you younger people she forgets to put herself to bed. What we talked about I would confide to you but don't want it passed on to those nosy, judgmental van Hertzogs—I keep wanting to write "warthogs."

You say Jan is "serious." Serious is the one thing he impresses me as *not*, from all I have been able to discern between the lines of your cherished and pondered, though short and infrequent, letters. He is a floater, dear—a fleck of suds on his father's malodorous fortune. A generation ago he would have been rioting and making plastic bombs and wearing filthy floppy rags; ten years ago he would have been doing the disco scene and jetting to Bali with all the other children of inflation. In these more straitened times he comes to Oxford to study economics and just happens to make the acquaintance of an innocent golden American girl whom he of course wants to marry and not just incidentally thereby get himself his green card. They all love their green cards, these foreigners—Durga and Vikshipta have an incessant problem, and keep getting these badgering letters from the Immigration Service, and even our miraculous Arhat, who has brought so much wealth and profitable enterprise to the nation, became rather mysterious and irritable when I once asked him about his residency status.

But I mustn't mention the Arhat, as that offends you. You write rather wistfully of your father's visit this summer. You say he spoke fondly of me—as if that amazed you. You say he seemed in a forgiving mood— as if there was much to forgive. You write that he keeps our old home up, mostly by not living in most of the rooms, and has no conspicuous girlfriend—as if that will gladden my heart or shame me or do *some*thing to me. It does nothing. Nothing but make me feel a quite unnecessary estrangement *between you and me*. You write of him as of a lumbering fuzzy old bafflingly wounded teddy-bear at the same time that he and this shyster Gilman he's hired are bombarding me with the most preposterous legal documents, all meant simply to terrify a defenseless woman, who has for a lawyer that wimpy if formerly superficially attractive Ducky Bradford; *he* is so preoccupied with coming out of the closet as a middle-aged gay and humiliating poor Gloria and then discovering that life out of the closet is no picnic either that he can hardly lift a legal finger. (None of this came directly from him but from Midge, who on her last tape painted a pathetic picture of Ducky slowly realizing that the only market for an aging American man is with American women and that he should have announced himself when he was young and slender or kept quiet forever—he's Grecian formula-ing his hair and wearing closer-cut suits, but it's not nearly enough.)

You write of what a tender and attentive father yours was when the sad truth is he hardly bothered to kiss you good-night most nights let alone read a bedtime story as you and he both seem to be fantasizing. Worse yet, even when you had a cold or mumps that time your face looked like a gourd, or that very odd fever up to 104.5° that had me so worried about possible permanent brain damage, your father the big Boston doctor couldn't be bothered to doctor his own daughter but had me drag you over to the Beverly Hospital and sit there in the waiting room with the television turned up so loud and the air so thick with germs you refused to breathe and turned bright blue. Precious Pearl, make no mistake: *I* nursed you, *I* changed your diapers. I dried your tears. I sang you songs when you were nervous at night, on and on until my own eyes could hardly stay open. You sucked milk out of *my* breasts, took hold of life in *my* belly, not your father's. All he did was clumsily contribute his sperm (I had no climax when you were conceived; I rarely did in those virtually virginal days) and show up at your graduations (and in fact, having written that, I just remember that he missed the one from Miss Grandison's in the sixth grade—said he had a MSPCC board meeting—likely story!) and condescend to keep your picture on his desk (along with his boyish self in his Boston Latin baseball uniform and that one of me I always hated, in that foolish garden hat standing there tipsy and tense at one of the Hibbenses' gauche lawn parties worrying that your father was going to lose the lens cap). Now of course that you're a stunning woman and he's a well-dressed man in his forties who hasn't let himself go entirely to pot it's all very cute for the two of you to trot out to the Queen's Arms or the King's Joint or whatever the most expensive restaurant in Oxford is and split a carafe of an amusing dry Beaujolais and discuss in tiddly cozy fashion how far poor old Mother has wandered off the deep end: but *raising you was not an equal partnership*, and I *am* hurt, dearest Pearl, by what seems to me not so much your divided loyalty—that perhaps is to be expected and is healthy—but what can only strike me as *dis*loyalty. Be true to yourself, and you will be true to me. I did not raise my flaxen-haired darling to be her father's cat's-paw or for that matter some minor princess of malt.

On top of all this paternal interference, you say my *mother* has written lachrymosely to you. Of course you can see that what meager sense senility has left in Grandma's brain the sun and saltwater have quite vaporized. I do believe she has goaded your Uncle Jeremy into writing me a somewhat harassing letter as well. What *do* you all object to? I know the answer: my attempting to become anything other than your (plural) obedient servant and flattering social extension. *Perish the thought* that I and my shoeless friends would for a moment cause a frown to cross the stately brow of the beer count where he sits enthroned amid his mighty vats of boiling mash! Not to mention his fat Katrinka of a countess and their wispy dilettantish son, who led you to waste a whole glorious English summer, the kind that Browning wrote about, on dreary flat soggy Holland—forgive me, I just get frantic fearing that Jan won't let you *grow*—that you'll allow him to put a permanent cramp in the ongoing splendid adventure of your womanhood just as your father with the connivance of *my* parents did to me twenty-two years ago.

To Pearl

Do forgive me. How your mother does go on with her "wiggles"! Think of these letters as what I do now instead of embroidery. But isn't it better not to pretend I wasn't hurt by the really very delicately but unmistakably challenging tone of *your* letter? I've been under some stress here, too, aside from worrying about my priceless elf-child. Pressures from the outside are producing shifting allegiances within. It turns out that Ma Prapti, a rather stern sad mustachioed soul whom I formerly admired, as a kind of Albert Schweitzer or Mother Teresa, has really *been* rather indiscriminate in her distribution of prescription drugs. Vikshipta left, it turns out, because he was convinced he was being poisoned, I was recently told (by Yajna, the boy about your age I playfully offered you but who for the moment seems to be involved with Satya and Nagga and their crowd of PR glamour girls, who really could be professional football cheerleaders from the uniform glossy look of them). There *are* days, especially after the cafeteria has served one of those cruelly hot curries that disguise every other taste, when people complain of wooziness and cramps and we all go about in something of a daze—I've been blaming it on the heat, which even though we're almost into September has not let up. There is so much suspicion around in fact that I don't like to mail personal letters with the Uma Room mail but I *must* get this on the way and *do* hope it will still reach you at the Iffley Road address. If not, they can forward it back to Yale, which begins in less than three weeks! I will ignore your passing mention of Jan's wanting you to take the fall term off so you and he can go to Crete and the Greek islands in the familial yacht. I know taking time off from college isn't the end of the world like it used to be but skipping out of your senior fall term for a Mediterranean jaunt with a Dutch playboy would be—how can I say this without giving offense?—unspeakable.

Still love me? Here's some kisses:

XXX

Mummy

September 2, 1986

Gentlemen:

Enclosed find endorsed checks totalling $66,403.27 for deposit to my account, #0002743-911.

Thank you sincerely,

Sarah P. Worth

September 2, 1986

Gentlemen:

I am very interested in opening a credit-deferrable charge account with the Arhat Book and Gift Shop of

Samana Cay. My understanding is that a balance in excess of charges will accumulate 6% interest compounded monthly, while a debit of more than thirty days' standing will be penalized at the rate of 12%, also compounded monthly. Though I am temporarily an executive assistant at Ashram Arhat here in Arizona, my account, I wish to emphasize, would be a personal one, for my use only. I look forward to receiving whatever information you can send, mailed to me in care of this motel, along with relevant currency and investment regulations in the Commonwealth of the Bahamas.

With sincere thanks,
Sarah P. Worth

le deux septembre 1986

Monsieur,

Je voudrais ouvrir, peut-être, avec Crédit Suisse un compte identifié seulement par son numéro, un numéro qui soit secret. Envoyez-moi, s'il vous plaît, à l'adresse cidessous, les formules nécessaires et les règles qu'il faut qu'on observe concernant un tel compte.

> Agréez, je vous prie,
> l'expression de mes sentiments distingués,
> Sarah P. Worth (Madame)

Sep. 2

Dear Dr. Podhoretz—

I'm afraid an October appointment won't do either. Tell your secretary to put me in the inactive file. I'm still flossing, though. Do you think an occasional twinge in the left eyetooth means anything, or is it just the enamel wearing thin with old age? I notice it most with iced tea, though very hot curries set it off too.

Warm regards,
Sarah Worth

September 2

Dear Martin—

Well, I'm enchanted that my little postcard meant so much to you. Your generous response—longer, I fear, than I can answer in detail—was waiting for me here at the motel. I don't live here, I live forty miles away with a lot of other people seeking the inner peace that comes with the good life. When I wrote you that all the material world is a jail I did not mean to make light of your predicament or the terrible conditions of incarceration in Massachusetts but to offer a consoling general premise—that for any of us to be alive is to suffer pain and limitation. We are born into a certain body, with a certain sex and color of skin, etc., at a specific time and place, of parents who shelter us and damage us according to their capacities, and as we grow we attain a certain height and degree of intelligence we can't do much about, and fall into some job or rôle—in your case, into drugs and burglary—and from a certain angle one could become intensely claustrophobic about all these circumstances, which are more constricting and harder to escape from than any cell. And then the body and with it the brain begin to age and malfunction and eventually to die and the constriction is very tight indeed. But there is a way out, the way of the spirit, of accepting that little unchanging viewpoint or "I" inside you as part of a larger spiritual reality, which we call *purusha*, in relation to which material reality with all its confining specifics is mere illusion, called *maya*, which also means deception. And there are exercises and disciplines which enable men called masters *(gurus)* to attain release *(moksha)* from the material world and the bliss of pure spiritual being, *nirvana*, which doesn't literally mean nothingness but "no wind"—we will get out of the wind, Martin, and exist in a place where everything is still and shining and eternal. The orthodox path to nirvana is long and tedious (you begin by thinking of a point just behind your forehead, at the bridge of your nose) but it is not the only way, there are shortcuts that suddenly open to people—even and perhaps especially to foolish and miserable people—and there is no reason why at least the beginning of enlightenment—a little fascinating pinprick—won't come to you in jail just as one came to me in my nice suburban home (which in moments of weakness I still miss). *But you must look within for what is real.* You tried to look within with drugs but what they gave you was not real, they just suppressed part of *maya*. There is a better way out, which does not lead to jail and early death. This Way embraces everything: it is the Way of striving and sur-render, of action and inaction, of good and bad, of the senses and their absence. Whatever name you give this Way, whatever images you use to help you visualize the Path, it is the Way that we all seek and that makes all our seeking one.

My fond regards to little Eldridge and your mother. Tell Shirlee my hair is stiff and brittle as burnt toast here in this climate and that I have given up Clairol so the gray strands are poking through, and I cut it short in a kind of scruffy mid-neck flip just to get it out of my mind and concentrate on higher things, but for all that there are still some here who find me an attractive bru-nette.

Your friend,
Sarah Worth

Sep. 6

Dear Mother—

Just the briefest note, to check in. They've given me more responsibilities here, and I'm up to my ears in legal and financial details. Of course I'm *horrified* to hear that you have cashed in all your CDs, even paying the fines to do so, and have sold those blocks of Daddy's lovely old IBM and AT&T, and put everything into the stock of this cosmetic company your admiral friend has heard is going to be taken over by Revlon. His grandson's being an investment banker doesn't mean a thing; or, rather, it *does* mean, if this is real insider information, that you and the boy and old Granddaddy will all go to jail. I recently received a letter from a man in jail and he says it's no fun—the toilet is in the middle of the cell and the white guards let the black prisoners rule by survival of the fittest and there's a two-year wait for the course in computer science. If on the other hand it's *not* real insider information, then you're holding a big chunk of some stagnant company (Visàge, Inc.—what kind of name is that, and who put on that absurd incorrect accent?) from Arkansas (Arkansas, Mother!) that will pay peanuts—not even that, peanut *shells*—for dividends and slowly sink into the swamp of what's left of Reaganomics. The CDs were safe, sure, and smart, as I told you before. You've obviously written me off as an adviser and probably even heir, but think of your own grandchild, pretty Pearl who adores you and who has let herself fall into the clutches of some loathsome Dutch pseudo-plutocrats because, no doubt, of financial insecurity. If she didn't have a grandmother who was squandering her eventual inheritance she might have the self-respect and self-confidence to stick with her education and independent development. She's even threatening not to return to Yale this fall! Isn't that incredibly self-destructive? Do phone her and tell her so, instead of commiserating with her over what a rotter I am and what a saint Charles is—she didn't *exactly* quote you to that effect but I can read between the lines.

Your involvement with this alleged admiral I find, of course, alarming. He sounds like a typical male exploiter, hunting for a cook and a nurse to see him into the grave. Don't be conned, I beg you, and don't tell me how dashing he looks in a double-breasted blazer and old-fashioned cream linen pants with broad cuffs—I can't imagine what's come over you. After Daddy, this clown in a sailor suit? I don't think you realize how humorous and pathetic your description of his rapping night after night on your hurricane shutters is. I guess it's not in the nature of women to learn. Seduced and ruined by an octogenarian swindler—is that what you want your epitaph to be? I know you have been teasing me about this romance, egging me on to overreact, so I have tried to be circumspect. It *is* your life—just don't ever dare say a word of criticism to me again about *anything*. And don't get Jerry to write me any more platitudinous chummy letters. It was embarrassing for both of us—he didn't know what to say and I didn't either. My brother is part of me but I have no more to say to him now than to my own left foot.

But *do* sell that preposterous Visàge and put everything into a 6% savings account. Even under your mattress would be better. *Don't discuss money with this ancient mariner.* Or if you do, ask about *his* money—find out if he has enough of his own so that he isn't after yours. Do take your vitamins, especially A to combat aging and brain-cell loss. Niacin can be very effective in reversing delusional thinking. A lot of Alzheimer's, they think now, is caused by aluminum salts in the blood. Aluminum turns out to be in *everything*—toothpaste, aspirin, water. And of course you cook with pots of it. I forgot— you don't cook any more, you and the Admiral eat out, champagne and oysters and chocolate cake every night. I told the Arhat what you were up to, and he laughed and laughed and said, "Women are the gods!" He joins me in sending you *strivyatireka* (love).

Sare

Sep. 28

Dearest Alinga—

Tena tyaktena bhunjithah. I fear, my darling, we have reached our quota. These months living with you have been the happiest of my life, as far as cohabitation goes—the most *harmonious*, as if we were two upright notes, one blond and one dark, forming a single chord. No pulling and hauling, no serving and being served—or, rather, *both*, so carelessly and lightly blended that there was no knowing where the serving left off and the being served began. Our time together has in my mind a precious fine fragility, a crackled gold-rimmed rightness, that makes me hold my breath as I try to set it down.

This break with you is, as I conceive it, a delicate one, scarcely perceptible but to us. We will still share the ashram, and our love of the Arhat, and our work in the Uma Room, and why not then some hours of private talk and even rasa as before? Do please keep thinking of me as your lover—your dark and stormy prince, you once called me.

But I must feel *free*, to continue what let's call my ascent toward the unconditioned. I do not want to make you my prison warder as I did Charles—the guardian of habit, of limits, the enforcer, albeit for my good and out of affection—he *was* affectionate, I can admit that now—of a system in which my function is simply *to hold still*, to be the same day after day. Durga's madness and the siege from outside have thinned the population of the ashram so that there are plenty of empty beds. Vikshipta's old A-frame is vacant, though my moving in there risks stirring up ugly memories, like some dust rich in allergens. He wonderfully managed to make heterosexuality ugly and yet for me this hard, silent other (shunya = void = diamond = vajra = thunderbolt = linga) with whom we must share our species still retains the fascination of a challenge, the task set for *us*, the basic duty. In this sense perhaps I was always a bit unfaithful to you, harbored a bit of reservation, so that all we enacted together, gracious and blissful as it was, had a certain quality of foreplay, of something less than full seriousness, the seriousness that leads, biologically, to that tremendous bloody ego-splitting death-defying bearing of a child.

Now I fear I have set down the gold-rimmed vase with a crash. But honestly, didn't it ever feel to you as though I was nothing but a strangely weak man? Of course we must honor those who stand aside—the sexual saints, the little roundish men who would rather collect books or jade elephants, and the handsome Hepburnesque women not meant to be mothers—many of whom, so unfortunately (I think of my serenely selfish own), become mothers anyway. Actually, this ego-splitting I seem to extol doubles rather than halves our natural selfishness and selfish frenzy. Without a child, women are free to mother others—you, for instance, mothered me. And what a child I seem to be!—willful, needy, exhibitionistic, compliment-seeking, petty, jealous. Jealous, as we have discussed, of you and Durga in the time before I came here, when she was to you something of what you have been to me—an initiator, an apsaras, an avatar of Shakti. Even now as she in her drug-riddled fury brings down the paradise that the Arhat's beautiful energy crystallized, I feel in you a certain lackadaisical fondness for our Celtic destroyer, a passive willingness to "let it all go" as one more meaningless ripple of maya. Your energy exchange with

Durga, in other words, still proceeds, though you find yourselves in opposite camps during all this scheming, feuding, poisoning, and mutual manipulation as the implacable outer world closes in.

This is not a complaint, but a halting explanation, much longer than I meant it to be. I know how you hate to read, how content you were to betrance yourself in front of our feeble old Zenith with its ghost images shuddering as if the mountains between here and Phoenix were always in motion. I love you. But not *only* you, so I can no longer accept your roof, your A-frame. I am writing you in the rock garden, and will miss this shady spot beneath the box elder—the nirgundi, you taught me it is called in Sanskrit—and the garden's crowd of funny little scrunched-up cactus-faces, like the rumpled faces of pug dogs or of whiskery cartoon cats. The tree's seeds spin down on me, the wings of the twin samaras not outspread as in the energetic flaming maples of New England but folded down, as if still asleep and dreaming of, instead of experiencing, flight. And the rising sun like a vast high press squeezes from the air that desert spiciness, that very fine powder in the air like the substance of purusha and like something—some dim closeted seasoning—I used to smell in my grandmother's kitchen in Medford.

Darling, it is nothing you have done—you can do nothing wrong, because in a deep and very soothing way you are beyond attempting to do anything *right*. You accept. In the sthula sphere you were all padma and I the mani, the flawed jewel to your perfect lotus. The way you would let me brush your silky long hair on and on in the dark as the blue sparks flew about your head and my hands. And the way the top of your head would show an utterly straight parting, like a chalk-line, scalp-white, when in morning light you would shadowily kneel to give me a "tummy kiss." It is nothing you have done and nothing I am doing—it is Kali, dearest, time undoing and destroying so that the new weave can be begun. Kali who moves through all our passions, momentous as they seem, and tugs them toward the wheel's next turn. My worst fear as I write—how close I am to tearing all this up and sparing myself the pain of packing and saying goodbye to the rooms where, once frowny twitchy guilty Nitya's discordant note was gone, we made our harmony!—my fear is that you will shrug me off, you will shed me, that is what we do with one another, all of us, but it never seems right, never seems natural, though it is the most natural thing in the world.

Be a lamp unto yourself,

K.

Oct. 1

Charles—

I am living alone again and unable to sleep tonight. Your barrage of Gilmanesque legalese has left me unimpressed. If you can arrange my arrest, go to it. Pearl can add to her distinctions that of her mother being put in jail by her father. Actually, you never hear of that, do you? Halves of a couple can murder and desert each other easily enough but legally I believe we are somehow one and therefore have oddly little legal recourse. Anyway the courts are bored with couples. The whole world for that matter is bored with couples, and if a couple doesn't take an interest in itself no one else will. All these lawyerly threats and bluff I take to be your stiff and clumsy way of expressing continued interest in me.

But I would never do as your wife again, having so wildly fallen. To my derelictions I have recently added a lesbian romance—delicious and comforting but rather, for my Yankee tastes, lacking in fiber. It did helpfully clarify what men see in women. The lady, in posture and offhand affect and even in a certain disarming flatness of accent, reminded me of Marcelene Rabinowitz—remember her? Women of course *are* divine energy—without Shakti, as they say here, Shiva is a corpse—but, so satisfactorily endowed by the cosmos, they tend to be conservative—reconciled to the cycle, hypnotized by the days, the days in all their rasas (shades, feelings, bliss). The days go on without you. I seem myself to be involved in an ascent, or at least moving down a one-way street. Women *do* tempt the pilgrim to rest and that is why holy men have tended to hate them. Holy men—not the gods. Zeus, Christ, Buddha loved women. But not their philosopher-followers. No? I see you, dear Charles, as something of a holy man, really, with your white lab coat and your hands chilly from their last scrubbing.

To Charles

So truly you must consider me lost to you. When I left you last spring and wrote that long frightened letter on the plane it was like a prank I was carrying out under your auspices, under your giant parasol, and I was like the id in a dying body, that cannot admit it is dying. But now I can admit it: I was *dying to you.* Have you ever noticed, in all the dead people you have seen, how *small* they become? A dead face is no bigger than a dessert plate. I see you now clearly, reduced to your actual size. These legal pranks of yours are pathetic. Tell Gilman I will settle for half the value of the two houses as appraised *for fair market value in today's sky-rocketing New England real-estate market,* half the New Hampshire land ditto, the stocks and bonds as I divided them, my Mercedes (I hope you rev the engine now and then), all the silver and furniture that came from my ancestors with their single insistent initial, and all my legal expenses. The more or less modern furniture we acquired together I grandly waive—your next victim can live with it, and worry about the slipcovers and the loose legs. I think I'm offering a good deal—most wronged wives get 100% of the primary residence at least. And I *was* wronged, of course. Don't make me interrupt my lessons in non-involvement by coming east and collecting depositions from a bevy of fucked nurses and other helpless inmates of your hospital harem. Maybe we can work up a scandal for the *Herald* or at least *The New England Journal of Medicine.* Midge suffered your affairs through with me for these last ten years—I see her, really, as my human archivist. I told her everything, back when I cared, through storms of tears. Gilman should contact Ducky Bradford when he and you are ready to talk sense.

And do lay off little Pearl. Try to think like a father instead of a strategist in the war between the sexes. I ask your help in warding off what I think is her very demeaning involvement with this gross Dutch bunch. They are everything Americans left Europe to get away from—materialist, class-obsessed, cruel in their smugness, and smug in their dullness. The boy naturally has an unearned sophistication that would dazzle our wide-eyed daughter—flats in Paris *and* Venice!—but once the tourism is over, the leaden weight of age-old sacrosanct male supremacy will descend. Europeans are always bragging how their pedigrees go back to cavemen, as if this entitles them to still think like cavemen. Behind that superficial savoir-faire they are cynical slobbering brutes, and nothing delights them so much as the destruction of a beautiful innocence like our daughter's. Pearl needs nice shy American boys, awkwardly full of drive and idealism, eventually; but for now she should be allowed to study, to soak in the great poems and novels of the past if that is where her atman feels itself expand. Her not going back to Yale is tragic, and I blame you. Through this effete Jan you are acting out your own fantasies of seduction—Dr. Epstein and I often discussed your scandalous incestuous flirtatious behavior toward her, even when the poor little soul was still an infant. You are using your paternal power over her to seduce her into "showing me up" by getting married just as I am getting *un*married. I *feel* you, out there, as a dark packet of wounded maleness spitefully taking any tack to "get at" me, even if it means ruining your daughter's fragile young life. I can only hope that this sensation of mine is paranoid.

It is not too early to think about having some fall fertilizer spread on the lawn—they say the acid rain makes it more important than ever. Lawn Craft makes a 10-6-4 mixture called Turf Food that should go on with the spreader set at notch 5—tell the boys to move *briskly* doing it, last year they left burned patches wherever they turned the spreader around. Also tell them not just to *blow* the oak leaves—they love pushing that big blower around, of course—into the bushes in the circle and the ivy over on the rocks—but to carry them down in those dirty old sheets we keep in the tool shed to the compost pile, and to *dig* them out from under the bushes *with rakes*—the little hedge rakes that look like children's toys are actually best for this purpose. You *must* get Mr. Kimball when he does the storm windows also to clean the gutters—otherwise all winter there are those dreadful orange stains down behind the drain pipes. Remind him to turn off the outside water at the underground valve behind the lilacs. I usually do it, and you need an adjustable wrench for the big nut that turns the lid of the standpipe, and a flashlight to see in, otherwise you grope forever with that long rod with the two-pronged grip on the end. Make *sure* he takes the windows *out of the frames* and Windexes—or uses a squeegee and ammonia water, which is actually better—*both sides* instead of just the outside, which is easy to reach from a ladder—he *hates* doing it and who can blame him but it must be done. Remember, those first years after we bought the house from old Mrs. Pyncheon, so young and frightened that $56,000 might have been impossibly too much to pay, how we used to wash the windows together on a weekend, the warm early fall wind blowing the sailboats along on the dark-blue ocean with its whitecaps and the whole world so new to us and clean, clean, *clean*!?

Love,
S.

[*tape*]

Are you there? I guess it's working. Midge, you wouldn't believe the goings-on we've been having here! Maybe some of it has been getting into the Boston papers, but no doubt hideously distorted. Well, I'm not sure anybody can give an account that isn't somewhat distorted—even Durga, who is at the center of it, probably couldn't tell you everything, because she's been so crazy on all the drugs that Ma Prapti's been giving her and *e*verybody, it turns out. I told you—or did I write it to somebody else?—how funny people have been feeling after some of the meals, and how Ma Prapti has been complaining about running out of tranquillizers, out of Percodan and Valium and Demerol, over at the clinic—well, the reason she kept running out is it's all been being sprinkled into our vegetarian curry, like they used to put saltpeter into prisoners' food, to keep them from being too sexy—in our case the idea seemed to be to keep us all calm and passive, since Durga had this idea everybody was conspiring to take her power from her. It's true there's been a lot of complaining about things running downhill, but her notion of a coup was quite fantastic and insecure, since the only real power-source around here is the Arhat's spiritual beauty and condition of moksha, which can't be stolen or changed. But the numbers of reporters and county officials and state cops and FBI men and men from the Immigration Service that kept filtering through made her feel she was losing control, I guess—it turns out that Durga, who as I must have said before is Irish, from one of these charming little villages in the western islands with muddy paths and stone walls where things haven't changed for a thousand years and people go about singing to their cows and sloshing down usquebaugh neat in pubs, was terrified of having her green card taken away and being sent back there, and also Vikshipta, who couldn't find a job in Seattle and is back here now, is from West Germany, and Ma Prapti from Rumania by way of England, and the Arhat himself of course from India, though funnily enough he's the only real Indian, the others stayed behind when they had to move the ashram out of this hilly remote place full of carved caves called Ellora—so this threat of deportation really hung over the inner circle in a way that those of us who happened to be American citizens and never thought much about it couldn't really appreciate. And so Durga was becoming more and more insecure, so that every official terrified her, even the nice little old electrical man who came around to inspect the wiring and stage lighting in Joy-Six-Oh, and when they'd offer these poor men—these really touchingly straight young guys from the IRS or the INS, usually Mormons with that intense religious background—who came around to ask some more official questions herbal tea or whatever, they'd put in something, heaven knows what—I don't know half the chemical names, and Ma Prapti was willing to try anything as an experiment, even ground-up mesquite leaves and creosote-bush twigs, to make them confused and forgetful, but it mostly just gave them terrible diarrhea two hours later. She's confessed all this to the authorities, she talks to them day after day now. I don't think she felt around here anybody ever listened to her. So now all these men, including the lawyers for the ranches and the land-use clique from Phoenix, which is entirely retired Northerners with nothing else to do, and a lot of petty bureaucrats hoping to get their faces on television—this state is so square, Midge, the governor is called Babbitt!—have been milling around and commandeering desks in the Uma Room and putting their feet up and trying to be friendly, saying we don't seem to be such crazies as they had thought and dribbling cigarette ash all over everything, and half the sannyasins that hadn't already left are leaving, and Durga and the hard core around her, Satya and Nitya and Vikshipta and Agni and the security-force boys, have headed up the Sachchidananda to where it becomes a kind of canyon and have holed up in the trailers that were there as a last-ditch security compound, with evidently a ton of weapons like Uzis and Galil assault rifles and even some bazookas to use for anti-aircraft. There're these government helicopters that have been flapping back and forth overhead for days but they never seem to land, just come down and hover, stirring up the dust and blowing all the leaves off the few trees we *have*. Funnily enough, though, now that the roof's fallen in in a way, there's a sort of up mood among those of us still around, a kind of, you know, prakhya feeling that a really immense amount of garbage has been finally disposed of. And I must say that Durga, the last time I saw her, looked terrific, in lavender jeans and denim ranch-hand jacket dyed to match and with a lilac silk scarf at her throat like a British paratrooper and, believe it or not, paratrooper boots as well, and this swanky big black revolver holster strapped to her hip. She's taken to smoking tinted cigarettes in a long ivory holder and the only thing she needs is a black eye patch. She has, I guess I don't have to remind you, this spectacular flaming red hair and pale-green eyes and one of those milky slightly freckled complexions that when I was little I used to envy so—my mother has one and always thought I was disgustingly dark.

Ooh. What was that? Nothing, I guess. Distant shots. I've made myself this cozy nest in Vikshipta's old A-frame—he left his blankets, and a lot of Löwenbräu in the fridge, and all this Freud in German that I can't read. And, Midge, I found a little *whip*, and some funny black leather outfits I can't even figure out how to put on, all straps and rings. Maybe *he's* supposed to put them on. I feel rather hurt, that he never shared this with me. I wonder if that's what he and Durga had between them—when he came back from Seattle he went straight to her and didn't give me the time of day. At any rate—

Uh-oh. There it was again. It sounded closer than way up the canyon, but then that's how sounds are out here—the spaces are so huge and the air so dry, it's hard sometimes to know if a sound is up in the hills or right around the corner. Anyway, this harness or whatever it is is held together by big brass buckles and rings with these designs that if you look—

Oh no. *No.* That was *def*initely footsteps outside, on the gravel. Now something's fiddling at the door! My God, Midge, what shall I do? Somebody's coming in!

[*Amplified clatter and scraping as of drawer being opened and shut. Subsequent conversation faint and transcribed with difficulty. Male voice in italics below as before.*]

Master. It's you.

Who is with you?

Nobody. I'm alone. All alone. You scared me. My heart's pounding.

I heard your voice talking.

I often talk aloud, before I go to sleep. It empties the mind. It's like saying a mantra.

To whom do you speak, Kundalini, in this spiritual exercise, since God in the Occidental sense does not exist?

My daughter. My old friends back home.

They are still real to you?

No, Master, only you are truly real. It's just I have to relax my chittavrittis away from all this disturbance lately.

Let me feel your heart pounding, my dear. It is true. You are afraid. Whenever we talk, it is of fear. Yours or mine. We should attempt to talk of joy. When you speak in solitude, is it also to your husband, this Charles?

Rather rarely, Master. For years I didn't much interest him and now he doesn't interest me.

Perhaps you both self-deceive a little in this. You said he admired your breasts. He was correct. They are admirable.

I usually wear a nightie, but it's been so hot lately—
Kundalini blushes. Also she smiles. It is good, to be admired. I think despite your shyness you like being admired. I admire your smooth darkness, your old-fashioned upright way.

I find your kindness to me rather stunning, actually. I mean, I'm forty-two and just a former housewife—
Please. No fishing, Kundalini. You are magnificent. Your breasts are magnificent. Once, you did not let me caress them. You did not let me caress them like this.

Perhaps the context was different. Time has moved on. I was then in your abode, now you are in mine. You are my guest, one refuses a guest nothing. Master, why have you come to me?

I was alone. I was nervous. I thought of you, perhaps also alone. There has been so much disturbance but I am left alone, at the hurricane's eye—is that an expression? Ma Prapti has the many reporters to fascinate with her horrifying confessions. Durga has her fellow-warriors to exhort and imbue with thirst for glory. In my solitude I enjoy samarasa, the divine immobility. But for the condition of sahaja, of the non-conditioned and purely spontaneous, to reach that of advaya, of non-duality, and from this to attain Mahasukha, of which we once spoke, there must be yuganaddha, the principle of union, which implies an initial duality. I thought of you. My inkling has been that you, too, wish to confront the other, the opposite, and thus achieve advaya. It is perilous, because within it one loses the self.

You said you felt nervous. How can this be when you are a jivan-mukta, always in a state of samadhi?

I am Arhat, a follower of Buddha. The Blessed One did not leave the world, did not disengage himself from the confusions of jiva and ajiva and withdraw into nirvana like your cowardly Jesus. He stayed upon earth, instructing and consoling his disciples to the age of eighty. If we stay on earth, we stay in prakriti. If we stay in prakriti, we are subject to the vasanas and chittavrittis of other men. We are subject to nervousness in the forms of lust and fear. This is the great sacrifice the enlightened make, out of karuna, out of compassion. Indeed you are smooth, as smooth as black Kali. As smooth as Satyavati after bathing in the river Jumna. As smooth as Radha upon the flower couch in the groves of Vrindavan. There is that faint oiliness which I much love. It makes an iridescence.

My father had dark skin. My mother is quite pale. She takes a terrible tan, but keeps trying.

Yes. Your rich mother. We discussed her. I think you are very close, mother and daughter.

Not really. We got off on the wrong foot somehow, when I was very little. About your fear. Is it that you are afraid of death?—of course not, how could you be?—or of the troubles in the ashram sending you back to India?

To Midge

I am not so afraid of India. Perhaps I am afraid of non-India. I am afraid of advaya, of non-duality. For as long as there is duality, the spirit does not need to unrobe. I am not afraid of unrobing the body and will do so. But I am afraid, yes, of the spirit unrobing itself of the body. Of jiva shedding ajiva. That is what I promised you, I think. To turn your body into spirit, to have the great bliss, the Paramahasukha.

Do you think I'm ready for that? Maybe to start with we could have just a *little* sukha.

Let us concentrate, Kundalini. That is stage one. We will let Durga have her shootout on the hills and the FBI men shoot back and the poor little sannyasins run for cover while we enact maithuna. Maithuna is not what is called in this coarse country "fucking." It is cosmic play. It is lila. The soul's journey is lila. The emergence of prakriti from purusha is lila. From the truth of the body, bhanda, emerges by lila the truth of the universe, brahmanda.

I love it when you explain things. Would you like to touch me again?

That comes later, the touching. First is concentration, sadhana. We concentrate upon the beloved. It is best if she is parakiya rati—the wife of another. That is why I so much like your Charles. We need him. Otherwise you are apakva, unripe. Otherwise you are samanya rati, ordinary woman. We must mentally conceive you into vishesha rati—woman extraordinary, divine essence of woman.

Shall I concentrate on you, too?

It is not so necessary, what the woman does. But yes. I am nitya manus, eternal man. I am sahaja manus, man unconditioned. I am ayoni manus, man unborn. My linga is all lingas. My mouth is all mouths. My hands are all hands.

That idea gives me the creeps. I want them to be *your* hands, your hands only. When can you start touching me?

I am Krishna and you are Radha and we are in Vrindavan. Many flowering trees all about us. The smell of much mai-thuna all about us. The sound of water running. Birds unseen singing. All things rank, ripe, deep. We gaze and concentrate upon the other.

Is there a next stage?

Smarana, recollection. I think of Kundalini as when she first came in her rented Hertz, in a checked suit too hot for the sun, with the bold manners of a woman who thinks well of herself.

And I think of you as you were from afar, a brown face on a poster, on the label of a cassette.

Which cassette did you possess?

The one on yamas and niyamas.

Yes. That was a good one. An early one.

And then the one where you answer questions about the aham and the burning away of the vrittis.

I had stupid questioners that day. Stoned hippies and Vishnu bums. All squatting on the dirt floor in Ellora. Before the solid middle class discovered Buddha and pulled out their fat wallets.

Should we be proceeding with the ceremony? Should you have all your clothes still on?

It is not important that the worshipper be naked; only the goddess, the worshipped. Now comes aropa, the attribution of qualities. You are woman, nayika. You are tall. You are dark. You are smooth. You are splendid. You have limbs like thick luminous snakes. Your belly is waxen and long, long; under my eyes it has dunes and hollows like desert sands in moonlight. It

has shiny stripes like veins of expensive mineral. Your navel is
an eye without an eyebrow. It is elegant and long and was well
cut by the doctor the day of your birth. Bless that man. He is
present in your navel.

I was born in the war, in '44. Daddy was in the South
Pacific on a destroyer. The hospitals were understaffed
and the doctor on emergency was a black man my
mother had never seen before. Our own doctor had
collapsed; he hadn't slept for thirty-six hours, there
were fights and accidents all over Boston then, the soldiers and sailors and all these jazz places. It was war-
time. My mother said she was so terrified she vowed
she'd never bear another child. But she did, four years
later.

People forget pain. They do not so quickly forget bliss.

Oh, stop looking. I am so old. My poor saggy body.
My poor stretched belly, that's what those marks are,
from carrying Pearl. This Paramahasukha should have
come along when I was twenty.

You were not ready at twenty. You were only ready for
Charles.

I was ready actually for a boy called Myron Stern, but
my parents disapproved so violently I was scared off.
What a docile nitwit I was.

With this Myron, too, duhkha would have entered in. Life
is duhkha. Duhkha is incorrectly translated "pain." Buddha
did not say, "Life is pain." Duhkha is disenchantment. He
said, "Life is disenchantment." He said, "Life is a letdown."
With Myron, as with Charles, there would have been enchant-
ment, there would have been disenchantment. Even with Arhat.

Not with you, Master.

Why not? I am myself or another.

No, you are you. You have attributes. Let me see you.

I am afraid to disrobe. I am afraid of non-duality.

Don't be silly. Let me help.

[*Faint tumult.*]

I am fat, yes. My belly is in layers like a cake.

Just cozy. So much nice soft black hair.

My linga does not reach the sky.

It's trying.

In aropa, flowers are offered to the nayika. She is beginning to become a goddess. Her yoni is a lotus. Her mouth is a lotus.

You're so sweetly prim here. Like a little cactus. Without thorns. With a little bitter dewdrop.

Your breasts are fruit with tips the color of eggplant. Your shoulders are a silver yoke. Your jaw is a wing, beating slowly up and down.

Those are nice attributes. I like this aropa part.

When the nayika is not there, the yogi remembers her beauty. That is the fourth stage, manana.

Will you remember me?

Ah, your voice is dark and sad. That is the question women ask. They always ask, "Will you remember me?"

They want to know.

Their asking so earnestly plunges the lovers back into time, the sad time that does not exist in Vrindavan.

I think you have many nayikas to remember.

The vishesha rati is not jealous. She is Shakti and is all women.

How very convenient for Shiva.

You ridicule your Master. You are being wicked Kali.

I'm getting sexually frustrated. How many more stages are there?

No need exists to rush. That is very Occidental, your need to rush.

Couldn't you at least kiss me? Somewhere. Anywhere.

The next stage is dhyana, mystic meditation, in which the nayika sits upon the lover's left and is embraced, not for the sake of bodily pleasure but for the enhancing of the spirit.

That may be too subtle a distinction for this old girl.

No. Not subtle. Love is for bodies only when the spirits are in harmony. Love is more than fucking only when the god in the other is saluted. That is why we say, "Namaste."

I love the way you say "luff." I always have.

That is why we say, "So 'ham." I am He.

I'm supposed to say something back but I forget what.

You say, "Sa 'ham." You are She.

Sa 'ham. I am She.

Great Kundalini, stand so I may meditate upon your body, each glistening particle, each cell of skin, each hair and gland. Think with me of your body cell by cell, as something greater than galaxies, greater than all the jewel trees. You are like a Bodhisattva standing in the Land of Bliss, in Sukhavati. You are infinitely tall, infinitely splendid. You are immeasurably radiant, amitabha. You are amitayus, forever enduring.

Mm. That feels nice. Tickly, but nice.

I am bathing you with my tongue. I drink your perspiration, your rasas. This is puja, the sixth stage. The nayika is bathed as if she is a statue of the goddess. As I do so I repeat formulas in my head.

Must you go through this every time?

To make it holy, yes. To exalt us, yes. You may sit now. On my left. On the bed. The worship continues. Open your thighs.

That's nice too. Nicer, even.

Can you feel my inner concentration?

So that's what I feel.

I adore your yoni. I drink your rajas.

Don't stop. Must you stop?

Now the seventh stage. The adept lays the nayika on the bed and repeats aloud the sacred formula.

There is one?

Hling kling kandarpa svaha.

What does it mean?

Hling kling kandarpa svaha.

O.K. Pardon my asking.

Now sit on me.

It's too big. It *has* reached the sky.

This is stage eight, maithuna.

Oh. It's not too big. Not quite. Not quite quite.

Kundalini was impatient for this stage.

Keep talking to me, please.

Concentrate. Think of ida. Think of pingala. Energy is rising.

Mm.

Think of Muladhara to Svadhisthana. Now she leaves the belly and flies to the solar plexus, to Manipura.

Mmm.

From Manipura to Anahata, the heart. Up, up, to beyond the heart.

Nn.

Beyond the heart to Vishuddha, the throat. There are many throats.

N*nnn*.

Dombi dances in the sambhogakaya. The washerwoman dances in the throat. From Vishuddha—

[*Unintelligible.*] Oh. My God. Goodness me. Now you.

No. I do not do. You do again, Kundalini. And again.

Really? Isn't that unfair?

Unfair to you. It puts you into time. It puts you into the clutches of Kali, while I am in samarasa. I have the bliss of vajrolimudra. The energy of the suspended semen enters my spirit and makes me immortal. You die again and again. You are cruelly used.

If you say so. I keep going?

Keep going.

Mm. Nn. Oh. Oh yes, yes. God. How do you do it?

Advanced technique. It is called "ujjana sadhana," "against the current." It brings, through samarasa, sahaja. It brings the non-conditioned. It brings advaya. Shakti and Shiva, vajra and padma, jiva and ajiva are one. You and I are one. What I will, you become.

Yes, Master.

If I scratch your fat rump, it is pleasure.

Pleasure.

If I slap you thus, that too.

That too.

Come once more.

Darling, I'm exhausted.

Come. Come, you sopping cunt.

[*Click: end of tape, side one.*]

Midge, that was the most magical thing of all, the way that side of the tape got used up just as I did. I think my moan drowned out the click in the drawer, but *I* heard it. I really probably should erase that side, but I have this feeling about it that it's bigger than I am somehow, that my personal modesty is totally unimportant and it wasn't me in any case but a kind of goddess actually and that what really *is* important is the Arhat's voice on tape, his fantastic capacity for love. I don't know how he held it but it stayed just as hard as a rock, only of course smooth—a jewel just like they say. He was the jewel and I was the lotus. It felt just like that, on and on into eternity. And it wasn't just that once, I've been with him a few times since. I'm not sure, though, you should play the tape for Irving and the other girls— only if you think they can take it in the yogic spirit and not as just titillation and gossip. It *must*n't get back to Charles. I'll leave it up to you, I've been away so long now I can't be the judge of anybody's spiritual progress and maturity. Please keep it safe for me, though, so some day when I'm old and gray and sitting in some nursing home or Florida condo like my grotesque mother I can play it and remember the times when I was Shakti and Radha with the best of them. I wonder whose Radha *she* ever was, by the way. It's awfully hard to picture Daddy being Krishna.

What other news? I don't know what sort of stuff gets onto television back East—I suppose it depends pretty much on what the Russians and Iranians did that afternoon—but Durga and Agni and the rest of her hard core, mostly the guys from security and some of the younger women in PR, stayed up in the canyon a few more days, until their pills and water ran out, but when nobody came after them they began to dribble back to the Chakra and the cafeteria, looking dusty and under-weight and sheepish. Durga had expected some kind of shootout, like they have I guess in Belfast with the British soldiers, but the IRS and Immigration don't work like that, it's more a matter of form letters with that dotty kind of printer that only the government still seems to use, these utterly machine-made-looking let-ters you can keep ignoring because it looks like junk mail until some morning months later the sheriff shows up with handcuffs. These shots I kept hearing were I guess Durga and Satya and the guys having fun, prac-ticing with their infrared gunsights and these other fancy armaments that have been costing the Treasury of Enlightenment an arm and a leg. To avoid an ambush in the pass she came down the Sachchidananda on a rubber raft they had up there, and though there was her old kind of dash in that, she looks basically discouraged. She talks about deporting herself back to Ireland rather than fight the INS. We've had a couple of long talks, she and I, now that I use her old office in the Uma Room, and the odd thing is I'm beginning to *like* her, rather—though of course not the abso*lute*ly comfortable way I like you and Donna and Ann Turner and Liz Belling-ham. *We* have a language in common, we went to the same sort of schools and dated the same boys more or less and made the same klishta compromises, but a lot of the women here, frankly, are like people from the moon. It's like they skipped a beat somewhere, and

really don't much care about either death *or* sex. Maybe
it's an East Coast / West Coast thing, or a generation
kind of gap, but I don't think so exactly. Maybe I've
been standoffish. I came here, face it, to get close to the
Arhat, and now that I couldn't get any closer except by
crawling up his asshole—sorry, that's the way he talks,
once you get to know him, with almost a tough-guy
kind of American accent, God knows where he picked
it up—and now that I've achieved my objective and
satisfied my really pretty deplorable phalatrishna, I'm
able to relate to these people on more relaxed terms.
Durga's always frightened me but she says now *I*
frightened *her* from the start, and if you think of her as
just this little Irish village girl you can see I might be
frightening. She says she could see at a glance that I had
the kind of energy the Arhat eats up. She says he eats
people up, psychologically, without meaning to—it's
just that his prana and mahat are so strong they suck
you in and spit you out, he's so incredibly intuitive that
he gets impatient, and she and Prapti and Nitya and
Alinga and the inner circle were wearing out around
him. So she sensed I was going to take over, though of
course I haven't, I still don't know the half of what goes
on around here. She said, Durga, to finish up with her,
that she was raised with this terribly restrictive Irish
Catholicism and hated it and thought what the Arhat
was offering, this free-form Buddhism, would release
her but she wonders now if it didn't actually make her
more uptight, all these spiritual possibilities so she was
constantly having to choose, and maybe the real way to
be free is just to do whatever the priest or husband or

boss or whoever says while deep inside *scorn*ing it—that
this is *real* asanga, real detachment from your life, instead of coming here and trying to make a new social
model and the desert bloom and so on. All I could tell
her was that it's been wonderful for me so far but that
I rather did doubt if I or any woman would ever be able
to do vajrolimudra, because of the anatomical differences, and so would always be swept along by time. She
kissed me then, this big white face of hers swooping
down, she said I looked so sweet saying that, when I had
just been trying to be serious. I mean, *really* kissed me,
but it wasn't like with Alinga—I have the funny feeling
Durga doesn't have much of a sex life in any direction.
Her eyes get softest when she talks about Ireland and
her mother and the two cows they used to keep in the
village, the way their spotted big sides steamed just
after it rained. She was some sort of artiste in Dublin—I
don't know, do they still have music halls?—but it's the
village and the cows that turn her on. The warm milk—
that steamed, too.

I still love Alinga, by the way. I mean we don't live
together like we did but that lazy kind of deep affection
is still there. We're spending a lot of time in the Uma
Room together lately, still trying to straighten out the
mess Nitya left and to keep ahead of our mail. It seems
everybody is suing us, we're like a whale that's started
to bleed and every shark in the ocean has gone into a
feeding frenzy—I love that new term, don't you? Feeding frenzy. They use it a lot on television now, not just
the nature programs but the evening news. Not only

are all these governments—local, state, and national—
on our case but about three sets of parents are suddenly
taking us to court for brainwashing their children—
though I don't see how they can collect damages, since
these children are legally adult and if they weren't here
doing work as worship they'd be hanging around their
parents' homes soaking up money and wrecking cars
and running up psychiatrists' bills. Speaking of
Nitya—Nitya Kalpana, you remember, our former accountant—she says her head is out of the bad place it
was in and she can do with less meditation now—in
fact, she wonders if she wasn't being overdosed in the
clinic by Ma Prapti, who, even though she spilled the
beans for days to the FBI and everybody, is still under
a lot of indictments. The way Durga tried to explain it
to me, when we had our nice talk, it was more a philosophical inquiry Ma Prapti was undertaking. She was
asking, What is the mind? It can be altered by yoga,
O.K., to achieve samadhi, but also by drugs, by alcohol,
by fatigue, by hormones, even by things as innocent as
the moon and sugar. So why not develop a purusha pill
and get to nirvana that way? A lot of people do, of
course—like Marilyn Monroe and all these teen-age sui-
cides the TV commentators keep putting on long faces
about. This question of course is very troubling to the
old-fashioned rigid Christian philosophical framework
but it doesn't bother Oriental thinking at all, where it's
all maya anyway. Anyway, I really do resent Nitya's
coming out of meditation with all this officiousness. I've
pretty well got the accounts so I can deal with them and

I don't want her confusing things again. I feel invaded. No matter where you are, or how much enlightenment is around, human relations are tricky.

Midge, that is too bad, what you admitted, or really more implied, about you and Ed. You two always seemed so solid. I used to envy you, in fact—you seemed so satisfied, so unquestioning. I mean, you weren't expecting the world, and you saw Ed's limitations, and I know his drinking aggravated you more than you let on, and that loudmouth know-it-all manner that bothered me less than it did Charles because if you listened Ed really *did* know a lot of things, especially about electronic security systems and how car engines work and how the insurance companies and pension funds control the stock market, but nevertheless you never betrayed him by wincing or making sardonic eye-contact like, say, Donna and for that matter Gloria used to do, and whatever your differences your house was a *fun* one to be in. Those lovely lawn parties you two always gave. People are selfish, of course, and when a couple we know breaks up it's one less port in a storm, one or two less parties a year, one more house in town that begins to look weedy and sad. When I left Charles that was one of my thoughts—how sad it would be for the rest of you, not to have us to swell the scene, as it were. Heaven only knows what Charles is doing with his spare time now—not that he ever had much. Those little nurses and receptionists he used to screw so happily when he had me as part of his baggage I dare say look (and talk) quite differently now that he's, so to speak, free. Real freedom is within, Midge. You and I know that. This morning in darshan the Arhat shared with us Buddha's last words. You know what they were? See if I can recite them, without the accent. "Be a lamp unto yourselves. Be a refuge unto yourselves. Seek no refuge outside of yourselves." Seek no refuge outside of yourself, Midge—that's what I'm trying to keep in mind in these hectic last couple of weeks and you keep it in mind no matter what the future brings for you and dear old Ed.

I mean, it's been hectic here and it's been not. There's a lot of positive energy around since the scene thinned out. All along there've been a number of not-so-desirable types showing up here in dime-store sunset colors saying they were sannyasins, thinking from what they've seen on the news that this is a real gravy train, but now that all the papers are blabbing how we owe everybody fifteen million, or maybe it's fifty, they've pretty well split, and some of Agni's lavender cowboys too, now that the real fuzz in one form or another is always in and out serving summonses and repossessing computers and earth-moving equipment and running fingerprint checks on people and chemical checks on the cafeteria lemonade and ripping out illegal wiring and I don't know what all else to protect us against ourselves. Some of these outer-state types are kind of cute in their way and, you know, curious about us, and more open-minded than you might think. I don't really think you can say the world has subdivisions any more—what with television and modems we're all operating on the same sattva, and my conclusion so far, after being six months out of our own little North

Shore ghetto, is that the world *is* really slowly getting to be a better place, provided we can keep the population explosion from turning all the land into deserts and asphalt and if the destruction of the ozone by aerosol cans with the greenhouse effect doesn't melt the ice caps and flood every coastal city out of existence, not to mention the Bomb, which seems to be the least of the problems because at least people agitate about it and picket Army bases.

God, listen to the big philosopher. But one of the things the Arhat has done for me is encourage me to let it out, let out the feelings and thoughts both and get rid of the conditioning that had us trained to keep quiet while all these fathers and husbands and sons and lovers and lawyers and doctors and Indian chiefs talked. All this trying to be not too smart, not too loud, not too sexy, not too wonderful or else we'd overwhelm men that we were subconsciously taught to do like children in Hong Kong apartments trained to live in two cubic feet of space—I say, "Fuck it." "Fuck it" is what I say now, Midge.

But what I *start*ed to say, about all the repo men and sheriff's aides that are crawling around here, is that among the equipment they repossessed was that at the dental clinic, which was run by an absolutely cool old saint called Ganesha, older even than me and here because his practice in Boise began to remind him of death, so when I went with this lower-right molar that's been slowly going funny ever since I absent-mindedly chomped down on a betel nut, he said it looked to him like a root-canal candidate, it had been "insulted" so often with old silver fillings, but he didn't have the X-ray machine any more so I better get it looked at in town. By "town" around here they mean this dusty strip called Forrest that I think I described ages ago when I first came, full of retired people and old ranch rats and a few stray Navajos and these born-again creeps that attack the Arhat whenever he shows up for a Diet Coke—I was surprised they even had a dentist there. So I have to go in there tomorrow, if I can find a pickup truck or limo with some gas still in it. We have this five-thousand-gallon tank buried underground but Mobil refuses to fill it until we pay our bill. At the same time they keep sponsoring these holier-than-thou eco-logical documentaries on saving the whooping crane and the Salt Lake pupfish on television. How's that for corporate doublethink? Save the pupfish and let people on the path to holiness go hang.

Well, what else? What have I left out? The beauty of it here, maybe, now that what they call fall has come. Not fall like *we* have it, of course—nothing like all that glory of the leaves, the maples and sumac and ash, and the smell of burning applewood out of people's chim-neys, and the ocean turning that almost vicious dark-gray greeny-blue color under the heavy autumn clouds. Here it's more of a delicate change, like a piece of trans-parent, slightly brown film placed over everything. The nights are getting cold again, but the days are still hot. A few of the trees do have leaves that turn yellow and drop—there's the willow wattle, and Australian acacia, and a kind called shoe-string acacia—but by and large they never had much in the way of leaves to begin with, since the trick of the desert is not to gather photons, of which there are billions and billions too many, but to hold in moisture. The smoke tree and the paloverde hardly have leaves at all, just these threadbare skinny things that show up in the spring before the flowering and then drop right off. So you get this feeling of vegetation that already lives in purusha, with just the tiniest delicate grip on the surface of prakriti, without any of the turmoil and violence of our Eastern weeds and bushes and vines battling it out with all of their egos on every square foot that isn't absolutely rock. Here it's mostly rock, red rock and sand, so you're very grateful and aware of the slightest living thing—a lot of the desert flowers are almost microscopic, the size of pinheads practically. I love it, Midge. I love the freedom of the almost nothingness—the hills with nothing on them but wisps of golden grass, and the skies with only some jet trails and the highest little tentative horsetails that never seem to come to anything as far as the weather goes. We had an hour of rain the other night and everybody came out of the Kali Club and danced naked in it, though it was freezing, really. Where it's so dry, water evaporates on you so rapidly it *hurts*, you can't help but chatter and shiver and jump around.

My dreams, Midge. My dreams get more and more intense lately. It's frightening. And a lot of them are about, of all people, Charles. I've totally stopped thinking about him consciously—we've stopped communicating; let Ducky and this vulture Gilman communicate—but in these dreams we're making love the way we did the first years we were married. They say people in dreams are displacements and it must be that it's really the Arhat I'm dreaming about but it seems so vividly Charles—the flat hard body he had and still has, considering his age, and the way he did everything in silence and seemed a little offended if I made any noise myself, and certain little things I won't go into but that definitely identify him as Charles, a smell even, I know you're not supposed to smell in dreams, but he smells like the desert, or at least I wake up with the spicy musty fragrance all around me, and the moon on the tangled sheets, here in Vikshipta's A-frame. And *he* was another, come to think of it. Another severe man. Without wanting to be, I seem to be attracted to that type. In the dreams Charles and I are usually in a bare room, a room without furniture. Almost like an operating room, except there's not an operating table or the bright lights. There must be a bed, we have to be lying on something. He's pushed himself up on his arms and I see his bare shoulders and his chest, smooth and hard and almost hairless the way he was, just a few hairs that turned gray eventually over the sternum bone and around the nipples, the plane of his chest slanting down to where our bodies join, and I'm aware of his excited breath, the warmth of it, and this dry desert sweetness like the fragrance of mesquite pods, and I'm very young and tight and worried about getting pregnant, and at the same time I'm myself as I am now, and even know that sleeping with Charles is *wrong*, a betrayal of the ashram, but this sense of fatherly forgiveness and understanding enclosing me is coming from him, pouring from him like chakra energy from the Sahasrara lotus, so I know it can't be Charles really, since understanding he never especially was and forgiving he certainly is not now. It's strange. But I wake up overwhelmed. He seems just enormous, and flooding me with these spiritual waves. It must be a transposition of my experiences here. We're all just masks anyway, don't you think? I mean masks of the archetypes. My best to Irving and Ed if he and you work things out and Gloria and Donna and Liz and Ann and the others but abso*lute*ly—I *trust* you, Midge—*don't* let them listen to

[*end of tape*]

Nov. 12

Dear Dr. Podhoretz:

Just a note to bring you up to date on my dental adventures. I think I mentioned some months ago the sensitivity, an elusive "punky" feeling, in the lower-right quadrant. The molar—it was hard to know which it was, under the crowns—has been getting slowly worse, but not so bad that I couldn't ignore it, blaming it vaguely on the general nervous and spiritual stress I've been under recently, or even on the altitude here, which I imagined might function somewhat as an airplane ride does when it gives you an earache or a sensation of pressure in the sinuses. But lately the feeling *has* become unignorable, and I've come forty miles to a dentist here in Forrest, the town nearest the kibbutz-like community where I now reside.

But this dentist, a much more gracious and efficient practitioner than I had expected, with a definite English accent, of all things—the British seem strangely attracted to this part of the world, the opposite of their own dreary climate, I suppose—said that I didn't need a root canal but that the crown had been badly designed and was occluding in a way with the upper teeth that was applying torque and giving me soreness along the gums—*voilà*, the "punky" feeling! Well, of course I defended your crown, said you were considered among the very best in Swampscott, etc. But with this tranquil little supercilious smile he had me bite on a piece of red wax-paper and grind my teeth and then did some very delicate drilling (I didn't even have Novocaine) and I must say the trouble seems miraculously to have vanished! And he only charged me $45 for the appointment, as opposed to the $125 that you have been asking. But of course a lot of the things you buy here are cheaper than in the East, except for what has to be flown over the Rockies, like lobsters and cranberries.

Just thought you'd like to keep abreast of my mouth and make a mark on my chart. You have several sets of X-rays; perhaps you can tell from them whatever it was you did wrong.

> Happy Veterans Day,
> Sarah Worth

November 12

Gentlemen:

Enclosed find endorsed checks totalling $157,634.26 to be deposited to my charge account with your book and gift shop. I look forward to visiting Samana Cay some day and using my accumulated credit to make some purchases and enjoy some leisure there.

Yours sincerely,
Sarah P. Worth

le 12 novembre

Monsieur,

Voici les formules et les renseignements nécessaires à ouvrir mon compte, et aussi un chèque, tiré de mon compte à la Bank of Boston, pour $200,000. Faîtes-là mon premier dépôt, s'il vous plaît, et

Agréez, je vous prie,
l'expression de mes sentiments dévoués,
#4723-9001-7469-8666

November 14

Dear Mr. and Mrs. Enright—

We have been slow to respond to your several communications not because we have been taking them lightly but perhaps taking them all too seriously. Over the years a considerable number of properly concerned and loving parents have written us, threatened us, and even appeared at our gates with complaints such as yours; we are often besieged by lawyers and psychiatric "experts" and prejudiced journalists over these issues of "brainwashing" and "child abduction." Never mind that the "child" was as old as thirty-four in one case, and in almost all cases well above the legal age of consent. Never mind that "brainwashing" is a nebulous term that could with justice be applied to our elementary-school introduction to the history and the capitalist, "freedom-loving" values of the United States; or to the religious rubrics pressed upon the child not only by church, synagogue, and mosque but by home influence and certain sentimental strains of popular entertainment; or to the massive inculcation of consumeristic hedonism sought by the relentless barrage of television commercials and printed advertising. Not to mention the habituation to violence and vice that follows from even modest exposure to the televised dramas sandwiched between the insidious commercials; and the absolutely pervasive and irresistible rape of adolescent minds by the nihilism and eroticism of popular music;

and the more specialized forms of brainwashing undergone in military and corporate indoctrination programs.

Our brains are there to be washed, Mr. and Mrs. Enright, by everything from elevator music to bumper stickers, and amid this polluted tide of bobbing, jostling, oozing propaganda a few souls elect to discipline their egos and follow the Master. Our way is not easy. Many fall away when they realize that the death of ego is the price of happiness. Many desert when they discover that cherished possessions must be sacrificed to non-attachment. Many have lately defected, rather than face the true richness of paradox which the Master has prepared for them. Openness and spontaneity are our watchwords, not control. Your son Kevin, or Yajna as we call him here, came to us freely and is free to leave. Though appreciative of all you have done for him, from nursery school to business school, he does not want to return to your big sandstone house in Saint Louis with the mansard roof and porte-cochere, on its archaic private street, though he thinks back upon it fondly, as we all should upon scenes we have outgrown. He is not brainwashed. He is adult, and at peace, and on the road to nirvana.

Look into your own hearts. Our Master advises you to consider this text from the blessed Dhammapada: " 'These are my sons. This is my wealth.' In this way the fool troubles himself. He is not even the owner of himself: how much less of his sons and of his wealth." In demanding we return "your" son to you, you become "fools." A semantic misunderstanding lies at the heart of your confusion: when we speak of "our" or "my" son or daughter or wife or master, we are not expressing ownership but by a grammatical shortcut a certain intuitively felt connection: these persons or manifestations of enduring modalities have wandered into "my" sphere of apprehension, the possessive pronoun being used merely to locate the subjectivity. But people do not own people. Your son is not "yours" even though you carried him in your womb and paid for his extensive education, frat fees, auto insurance, etc. Though for a time he was "yours" to imprison within your Richardsonian mansion and perhaps to bully and beat and certainly to manipulate with the psychological blackmail at which the nuclear family is so adept, he is not "yours" now, to reflect creditably upon you in the eyes of your equally narrow-minded and proprietorial acquaintances, or to reverse the declining trend in the railroad enterprises that made your family fortune, or to extend your genes and generations further into the void of maya; he is, instead, "his"—or, to put it more exactly, his ego or aham is at the service of his highest self, the atman, as it merges with purusha, the changeless and featureless spirit which at the beginning of phenomena allowed itself to be clouded with the emergence of matter and its complicated turbulences.

To make "your" son truly "yours," come join him and us in this besieged place of pilgrimage and study, or, if you are too deeply mired in the illusory—too "brainwashed," so to speak—come join us in the sense of making a generous gift to the work of the ashram, in the form either of a direct cash donation (in this last year of the full 50% tax bracket) or a gift of stocks, bonds, or property.

                     Most sincerely,
                        Ma Prem Kundalini
                        Executive Assistant to
                        Shri Arhat Mindadali, M.A., Ph.D.,
                        Supreme Meditator, Ashram Arhat

Nov. 16

Oh my darling dearest Pearl, my only child—

How could you do so many vile things to your mother at once?

(1) You turned twenty-one—for this I cannot exactly blame you, though it means I have not even a vestige of a child now. I trust you received the sandalwood mala with the tinted miniature of the Arhat and the quite expensive snakeskin sandals that I sent off a month ago to make their way across the desert, the mountains, the plains, our good green East, and the blue Atlantic Ocean to *you*; you didn't thank me in your otherwise news-laden letter. The snake is the Arizona coral snake, which has this remarkable alternation of broad red/ narrow yellow/broad black/narrow yellow/broad red etc. stripes, all so mechanically perfect it looks a little cheap and plasticky—one of those natural effects too good to be true. The snake itself is rather rare and shy

and small (which makes the sandals both expensive and illegal) and highly poisonous, and has—all this from Alinga, who seems to have made quite a study of desert life in her years here—an endearing trick of, when threatened, hiding its head in its coils and lifting its tail and popping out its anus! That makes a distinct and alarming sound, she says. Really, prakriti is just so irreverent—it's all lila, as the Master often reminds us.

(2) You say you are not only taking the fall term off but may likely *never* come back to Yale and finish your degree. I can't *tell* you how much of an utter mistake this is. Your doubts about your major—whether or not this M. Derrida and his deconstruction are actually anti-phallic and whether or not this Mr. Bloom twiddles too much when he lectures—are really beside the point; you can major in chemistry or basket weaving or home economics (which used to be a course seriously offered to young women—how to sew and cook, mostly—wifemanship with sex left out) for all I care, but you *must get your degree.* If you don't you can never hold your head up; a college degree is the invisible tiara a woman must wear now, otherwise people write her off as a bumpkin, an ignoramus, a throwback, an archaic creature. Look at Princess Diana, how people snicker even at her. Look at me, whose greatest mistake in life was to leave Radcliffe at the outset of my junior year to marry your father—*how* I secretly suffered all these years, how I *cringed* whenever the subject of colleges came up in conversation. I vowed you would never make my mistake. Well, you *did* get through one more year than I did. So close! You say that in Europe it really

doesn't matter so much and if so that proves my point that Europeans are at bottom grotesquely primitive cavepeople who believe that everything comes down to entitlement by birth. The ones who stayed there chose to hang back from the great spiritual adventure America was and is and I fear I can't *bear* to think of my Pearl wasting her precious life among them. The Europeans here at the ashram, most of whom have been deported or gone into hiding, were a fascinating study in how intelligent and attractive people could go through all the correct motions and yet all the time be *missing the point*. They kept trying to make a formal church or a military organization out of it all; the *delicacy* of our American reality keeps escaping them, the way our whole lovely nation is founded on the edge of a dream, on the edge of purusha. I don't include the Arhat; he is not European but Indian, an Aryan with something else added—sun, centuries of terribly much sun, and also something religious from the Dravidian South, with its murderous worship of femaleness, like a wonderful gluey dark honey poured into milk. Jan sounds *totally* milky to me, and his parents too, though they've curdled into butter—little square pats stamped with some phony armorial seal. Darling, believe me, not going through with Yale, however much of an awkward bother it seems now, will destroy your life— you'll limp forever, my dear tall-striding beauty.

(3) You tell me your father, who has flown over again, likes Jan very much and finds the van Hertzogs jolly fun and wholeheartedly approves of your engagement. Don't you *see* he's doing exactly what my father (whom I

loved too—how can we *help* but love these fathers, the way the sides of their necks smell of sweat and aftershave when they pick us up off the floor and give us that squeeze that knocks us breathless?) did—pass you on like a manacled slave to another *man*? Men don't much like other men—all organic things intrinsically hate one another, except as food—but they're used to them and they're *not* used to free women—women standing upright and having ideas and walking up the middle of the sidewalk with unpinned hair bouncing and flowing behind, the way I've always pictured you. You can say I was trying to live my life through you in a way I never lived it myself; but that is what women must do when they knuckle under as I did through not knowing any better—and now as *you* are doing *though knowing better* and having other alternatives but spurning them. Of *course* your father would think it very cute having this bogus nobility with their unicorn and lion or whatever it is on every bottle as kin and connections over there so he can casually drop word to his posh surgeon pals of his jetting back and forth. New England snob as he is he imagines he always *did* have a foot still in the Old World. But what he *really* likes is that European dungeons are deeper, divorces are harder, and you are more securely locked in where he *can get at you.* There is no escaping Daddy once the van Hertzogs sink their claws in, and of course (you'll all say) poor Mother—she can't manage to leave her dreadful guru and always was a bit of a misfit. . . . Sweet little Pearl, this is our goodbye. Those round blurry spots in these "wiggles" of mine (remember, your calling them that?), are tears, actual tears.

I'm making such a mess, I had to lean back with folded hands and let them drop into my lap. The tears. I'm wearing the silk sari, in case the Master comes in. Water is bad for silk and saltwater must be worse. But it felt good to cry. The Master has given me so much of his own peace I'd almost forgotten how to manage a good old Occidental convulsion—a *Schmerzfest*, a purgative *déluge des larmes chaudes*. So, then, to continue,

(4) You are pregnant. After wounding me in these various other ways you want to make me into a *grandmother*. White hair, trifocals, rocking chair, crewel work. Passing down wooden toys and family lore before winking out like a frosted light bulb. And I have *never* felt younger—the bride I was at twenty was a timid hidebound crone compared with the woman I feel myself now to be. And you've decided—though I don't see how anybody of your age and position, with all the contraceptive gadgets and creams and foams they have now, not to mention all the non-procreative ways of "getting off" that were terribly hush-hush and taboo in the dark age when *I* was young, could *decide* anything of the sort; you both must have been stoned or coked or whatever out of your fuzzy heads—to make me an *ancestor*, ashes and bones in a sacred urn, some yellowing photographs in the family album, a filled-in slot in the genealogical chart, a sad old story buried amid the rubbish in the custom-house attic. I'm not ready, I'm still learning how to live, to *be*. I've reached the solar-plexus chakra and I'm still climbing. I'm having *fun*, honey.

People are supposed to rejoice at a pregnancy, however inconvenient it is. At least the Pope wants us to.

I wonder why. You were always a healthy normal girl so this event physiologically is no triumph against the odds. You would have been able to pull it off at thirty, at forty even. Why so early? Naturally I blame myself. My running off—deserting my biological post—made you think you had to man—why isn't there a verb "to woman"?—the ramparts, the reproductive barricades. Or am I giving myself and the old riddle of mother-daughter relations too much credit? Most pregnancies, like most wars, are totally *silly*, and aren't intended at all—they come about in a long blink while the mind is essentially asleep. With so many of these teen-age pregnancies now it's obviously a childish way of punishing the world. Consider me punished.

Consider me cheated of every woman's most harmless fantasy—to stage-manage a wedding, to be the mother of the bride. I suppose that the van Hertzogs and your father have the situation heavily in hand. By even the fifth month you might get by with an A-line tulle-and-satin gown, and if it's only the fourth you could even have the dressmaker give you a bit of a waist. I *love* the look of a lace bodice, and a long stiff train, and a garland of real flowers that will wilt in an hour, and a veil with the bride's head obscured and vague like that of a goddess, a sacred statue, or a corpse—the *menace* of a bride coming down the aisle, to gobble up the quaking groom and, for dessert, his best man. It breaks my heart not to see my daughter married. But I disapprove so thoroughly of this particular ceremony whereby your lovely erect and shining womanhood bows low to this callow spoiled Dutch boy (his finger in quite the wrong dike) and his obese parents that my presence there would create a spiritual irritant if not a vocal objection ringing off the scandalized church rafters. You don't say what kind of church the vain Warthogs favor; my intuition says not the sturdy Reformed faith that gave us all those gorgeous Rembrandt blacks and tidy tiled interiors but sneaky snobby Catholic, so watered down by these Dutch theologians one reads about being nearly excommunicated all the time that you've never *noticed* your in-laws' Papism until now that it's too late, and no doubt they'll want you to convert, smilingly assuring you that it's just a formality and doesn't mean a *thing*. Thus the Old World reclaims the New and rescinds its beautiful promise of liberty. What Catholicism means to you, my dear, is incessantly more pregnancies—Jan is himself the baby of six, you told me—until by mutual understanding your husband wanders off to deposit his sperm in the famous red-light district or else in some querulous but spermicidal mistress whose progeny are no priest's business. And you, my poor Pearl, where will you find happiness then, as the little warthogs swarm around you and their paternal grandparents, smelling of rancid hops, lower over you like two rainclouds and all around you the air is thick with the ugliest language in Christendom? If you ever seek to vary your entertainment as Jan does his, you have a world of flat-headed Dutchmen to choose a lover from. You will be saddled with *respectability*—respectability more oppressive and muggy than any form of bourgeois self-enthrallment that has ever taken root in America, where at least one can always go west or make a wisecrack. No wisecracks in Holland—just boors and beers and burghers and bores.

Let's hope I'm quite wrong. Have a lovely wedding. At some point in life a woman becomes her own mother and you have reached it sooner than I did. Even if I could stomach the jet lag and Lowlands humidity I by no means wish to encounter your father, who might slap a subpoena on me before giving the blushing and bulging bride away. He imagines all sorts of legal wrongs from his helpless old helpmeet. So let this be his circus, while I watch my gallant circus here slowly fold its tents and put its elephants to bed. The ashram's days feel numbered. Do drop a note to your grandmother to tell her she's becoming a great-. *She* is being romanced by some antique fraud the Navy let out of mothballs and may have some rude news of her own. For the baby's sake, take lots of vitamin B-complex and *zinc*— zinc for all life-changes that involve metabolism.

See? For all your naughtiness I am still

Your loving Mother

Nov. 22

Dear Mother,

Your daughter has been most cruelly deceived! Thinking I was achieving vidya, I have been floating in a sea of avidya. My disillusion came about in this way:

There have been officials of all stripes and flavors hustling in and out of here legally picking the bones of our beautiful disintegrating Buddha Field. Prominent among them have been these men from the Immigration and Naturalization Service of the Department of Justice accusing us of immigration fraud. Our dear U.S., as you in South Florida know, has gone from being a global void that had to bribe people to come or else drag them here on slave ships to being a kind of last chance in a world of economic misery. Maybe the world has always been economically miserable—why would anyone *work* otherwise?—but people didn't use to know it and now they do. Rather close as distances go out here is the border with Sonora in Mexico and apparently a number of our sannyasins were wetbacks of this utterly dry kind, since they've come in across the desert, smuggled in trucks and boxcars and some of them fried to death, poor souls. Also, from the India days, the ashram has a number of Europeans—mostly West Germans, Swedes, Danes, and Walloons—somehow Mediterranean Catholics don't need Buddha, maybe because they have the Virgin Mary with *her* sweet smile—who evidently pretended to be married to American sannyasins or who really *were* married but the INS claims insincerely, just to get by immigration. How they measure the sincerity of a marriage I'd love to know. So as all these people were being grilled and weeded out and tagged for shipment back to place of national origin I began to wonder why the Master himself, the Arhat, seemed immune from deportation even though he was from India, which I am sure is near the bottom of the list of the Immigration Service's favorite countries.

Well, I was with my dear friend Alinga—I think I wrote to you or somebody all about her: from Iowa, lanky, spacy, pretty in a willowy pale way, very supportive to me back in the days when I was being promoted from the backhoe and the artichokes—and I mentioned this minor miracle to her and the corners of her lips turned up in a provocative way she has and she said she'd assumed I knew by now. Knew what? *Knew that the Arhat's real name was Art Steinmetz, and that he was from Massachusetts*—Watertown, to be exact. *Watertown*, Mother!

Actually I make it sound as if she told me on the spot but it took several days of campaigning on my part, playing it cozy and not pressing until we were really relaxed together and it could kind of slide out. Evidently he *did* go to India and did learn Hindi and Sanskrit and some Pali and study yoga but this was all from about 1965 and then all through the Seventies, but before that he was just one more bright good Jewish boy, who even put in a few terms at Northeastern studying sales engineering and business administration before the peace movement got to him and he took off. Just think, all those times I rode the Green Line out to the MFA to be ravished by the Impressionists once more I might have passed him in that crowd of sullen-looking students always clustering there on Huntington Avenue! Though I've always revered him as this ageless rishi he's actually not quite my age, a year younger if he was twenty when he went to India the year after I was married, which might explain certain things about our relationship—the way he somehow looked *up* to me as well as down, and brought out my mothering instinct as well as being my Master. I'm all confused. He's not even Jewish, technically, since his mother was Armenian—you know there's that big Armenian community in Watertown, just as you cross the Cambridge line along Mount Auburn Street, past the Cemetery—and that might give him that Asiatic quality I was so sure he had. Unlike Daddy, I never was much good at identifying ethnic types. Remember how he could tell all the way across a ballroom an Irishman from a Yankee, and spot Jews where nobody else saw them, without really being nasty about it (Daddy) but just factual, by his lights? I'm truly confused but as Alinga says, *Ko veda?* The Arhat either opened us up and got rid of our ego garbage or he didn't, and if he did (and he certainly did in my case) who cares about race or place of national origin?—it's all maya anyway. I know she's right intellectually but still I feel *deceived*. I gave myself to him *totally* and where I thought there was this great everything, this mahat, there was nothing—*shunya*. Of course one of the truths of the Eightfold Way is that the void is the plenum and vice versa, but you probably don't want to hear about that. Maybe thanks to you and Daddy I'm such an incorrigible snob it's simply the idea that he's from Watertown—if it were Newton or Belmont or even Arlington I might not mind half so much. But I can't believe I haven't burned away even that much petty prejudice in these seven months. I still love him, of course. Maybe it's the idea that in all our intimacy—I've been seeing him nearly every day, composing letters and consulting and lately just commiserating—he kept up this pretense and said everything to me in this funny high-pitched sing-song accent. While I was responding with my whole heart, with my honest voice. I mean, how big a fool can your daughter be?

Now that I know, he *does* remind me a bit of Myron Stern, and that must churn up a lot of old rage and frustration in me. Not *at* you and Daddy any more—you were no more to blame for squelching that romance than a cat should be blamed for tormenting a mouse; it was just your creaturely nature, and I, I suppose, down deep wanted you to do just what you did. My anger is at myself, all the worse in that my recent attempts to squelch an infatuation of *my* daughter's have proved totally ineffectual, thanks in part to the transatlantic meddling of your groom-of-choice, the impeccable Charles. Did you and Daddy ever feel even the *littlest* bit guilty about nixing the love of my life? Maybe it would have been a sociological misfortune but a healthy cross of genes. You shouldn't interfere with natural processes—that's called pollution. Now that I look with vidya, the Arhat has Myron's wonderful little way of cocking his head back (I thought it was the itchy beard made him do it) and lifting off his heels like a bird preening and about to take wing: king of all he surveys, adding a cubit to his height, cock of the walk, whatever. And his hands—those subtle tapered fingers, formed by generations of watchmaking and counting gold and not being allowed to own land or farm—like trickles of warm oil on your skin. Though Charles had done all those million stitches and palpations, his hands felt always a little rigid and clumsy, and *cold*—I used to think in bed my skin would warm his touch in a few seconds but it would take *minutes* and by that time this anger would be rising in me and everything would be against the grain, as they say around here—there's even a word for it, *pratiloman.* It's what happens when you stroke a cat against the fur.

Forgive me, you don't want to know any of this. This is my garbage and you have your own life. Somebody said to me the other day that at some point a woman must become her own mother. But it's hard when you still have one alive and well. That is *amazing* about the Visàge buyout by Revlon, and your making all that scrumptious money! But now *do* put it in some safe securities—utilities pay the best dividends of course and are not apt to go down unless the company overcommits to nuclear power—or CDs and don't listen to another word the admiral whispers into your ear. *You were lucky.* It seems to me that if the SEC were to investigate you could both go to jail for that tip and his son too. How old is his son? Forget I asked, I'm not on the market, but I can tell you entre nous it's only a matter of time until I am disparue from this place. The only people left are those with nowhere else to go, or those who *did* attain near enough to vairagya and samadhi not to give a hoot about their surroundings. Almost all the stores in the mall are shut down, and the Karuna Pharmacy is under a heavy indictment from the narcs, and even the sweet little Sachchidananda River has dried up—I guess we *were* depleting the water table, with the irrigation and all the flush toilets people insisted on having. It used to be called Gritty Creek and now we can see why. Even the days have turned unfriendly— the sun is bright but not warm and the nights are viciously cold and somehow frighteningly *enclosing*, like being inside a black crystal or a cage of stars. So many stars!—an impossible dust of them that you never see in the misty polluted East.

If you and your voracious boyfriend are going to keep eating out at Polynesian, Mexican, and Cajun restaurants every night you shouldn't be surprised by an irritated duodenum or even diverticulitis. What you need is *bran* and raw iron-rich vegetables (dark-green leafy ones—*not* iceberg lettuce) and eggs in moderation, and to cut out all grease and fatty meats, except maybe liver once a week for the iron. *Don't* tailor your diet to the Admiral's—he is a man and has altogether different needs, since he has a prostate and you don't and you have smaller bones. Men can absorb much more calcium than women, and you should never drink milk for a pre-ulcerous condition—milk, it turns out, is rather *hard* to digest. Try Gelusil—Maalox somehow has a bad aura, a faint vibrating violet glow like those public toilet seats that supposedly sterilize themselves. *Please* don't tease me about your marrying this sailor-boy—it would be much kinder to the heirs and save a lot of legal fees if you would just live in sin. Couldn't you find another condo, with an elevator and a peek at the sea? Or get used to the pool view from his, and ignore the rattle of the diving board and the sound early in the morning from the sprinklers? If you wouldn't wake up at four in the morning you wouldn't hear the sprinklers. Have you ever tried wax earplugs? The best are made in Europe, Oropax—little fuzzy balls that go deliciously soft from your body heat—but Flent's from any old American drugstore might help you. Warm them in your hand before poking them in, otherwise you could break an ear drum. I'm sorry your know-it-all swain thinks the real-estate action is moving inland and that your place is depreciating. In Florida housing may be more like cars than in the North—new is best and almost-new is second-best and then it's all downhill. Also I suspect there's a subconscious pull away from the seaside now with the icecaps melting from these holes in the ozone. But what would the two of you do with a view of a golf course? Balls through the window, and electric carts being driven right through the yard. As I remember, you never liked men having fun by themselves. And think how you'd miss the little shops at the Palm Royal Plaza—you *know* you didn't like Del Mar Village near as well. We Price women need to see the *sea*. That *was* a rather funny cartoon from the Miami *Herald* but men never wear those dots (tikkas) on their foreheads, and he never claimed to be a Brahmin, only an honest Shudra (the artisan caste).

Happy Thanksgiving, and even Merry Christmas. I don't know what will be happening to me. I have to confront the Arhat and do dread it. I waited twenty-two years to confront Charles and then it was by being out of the house when he came home from work.

Thanks for letting me cry on your shoulder about Watertown, etc. You were a good mother, given the vikshipta (scatterbrained) style of your generation. I guess that's all any of us can do, follow the fashion and trust biology to override culture—if we try to be better parents than our peers, our children will feel uneasy. I mean, children aren't *entirely* the point of a woman's life, are they? But if not, what is? Tell me if you've learned.

Addled love,
Sare

[*tape*]

Namaste, Master.

My little Kundalini has been avoiding me these past days.

These past days have brought many duties and distractions.

And disasters.

Disasters only to those who have not yet disengaged from prakriti. Whose vasanas still harbor phalatrishna.

That is well spoken. You are wearing Western dress. It has sharpened your tongue.

Now that it is almost December my saris seemed thin.

Your sweater indeed appears bulky. It conceals the shape of your beautiful breasts.

I blush to hear you call them beautiful. Only Buddha and his peace is beautiful.

Within his peace there are a million million jewels. It is one of the priceless insights of Mahayana that particulars do not cease in nirvana. They are simply at last freed from disturbing motion. The wind of decay no longer caresses them.

As executive assistant, I have a number of sorrows to report, and one cause for joy.

I wish to hear the cause for joy. Let our lawyers deal with the sorrow. Sorrow is their trade.

The joy is that Melissa Blithedale, after months of meditation and growing disenchantment with the Presbyterian Church and her mirthless financial advisers, has experienced a change of heart. In our letter of late May she was told she would be welcome back here. Now she wants to come. And to secure your benevolence she not only offers to cease demanding return of the loan she made three years ago but wishes to kick in another five hundred K. What shall I tell her?

Tell her of course to come. Write and say, "Come, ineffable Melissa! Be no longer buffaloed!"

She will find the puram much diminished since her last stay. Then, I believe, she was thoroughly coddled.

We will coddle her again, the good Mrs. B. We will take her into our innermost councils, which since Durga's departure are underpopulated. We will house her in high style, in her choice of abandoned A-frames. She will find spiritual advantage in the many challenges. You have never met her, Kundalini. Her ashram name is Mahima, which means "the power to swell to enormous size and touch the moon." She is quite short and squat, yet with a charm, a monied bounce. She has that sexual

confidence of rich women. She is of an old San Francisco fam-
ily. You will enjoy her. She is amusing. You and she will speak
the same language, that of the manner born.

I am not sure she and I will speak any language.

How is that, my most precious?

No. Don't touch me yet.

As you wish, my nayika.

When I first came here, my leader in dynamic medita
tion kept shouting at me, "Who are you?" Now I ask the
same question of you, Master. Who are you?

Who do you think I am?

I think you are my Master and love and my living
path to Buddha.

[*Silence.*]

But now I have been told that you are not a holy man
from India but a Jewish Armenian from Watertown,
Massachusetts.

[*Silence.*]

Which is true, Master?

Wherein is the contradiction? Why may not a holy man come
from Watertown? Why may not the living path begin there?

Perhaps there is no reason.

And yet you feel one. You feel deceived. Worse, you feel
mocked.

Yes, I suppose.

Our tantric lovemaking, the highly successful technique of
vajrolimudra, now seems a mockery, a loss of your dignity
because behind the mask and accent of the guru a pair of
Western eyes watched, and a brain thinking with a coarse
American accent?

Something like that. Let me hear your real voice.

I'm not sure I can still do it. Even my brain now, when it talks to itself, has the Arhat's voice.

When did this incredible imposture first occur to you?

I resent the word "imposture." I grew into it organically. It's a phase of my being, a karmic reality. In India I became Indian. I never applied for citizenship, but the rest of it—the diet, the clothes, the languages, the mind-set—just came and filled me in. But they didn't forget—the Indian authorities. They remembered, and when enough little embarrassments at Ellora had piled up—injuries, bad trips, complaints from parents, complaints from neighbors—they kicked me out. The wogs deported me.

Why isn't this generally known?

I wasn't getting stateside publicity in those days. I was just one more guru obscuru. Coming to the States was Durga's idea, and she was right: this is the place to score. This is the place where duhkha translates into money. Back in India, once I was gone, what did they care? To them, I was one more piece of foreign klishta—as long as I left and the ashram dissolved, they were happy enough. Their dirty little secret was, our farmhouse and its bit of land was where they were putting one of their cardboard-and-plaster housing projects, with rakeoffs for everybody. Our getting out quietly was part of our price for not balking at their price. What you got to realize about India, it may be poor but it's a capitalist country. People are on the take. For peanuts by our standards, but on the take.

But how did you get into this country?

No problem. I had my old passport. Dean Rusk had signed it, that's how old it was. I went and got it renewed at the consulate in Bombay and walked through controls at Kennedy.

Welcome home, Mr. Steinmetz. I didn't even bother to put on a suit. Durga and Nitya and Alinga knew, but that was about it. Ma Prapti maybe, but I think not; otherwise she would have blabbed when she got to blabbing. Not everybody came in the same plane, remember. You stand in the fast line, they look up your number to see if you're on the feds' shit list, and bingo, if you're not, you're in. Once in, I'm the Arhat again.

But how did you become the Arhat in the first place?

The story of my life. O.K. I was born on Elton Avenue, of these two crazy mismatched people. There wasn't any religion around the house, my parents cancelled each other out. They must have had great sex, because nothing else showed. My mother was actually a kind of anti-Semite. She couldn't stand my father's people, from over in the old West End, mostly. She thought they were pushy, greedy, slippery, and had crucified Christ. And him and the Armenians—he called them barbarians, he called them gypsies. He'd say the Turks should have finished the job, she'd say Hitler didn't have such a bad idea. I got nothing, growing up. No baptism, no bar mitzvah. My mother didn't even make choeregs for breakfast, she said my father could go out and buy himself bagels. People felt sorry for me. One of my mother's older sisters, Aunt Mariam, took me to church a few times at Easter and Christmas—to St. James locally and that new one they put up over on Brattle Street, right in Wasp country—but, Jesus, the services were endless, and all that incense and candle smoke did a job on my sinuses. I was one of those kids with tons of allergies. The desert here has been great for that, by the way. The same with you? I notice your nose runs a lot. O.K. Don't answer. Sulk. Make your guru squirm.

So: spiritually I grew up with nothing, just these ethnic slurs all the time and noises from the bedroom. But there was some-

thing—a blank little God I carried with me like a tiny teddy bear in my head, this little curved shadow like a husk clinging to the underside of my brain. I mean, it was me, yet something more than me, something I could appeal to—and there wasn't just input, there was output. I was transmitting and receiving. I could feel it at night. But also in the day, in the middle of the afternoon, out on the schoolyard, this terrific joy, this gratitude that kept spilling and spilling out of me like thread when the sewing machine goes crazy. But it had no face or name; it had no form. I was jealous and sore—my parents with their orthodox upbringings had been given something, it was part of their energy, and the other kids in school had been given the same sort of thing even if they took it for granted and didn't know diddledy-squat about it and even shat on it. The Catholic girls with the little gold crosses between their tits and the Jewish boys taking off a double set of holidays and even the Protestants, their faces would get a little stiff and guilty if the talk got too dirty—you could see some shadow coming from above, some message from way upstairs.

Well, not to make a sob story out of this, it got to be the late Fifties, the early Sixties. I read Alan Watts and Krishnamurti and Salinger and Ginsberg. I read the Upanishads and, right there, hit this terrific verse, where the King of Death says to Nachiketa: "The Supreme Person, of the size of a thumb, the innermost Self, dwells forever in the heart of all beings." That was Him!—my old pal God, the size of a thumb, and with just that backwards curve, you know, that a thumb has. I was at Northeastern at the time, reading poli. sci. and introductory psych., and a lot of other crap that was supposed to translate into some ass-kissing desk job at John Hancock or City Hall. Suddenly I was sick of competing with nerds. I could have been shipped to Vietnam but turned out to be 4-F—too asthmatic. I thanked old God and took off for India. Unlike a lot of the trash went there after the Beatles cruised Calcutta, I stuck. Where's the imposture in that? I found peace, I gave peace. India made sense to me—Buddhism made sense to me—the way you can take as much or little as you want, the way even nothing is something. After fifteen years I was Indian. The people that came to that first ashram in Ellora—there on the edge of town, this falling-down tin-roofed lime-green house—were almost all of them Westerners. Why would they want to come to another Westerner? Subliminally, of course, what attracted them was that I was a Westerner—my vasanas spoke their language. I spoke to their hangups. But up front I had to be strange—I had to look like something else, a fresh chance. So I gave myself an Indian childhood as a beggar boy in Bombay—what's the big deal? Maybe I once was a beggar in Bombay, a Shudra gone to seed, and not good enough even at that, so for my sins I got shoved into the incarnation of a messed-up little Armenian just across the Cambridge line, across the line from all those hotsy-totsy bits of ass like you. You've been bliss, frankly. The way you talk in complete sentences, the way you hold your head, your posture. Nice. I mean really nice. Now you begrudge me everything because of a little name-change. What's the point of living if you can't shuck skins?

No point, Art.

Come on, Kundalini. What's your old name? I've forgotten.

Sarah.

Come on, Sarah, put away that long face. Stop trying to lay a guilt trip on me with those big dark eyes. Guilt trips went out with the rest of the garbage.

Tell me. What is not garbage to you?

Purusha is not garbage. The eternal present is not garbage.
Don't touch my breasts. I mean it.

*What's this protecting your tits again suddenly? We've been
friendly—didn't you like it? Multiple o's, every time.*

They were lovely but, as you said, partook of flux.
Flux and duhkha.

*Fuck flux and duhkha. Listen. I need a vacation. Every man
needs a vacation. For a man, a woman is a vacation. I need
you to love me the way only you can.*

I do love the way you used to say "love."

*My luff for you wears a million guises. You are Shakti, I
am Shiva. I am Krishna and you are Radha, shlippery with
your own sweat and rajas, your hair all in shnakes and your
clothes torn in delirious disharray.*

No, really—hands off, Arthur. Arthur Steinmetz.

*My father used to say Steinmetz was a genius, my mother
would say he was a dwarf. The brains behind Edison. The
feeling of your ass in my hands, one cheek in each.*

Darling, I'm not kidding. We've had it.

*Why? Because of names? What does it matter, what name
I have? Or you have? A little flick of karma, and I'm a
centipede, and you're a chestnut tree in blossom.*

I can't exactly say why. For a woman to give herself—and it's utterly lovely, to give yourself—there has
to be an illusion, or it's no good. Maybe "illusion" isn't
the word, since everything is illusion. There has to be
an appearance—a possibility—of progress. There has to
be rectitude.

*We'll make progress. We'll have rectitude. The garbage's
gone, all that drugs and paranoia. Melissa's coming with her
moola. Stay here and we'll build it up again, along more classic*

lines. Hinayana this time instead of Mahayana. Less group stuff, more one-on-one. Cut out all the commercial crap, keep off TV. Just the how-to-live books and the less far-out tapes, and go for a more modest operation that won't make waves in the courts. Keep peace with the local squares. This is a great spot, if we don't abuse the water situation.

Why do you want me? In your philosophy, one woman is as good as another. We're all lotus to your linga. With this particular lotus, I fear the bloom is off. Though of course I do adore you. More this moment than ever; there're all these new layers of you to get to know.

But no rectitude. Who'd you ever know who had rectitude? Your husband—what was his name? Charles. Charles the Worthy. Whenever you mention him you get prim and cute and arch your back. What's going on between you two? I get the feeling he and I exist in some sort of symbiosis. It's making me jealous as hell.

Don't be ridiculous. I can't stand him.

You ask me why I want you. One, you're a knockout, with these super knockers and a two-handsful ass.

Keep your hands to yourself. Don't be so adolescent. I'm almost forty-three.

Ripe. That's nice. Two, you're every inch a lady, and I seem to be a sucker for that. My own social insecurity, no doubt. Everything goes back to having a lousy childhood.

Mine wasn't that great, you know. My mother—

Three, you know the ropes here, and, frankly, I don't. I reach into myself and say what comes but the organizational part of it has always been over my head. There's always been women to do the—

The dirty work.

Tape

The nitty-gritty, the sthula side of things.

You would have to do with fewer limos.

Absolutely—that was just an image kind of thing. The humor of it appealed to me, being dragged along these dusty washboard roads like they were Fifth Avenue.

And the diamonds. They should be sold.

Sure, sell 'em—though you won't get half of what we paid. Again, it was the symbolism, the Buddha Realm bit, the pari-nirvana part of it. It got people's attention: gave 'em a little shock. Stop people short for even a second, and you have that much more of a chance of enlightenment fighting its way past the aham and all that defensive furniture.

I understand the theory; but the practice has proved to be very expensive.

You may or may not believe this, but I really don't give a shit about any of this material garbage. It's all external, it's all just semiotics. I am non-attached, that's not just bullshit.

Then I, too, may be dispensed with.

To you I'm attached. Maybe not forever; as you say, I'm subjected to a lot of temptation. But for now I'd like you to hang around. I'd luff for you to hang around.

Don't *do* that to me. Say that word that sweet way.

Hey . . . Flash: Watertown boy confesses emotional dependency on North Shore matron! Ashram recovers, Arizona declares bank holiday.

Thanks, dear, but, truly, no thanks. I figure I've had as much sahasrara as I can stand. And if you or your other in-residence Shaktis try to keep me from going, I'll tell the world you're really Art Steinmetz. Now that *would* be a news flash.

Don't talk ugly, Sarah. We're trying to get back on an even keel, you and I. I don't know how good that is as blackmail—it might leak out anyway, if the media keep working me over, or Durga tries to make a killing on her story. It might not hurt so much. It might just stop people short for that second we were talking about and let in some light. You've heard me at darshan—you can say it's all bullshit and still they dig it. They think your saying it's bullshit is bullshit. Deep in Kaliyuga as we are, it's hard to come up with bad publicity.

Well, at the least you'd have to scrap a lot of T-shirts. I think you're a teentsy bit bluffing. I think you *like* being the Arhat.

All it means is "the deserving one." I deserve all I can get, after the lousy upbringing I had.

What do the scriptures say of the arhat? "In character as excellent as the gods, in meekness as the ascetic, and in wrath as the thunderbolt."

That's me. Speaking of vajra, let's lie down to talk. I got to get used to this idea of doing without my Kundalini. I'll miss those multiple o's.

I'll miss them too. But I think they were just a stage.

Sure. Use me and throw me away.

We throw ourselves away. All of us. Isn't that what you taught?

I forget what I taught. I get frightened, Sarah. All this spiritual responsibility is frightening. I need you to give me some structure. I need those big tits of yours to suck. I need to hold on to your ass.

Stop trying to sex me up. That's very chauvinistic, what you imply—that women don't get frightened too.

Buddhatvam yoshidyonisamsritam.

Oh sure. Women are gods. Women are dirt. It comes

to the same. Women are just like men are—little bits of purusha caught in prakriti, lost and isolated in all that duhkha. Why did it happen? How did purusha get so polluted?

The explanation is, it allowed itself a moment, just a moment in all that eternity, of self-reflection. And, whoomph, everything clouded over. Bingo: maya. But fear not, Kundalini. A way out exists. The thinking brain—buddhi—can lead man—and woman, if you insist she needs an out—to the edge of awakening. When prakriti is recognized as itself, it flees the spirit, the Sankhya-sutras put it, like a dancer who has satisfied her master's desire.

And isn't *that* a chauvinistic image, by the way?

Come on, ease up on the gender politics. I'm trying to answer your question. People want to confuse purusha with the chitta-vrittis, or with buddhi; but these are just the most complex and rarefied manifestations of prakriti. Prakriti, like purusha, is eternal, but it has a kind of incipient motion, a teleological instinct. Once it departed from its original state of alinga, energy appeared, monstrous amounts of it, called "mahat." And then evolution, parinama, took over. Come here, you sweet hotsy-totsy. Let me check if Buddhahood still resides in your yoni. I'll eat the bastard out.

Don't be gross. What I've never understood about nirvana—

Yes, you little yum-yum?

How does it differ from extinction?

Who says it differs?

All that Mahayana business does—but maybe that's just popular superstition, icing an originally austere cake. The same thing happened in Christianity. But I can appreciate how the popular mind works: why have all this religion to attain just what we're afraid we're going to get anyway? I mean utter death, utter extinction.

Cut it out, Sarah. You're frightening me. It was bad enough always having my parents threatening each other with genocide.

See? You're no help. You just reduce everything to the personal.

You haven't been a sannyasin long enough to understand. You haven't burned away your ego, your phalatrishna. You must become shunya. You must become emptiness. Shunya also means a girl of low caste, a slut. When you become an utter slut, then vajra will shatter you. Buddha will fill you.

When does he fill *you?*

When he fills you.

Thanks a lot.

Baby, all your questions—they are optical illusions of the mind. They disappear in the right light. You still have that Christian capitalist me-first mind-set.

Look who's talking—Art Steinmetz, the pseudo-Hindu.

Steinmetz, the Arhat, Krishna, Buddha—you're hung up on these secondary distinctions.

If your mind-set is so great, why do you keep saying you're frightened? Why are you begging me to stay?

Being a jivan-mukta, you're still a person. You're like the potter's wheel that keeps turning, though the pot is finished. I am not begging. I am respectfully inviting.

I respectfully decline.

We had such super maithuna.

We did, but funnily enough that's not a reason to stay. It's a reason to go.

Spoken like a man.

If you had spoken like a man you would have told me who you were.

I am what I have ever been.

A liar. A sham.

You know, you have gotten a bit butch since coming here.

I used to hear Durga call you Art and I thought I was mishearing her Irish accent.

So it's jealousy of Durga this is all about. She was in on something you weren't.

Shams. That's what men are. Liars. Hollow frauds and liars. All of them. *You're* the nothing, not us cunts. *You're* the shunya.

Ah, shit, Momma. Suddenly you're boring me.

[*end of tape*]

December 1
(New Moon)

Dear Mahima—

It filled me with limitless joy to receive your letter announcing your rebirth as a sannyasin. The shanti of the Buddha penetrates everywhere, and will redeem every atom before the end. Your supplementary loan of

: 248 :

five hundred thousand ($500,000) is hereby gratefully acknowledged and its instant repayment at your pleasure guaranteed. Its temporary repose within the Treasury of Enlightenment will go far to repair the damage in these past months done the ashram by its ego-ridden enemies both within and without, and to fuel the flame of dispassionate wisdom which we seek to set before the world. To quote the blessed Dhammapada: "It is sweet to have friends in need; and to share enjoyment is sweet. It is sweet to have done good before death; and to surrender all pain is sweet."

You will find many changes when you return. The security force, now called the Peace Patrol, has been much reduced, and no longer wears its lavender paramilitary uniform, with belting and epaulettes. Instead, our young protectors, no less healthy and vigorous than before, wear loosely fitting karate pajamas, and instead of Uzis and Galils arm themselves only with wands of hickory wood and attitudes of impregnable benevolence. Miraculously, the number of trespassers and spies they once had to repel has markedly diminished, and if you find the outermost sentry post deserted, have your driver himself swing back the de-electrified gate and serenely proceed.

You will find here a number of state-employed clerical workers and conscientious bureaucrats who are supervising the legal exactions made upon our properties. These alien personnel are non-threatening and, increasingly, sympathetic; indeed, a number of them have expressed interest in my halting preachments and in more than one case have succumbed to the inexorable appeal of the Eightfold Path. The Hall of a Millionfold Joys, whose foundations were merely a hole in the earth when you were led astray by the delusions of Presbyterianism, is now being dismantled because of alleged violations of the Arizona laws pertaining to zoned ranchland use, insurable electrical wiring, and required number of emergency fire exits. A small glassed-roofed shed, however, will be allowed to remain, in the position of the present entrance foyer, to be used as a combination agricultural greenhouse, tractor garage, and emergency meditation space.

The Fountain of Karma, which you will recall in all its multi-colored, round-the-clock glory, now plays for half an hour at dawn and at sunset, when the sannyasins, passing to meditation, darshan, and aerobic exercises, may contemplate its symbolism of endlessly restless prakriti. The other twenty-three hours, it rests, and allows the Sachchidananda River to replenish its depleted flow. To quote the sacred Upanishads: "This earth is honey for all beings, and all beings are honey for this earth. This water is honey for all beings, and all beings are honey for this water." Although unusually severe climatic conditions this past summer reduced our anticipated artichoke harvest, our agricultural expert Hanuman has exciting new plans for acres of xerophilous, oil-rich jojoba and therapeutic mescal bean.

You will find a great choice of accommodations when you arrive. Many former pilgrims have deserted the Eightfold Path for the vanities of secular life. A number of others have been restored to their native lands. Commodious trailers and air-conditioned A-frames stand empty for you; I recommend that you take up residence close to my abode, and to the Uma Room, where you will be working to help administer the revised fortunes of the ashram. Our sister Alinga, our brother Yajna, our vigilant accountant Nitya Kalpana, the delightful and energetic Satya and Nagga and many others await your healing presence and guiding counsel. Above all I await you. We shall resume, dearest Melissa, your ascent to samadhi where it was regrettably arrested at the third, or Manipura, chakra. Since this is the "gem center," the thought has crossed my mind that if you were to divest yourself of your own gems, secluding them within the impassive bosom of our Treasury of Enlightenment, you might be freed of the klishta they represent. Consulting your records, I am now inclined to believe that the burning sensation you often reported was the vain effort by your subtle body to remove this granthi with tapas, the cleansing ascetic fire. Lightened of the impure weight of personally retained jewelry, you should quickly rise up the sushumna nadi to the fourth chakra, Anahata, whose element is air and whose principle is touch and whose presiding deity is Isha. After that, as the sages say, "Ko veda?"—"Who knows?"

Anticipation of the bliss that will be assuredly yours fills me with immeasurable satisfaction. My colleagues at the ashram are of like mind. Even our little river seems to play a merrier tune and once again to merit its name. To quote once more the invaluable Dhammapada: "He [or she] who in this world has gone beyond good and evil and both, who, free from sorrows, is free from passions and is pure—him [or her] I call a Brahmin." I am eager to embrace you.

Yours most faithfully,
Shri Arhat Mindadali
Head, Ashram Arhat

/k

le 3 décembre

Cher monsieur,

Je vous envoie ci-joint un chèque pour cent mille dollars des États-Unis ($100,000 U.S.)—le déposez à mon compte. Ma nouvelle adresse suivra bientôt. Je ne me trouverai pas encore dans The Babbling Brook Motel.

Agréez, je vous prie,

l'expression de mes sentiments très amicaux,
#4723-9001-7469-8666

December 3

Gentlemen:

Enclosed find a check for $100,000 to be paid into my account with your bookshop. The address on this stationery will no longer be valid—in fact, I very much look forward to visiting Samana Cay in the near future, and perhaps taking up residence there. So you will know me when you see me—I am rather tall for a woman, with dark and abundant hair, touched with gray as yet but lightly, and with what has been kindly described as "a figure of perfect elegance on a large scale." Actually, I don't weigh a pound over one hundred thirty-five, which is still a bit heavier than perfection. I look forward very much to browsing in your store, drawing upon some of my considerable credit with you, and acquainting myself with your island and its idyllic (I have every reason to expect) climate.

> Yours in keen anticipation,
> Sarah P. Worth

December 3

Dear Jerry—

Please take this tape and put it in the safest place in Caracas—your lockbox at the bank if you have one, otherwise somewhere around the hacienda, maybe with your kids' rock tapes, like the purloined letter in that idiotic Poe story they used to make us read at Concord Academy. I don't hope ever to have to use it but there may be unpleasant developments where its evidence could be useful. *Don't listen to it*—it won't make much sense to you and doesn't show your sister at her best. And Esmeralda might be shocked—she's such a Latin lady.

I've decided to leave the ashram. I think the winter here is worth skipping—they tell me it's brief but raw, and there's nothing worse to a New Englander than a winter that doesn't pack any kind of picturesque punch but doesn't let you enjoy the outdoors either. I'm thinking of an island—just being on the same continent with the men in my life makes me feel crowded and harassed. Charles has been rather quiet, but now that I know the reason why, it's worse than the harassment. I'll get over it, of course. People get over everything, and that's the secret of all the persisting religions—God or whatever they call it gets credit for our animal numbness and reflexive stoicism and antibodies and healing processes, or else we die and that shuts us up as effectively as an answered prayer.

I'm sorry, I don't want you to think you have a bitter sister. But one of the things you as a male will never have to know is how much a woman can *suffer*—jealousy, humiliation, panic, sense of betrayal—such a churning would shake a man to pieces; his nuts would come off his bolts, and all the studs out of his dress shirt. I've had some disappointments and reversals lately, but not along the lines of your scoffing jeering letter last summer. The Asian part of my experience has been perfect—a whole new vocabulary to frame the perennial problems in, and a way of looking at them that makes them almost vanish, like those holograms—re-

member, the postcards we thought were so risqué from
that variety store in Roslindale?—that are somehow
printed onto tiny iridescent ridges and show you different things or the same thing from a different angle
when you very slightly move your head. Just as changing your head on the pillow gives you the strong sensation for a minute that you're about to go to sleep.

Mother, I've decided, is just beyond me. Why don't
you fly up with some of the grandchildren? You could
combine it with Disney World and Epcot Center. She's
playing these wild games with Daddy's stodgy old blue
chips and last month actually made a killing of sorts, so
you can bet she's going to keep at it until she loses
everything. I hope you weren't counting on much of an
inheritance—I'm sure not. Some of the Price and Peabody silver should be yours eventually but I'll keep
what I have for the time being—at least it's not tarnish-
ing black as lead like all that wonderful old Perkins stuff
she has sitting around on her wrought-iron glass tables
just *drinking* in the salt air and the acid rain from all
those space shots that now at least they've stopped trying. Whether or not she marries this utterly senile-
sounding admiral depends I think on how senile *she*
becomes and how successful *his* children are at prevent-
ing it. I think there are three, all in their fifties and no
doubt with expensive habits and stalled careers. She
ever so slightly mentioned them in one of her letters as
being "rather materialistic," and I dare say they see
Mother as a fortune-hunting vamp. Maybe she is, in this
newest incarnation. We all have a number of skins,
especially women I think, because society makes us

wriggle more. Do you remember how she used to go on and on about the *hateful* Prices and how her mother-in-law had once commented about the décolletage of some dress she wore going out to some dance or dinner with Daddy before they were married—this must have been in the Thirties, but I don't think there was still Prohibition—being rather too "staring," meaning there was too much bare skin showing, and Mother never forgot or forgave it, and used to tell us over and over how that remark ruined not only that dress and that evening for her but the whole idea of *ever* going out with Daddy and having a good time, and how she always got excited telling us about it, saying the word "staring" with this terrible mother-in-law hiss? These odd little passing hurts that echo down through families like cannon balls. I've tried so hard *not* to raise Pearl, as I'm sure you have your six, your dear little niños and chicas, so these petty old snubs and slights become grotesque be-alls and end-alls—the way, for instance, Mummy wouldn't let Daddy join his uncle over at Stillman, Ames, Hannicker & Price because she didn't want him under the influence of—to be *indebted* to—his own awful family, and made him stay on as a trust officer at the 5¢ Savings Bank where you and I know he never was happy or his talents, really, appreciated—that lovely intuitive mind of his which had to make do with the Metaphysicals since no *creative* investment decisions were ever entrusted to him, just buttering up widows and second sons—all going back to her décolletage being possibly "staring," when of course if you remember Mother as a youngish woman that was a perfectly apt description—she was always looking for excuses to take her clothes off. Not just on the Vineyard with those Social-ist nudists or up in Maine at Great-granddaddy's lake but I can remember her standing around in simply her girdle for hours before they were giving some party, so that these poor caterers' men dragging in these boxes and boxes of liquor had to keep averting their eyes, and as late as the Myron Stern days I remember him coming one time to the house for me and being embarrassed by this gray-haired—probably not much older than I am now, come to think of it—woman in that rather short terrycloth robe with no buttons, just a loose belt that kept coming untied, that she liked to sweep around the house in after having a bath, and his having to make some joke about it, to relieve his tension, out in the old blue Bel Air he used to borrow from his roommate. Now she's probably the oldest bimbo in a polka-dot bikini on the beach, giving herself skin cancer, and God knows how she lured this poor admiral into her sun porch. She said he kept tapping on her hurricane shut-ters but if I know Mother those shutters were up and all the lights blazing.

Didn't mean to run on nostalgically like this—the cassette's the thing. Guard it with *su vida*, as they say. You won't see this grotesque stationery with its faux-naïve logo any more, unless I steal some when I leave. I'm actually staying the night, tonight, which feels strange, since I've been using the dreary lobby, full of gun magazines, off and on these past months as a place to conduct my business. Some four-footed beastie keeps snarling and scratching and whining outside my sealed window, but if you turn the air-conditioner up to high it pretty well drowns him (or her—why do we always think predators are male?) out. The whole town of Forrest is sinister, in fact—the flattened-out flatness of it, the stagnant brook with its cottonwoods, and then in the distance these abrupt wrinkled mountains that seem pieces of another world. Pearl seems to be committed to a foolish marriage to some foppish young Dutchman—but who can say what marriage is more foolish than another? All have their merits and demerits and wear out before we do. Except in your case, of course. Maybe the language barrier you and Esmeralda had at first has lent a permanent touch of romance. It's really not wise for married people (or lovers) to understand each other too well—communication, I fear, is hideously overrated. An *abrazo* for the two of you, and six kisses to the little ones from their rather frazzled

Tía Sarah

December 7

Dear Ducky—

On the run, but I've been wondering how you're doing. I bet sometimes you long to be back in the closet. I know I do. Can you let Charles know ever so minimally, in that wonderful grunting way men have of communicating, that we're ready to talk if he is? As you know better than I, he is highly motivated now, and we can make the terms. I'll settle for half of everything but begin by asking for it all—the properties and securities, that is. On my alimony—would four thousand a month be too reasonable? I caught a cold in the Kansas City airport (semicircular, and drafty) and feel dismal. Let's have lunch again, when we're two totally different people.

Love (warmed over),
Sarah

Dec. 12

Dear Martin—

The conch is a big food down here as well as a pretty shell. When I have an address I can give you, I'd love to hear if there's anything *nice* you can say about prison. Security? Lack of responsibility? Friendships forged in difficult circumstances? I meant to answer your last good long letter but was *very* busy.

My best wishes,
Sarah Worth

Dec. 12

Dear Eldridge—

These are palm trees, common as telephone poles in this area. Their seeds are *entire coconuts* that ride across the ocean from island to island and take root. Isn't that amazing? The island I'm on is small but pleasant. I bet Boston is freezing now. But bells and lights everywhere! Merry Xmas,

Sarah Worth

Dec. 12

Dear Shirlee & Marcus & Foster & Annette—

You've got your troubles, I've got mine. Isn't that an old Beatles song? Don't know why it keeps running through my head. Actually this island is a little paradise. I swim at the beginning and end of every day and my hair keeps bushing out from the saltwater and standing up as if in punk spikes. I'm letting it grow long again. Happy holidays,

Sarah Worth

Dec. 21

Dear Myron—

How strange you must think this, hearing from me
after all these years! And I write inhibited not only by
shyness but by the fear that my letter and these two
enclosures will never reach you in care of a television
station in Los Angeles. But over a month ago, when I
was still living in the Arizona desert northwest of Forrest, as part of a religious commune you may have yourself heard about—*seen* about, I suppose one should
say—on television, I was watching with the guru, who
constantly hoped to see himself on the evening news,
and I saw your name amid the credits scrolling (isn't
that the word?) past after a fascinating and rather tragic
PBS show about nature, mostly the California condor
and its stupidity about not becoming extinct, even to
pecking open its own eggs, that we had tuned in the tag
end of. The scrolling was very fast but your dear name
jumped out at me like a snatch of an old song and I
remembered that the last thing I had heard about you,
about five years ago, from Liz Bellingham, whom you
may dimly remember from those college days and who
later with her husband—he works for a mutual fund—
moved to quite near me and my former husband on the
North Shore, was that you were doing television scripts
in Los Angeles. I was so pleased and proud to hear
it—you were always so funny and quick, in this totally
non-cruel way, and if you can't be Delmore Schwartz

or Norman Mailer (your idols, as I recall) what nicer than to mingle your sparkle in with the great electronic bloodstream of America?

So I thought it *had* to be you—the coincidence would be too great. I do hope I am right, and that the simple number of the channel is enough for the post office, and then that you are important enough for the channel to find you and hand you the envelope. It all seems rather a long shot, but everything in nature is a long shot, from our father's sperm breaking into our mother's egg to the California condor hatching its own eggs. Your mother may be still living in Dorchester but, to be honest, I've quite forgotten the number, though I remember the street—Juliette, my Romeo. It seemed likely that on the wings of your Hollywood affluence—not that condors are Bill Cosby, exactly—she had flown to a gray-shingled cottage in Quincy or perhaps Nahant, where my ancestors used to summer, when it was *the* North Shore and everything beyond it the forest primeval. I do hope she is happy and well. She used to be so nice to me, so cheerfully overriding my egregious goyishness, always asking after my parents as if she knew them, and as if they weren't a pair of insufferable Wasp pricks. Those little macaroons with the half-cherry in the center she used to force on me, saying I was too thin (my own mother constantly telling me I was too fat), and that nice blackberry-flavored tea she said was good for colds and cramps, and your little sister with the deep shadows below her eyes—such a solemn wraithlike relief from my jokey snobby towheaded brother—and your dead father, in his several framed pictures scattered around, somehow more *there*, emotionally, than my own father, who was certifiably alive at the time. Confession: it was not just you I was infatuated with, it was your family, tucked with all those others in this hilly wooden three-decker part of Boston I had never been to before, and that overheated long floor-through so different from the chilly bare Dedham house, so full of wallpaper patterns and kinds of plush and fat friendly knobby furniture and embroidered doilies and doodads still savoring of Europe, Europe as a place of actual living life and not just a vague distant source of authenticity and privilege. I used to love to step onto your tippy back porch, with its drying wash and cat and dog dishes and view of the gas tanks and Squantum and the harbor, and feel dizzy, as if I was on the prow of a ship that was moving, that was just docking in the New World. Your porch always felt thrillingly untied to anything, and there was this *tumbling* feeling in your apartment—words, cookies, souvenirs, meanings crowded one upon the other with this cheerful exalting intimate (though of course you weren't rich) *abundance*, a sweetly *crammed* feeling that made me feel crammed with my own existence, alive to all my corners and cherished or at least forgiven for being myself, my womanly self, into which I had rather recently grown and which I felt was something of a vexation for my own family, a kind of competitive messiness my mother didn't need. Puritanism in my parents had dwindled to a sort of housekeeping whose most characteristic gesture was to take something to the attic because it was undistinguished or vaguely reminiscent of some relative we preferred to forget. And I was so tall, and pungently healthy, and oddly dark—my skin was my father's but my mother often said she didn't know *where* I had gotten such broad hips, and blamed some aunt of my father's she had never liked, a poor soul from Bridgeport whose husband had given her syphilis and who died quite insane while he lived on forever, with a little pain in his spine but nothing more, it was said in the family that a Ziegfeld girl in New York had given it to him—I felt as if my femaleness was embarrassing to everybody and until you I had nowhere to *put* it, no place but your funny home in which I was *at* home. Don't be offended if I say that I think your Jewishness, though of course very bouncy and with its huge tragic history rather majestic, was the least of it—at that point in my life *any* family, Italian or Armenian or even Irish, would have struck me as a haven, a blessed relief from the terrible *sparsity* in which I had been raised, the curious correct emptiness of our lives as if half the normal human baggage had been left back in Suffolk, England, in 1630.

Or did I say all this at the time? Dear old Myron, can you really be baldish now, and with a potbelly, and three ex-wives, and wear safari jackets and sport shirts with an open neck and a gleaming gold chain? I try to picture it and still see that wiry bright-eyed fast-talking Harvard scholarship sophomore with a comic way of tipping his head back and half-closing his lids, as though I were some kind of blinding treasure who couldn't be appraised all at one go. Forgive me, now, for going on at such length, but if I have you—if you *are* at that channel—I don't want to let you go too soon. I have a great deal of time here, in my seaside cabaña. Other guests at this strung-out hotel go down to the beach all day and noisily play at wind-surfing and pedalboats, but I'm determined not to get all pruny and full of keratoses like my mother, who is having a second girlhood in Florida even sillier than her first. I sit inside and embroider my letters and read. Even so, just taking a dip early mornings and late afternoons, I've become brown as a Polynesian, and my hair is like thatch, stiff with saltwater. I wish you could see me. You'd be proud of how I've struggled to keep my figure and dignity, my feminine gentility, though I've stopped using Clairol and some gray shows now, amid the gleams of reflected sunlight.

This place, Samana Cay, is where some recent experts, working from the logs, think Columbus *really* landed, not Watling Island sixty miles to the northwest of here, and the locals hope to make a great thing of it, with monuments and a replica of the *Santa Maria* as a nightclub wing for the hotel and special postage stamps and so on. They want to take the name San Salvador, which Columbus gave his first island, whichever it was, from Watling, but I think the Bahamas government in Nassau is cool to the idea, at least until more evidence emerges. But what evidence do they expect?—things as they happen are always more confusing than they should be—maya is full of these airy holes—and it seems strange that if Columbus was to discover a whole new world he would blunder around in these Bahamas which all look pretty much alike and are just glorified sandbars really. When they taught us in school about

To Myron

October 12, 1492, I pictured the three ships just rolling right up to the East Coast, probably the pier at Atlantic City, and not fiddling around way out here on the edge of nowhere, where the Western Hemisphere thins out to almost nothing. Columbus called his island flat and green and that pretty well says it for Samana Cay. The only cash crops are dried conch meats and cascarilla bark, which is used to flavor Campari. The Indian name for the place, according to Columbus's log, was Guanahaná, and a little group of Indians gathered on the beach when the *Pinta* went ashore and were, according to the log, "naked as their mother bore them" and had the widest heads and foreheads Columbus had ever seen, because of the Lucayan custom of head-binding. The Spaniards evidently traded glass beads and falconry bells for live parrots and native spears tipped with fish teeth. Myron, what *language* did they talk to make these trades? These poor Indians, who were all to go extinct in a few more decades thanks to our diseases and guns, had never seen anything like European men and clothes and ships and yet didn't seem terribly surprised—it's as if somebody else, anonymously, had already been there, and paved the way. There are these *ghosts* all through the history of discovery, softening its shocks—a shadowy person who has been there before the ones who get their names in all the history books, a kind of nameless aura men throw ahead of them.

So mysterious encounters are the way of the world, including ours. Yours and mine. With our impossibly broad faces we were exchanging glass beads for live parrots. Weren't those nice times we had? Remember

Elsie's, that big black man behind the counter we called "Heavy" for "heavy on the dressing" on the Elsie's Specials, and the Hayes-Bick at two in the morning, and the folk-singing at Club 47 before it got too protesty, and downstairs at the Casablanca, where we felt we were somehow stepping into the movie itself, and Peter Lorre might sidle up to the bar in a white jacket at any minute, or Sydney Greenstreet in a fez or Claude Rains in a kepi, while time kept going by on the piano and Bogie and Bergman locked eyes in lost love forever? Can you remember how you used to adore me? I do remember, and in a sense have sailed through life ever since on the love you gave me then, though I suppose any post-adolescent young male would have done something like it—voted for me as I was, solid and sweaty, and not for some wispy docile entity caught in the webs of family and finance and whatever else gave me reality and justified my existence in society's eyes. I wish now I had given my virginity to you. We were like Columbus in a way, poking from island to island and never reaching the mainland. Maybe it was better; I used to feel you come through all our tangled clothes and be so proud of myself. Can it really be that nothing will ever bring us back, Shiva and Shakti for the first time in our lives, and that the overheated interior of that aquamarine Bel Air you used to borrow from your roommate has melted for keeps into the cold cosmic void, into past time? Our pastimes. I loved you then and would love you now and am truly sorry I didn't have the courage to defy my family and all that inherited silver and go off with you and be your woman forever.

To Myron

I would like Hollywood, I do believe. I have read somehow that it's a woman's town—the only town in America where women wield real power, though they tend of course by their sexist conditioning to hand it back to the male agents and those deplorable weak and grabby hanger-on husbands they choose—the stars, the gossip columnists, the porn queens even, enslaving themselves to these deplorable men when there seems no reason. Why are we—women—such a dependent and self-destructive lot? The act of childbirth is such a risk, I suppose, we build prapatti (self-surrender) in. The reading matter around here is rather limited (I've already given you the gist of a pamphlet they hand out about this being where Columbus landed) even though there is a so-called bookstore right in the middle of the village—hardly a village, just six or so tin-roofed shanties with this one new posh-rustic hotel and a few attached shops for the Americans and Canadians and this bookstore with almost nothing in it but last year's bestsellers and loads of Oriental mysticism—I've been driven to read a battered old college textbook on zoology some island-hopping camper left in the hotel lobby to lighten his backpack. The book talks about "the simultaneous eagerness of the female for sexual stimulation and her inherent fear of body contact with any other animal, including a male of her own species." I found that so touching. The story of my life and all our lives really. Scared of our species. It goes on to talk about how lady gray squirrels—and if you've ever seen them chasing around trees you'll know just what it means—"feel torn between two powerful instincts: they want to escape and at the same time they want to greet the male."

And so, having escaped over twenty years ago, I still greet you. I wanted to apologize to you for letting everybody bully me into marrying Charles Worth when you did more for my blood, my rajas, my ego, and the atman that lies beyond and within the ego. (My marriage, as you can guess, is kaput, though it produced one lovely child—a fair-haired daughter—and twenty-two years' worth of distractions and genteel pretense.) I wanted you to know, in case I die here or am put into prison for some technical reasons I won't bore you with, how your texture, your voice (so quick, and sensitive, and yet sweetly tentative, and even lulling), your chest with all its downy hair, and the milky musty smell of us entwined together were woven into my nerves and will never be unwoven. Having apologized, dear Myron, and having mailed you this rather heavy-breathing bit of the past (scientists, I just read in the Samana Cay *Gazette*, are doing things with "old air" captured inside hollow brass buttons and tightly corked bottles), let me ask you for two tiny favors: please stamp and mail the enclosed two letters. Again for technical reasons, I don't want the recipients to have *any* idea where I am, and a Los Angeles postmark would be a wonderful parting gift to

Your unextinguished old flame,

Sarah née Price

December 19

Revered Master—

To quote the blessed Dhammapada: "I have conquered all; I know all, and my life is pure; I have left all, and I am free from craving. I myself found the way. Whom shall I call Teacher? Whom shall I teach?"

Forgive me for leaving unceremoniously. Our farewell was implicit in our every encounter, and within the cycles of karma meetings and partings are hardly to be distinguished. If Nitya Kalpana is now recovered enough to resume supervision of the Treasury of Enlightenment, kindly explain to her that any apparent discrepancies she notices in the books must be blamed upon the irregular methods of accounting which I, having never attended business school, had to improvise; and if *that* does not explain everything, blame the diabolic machinations of the perfidious Durga. In return for this courtesy, rest assured that our personal relations and whatever revelations they brought are sealed in my vasanas, to remain there as speechless vidya forever. If not, not—if you take my meaning. Neti neti, that is to say, or iti iti. I think our mutual reticence forms a beautiful harmony—a balance of sublime negativities—and pray that you will agree. At our last, and frankest, discussion there was a tape recorder between my breasts, my breasts which you were always kind enough to admire. In my allocation of recently received artha, more than half has been left in your discretionary fund. 300 K ain't hay. May the ashram prosper, along the lines of Hinayana as you mentioned.

Where am I? I feel you asking "Where are you?" much as I was asked, on arriving at the ashram three seasons ago, "Who are you?" We know now who I am: I am Kundalini, the energy-serpent that rises. Master, I have come to that place which always interested me—where purusha, in its eternity, immutability, and utter freedom, *very slightly* wrinkles (as I picture it) and makes the infinitesimal concession whereby it permits itself to be wed to prakriti in all its tragic tumult of phenomenality and flux. Or perhaps (the distinction, like so many in your teachings, remained a bit obscure to me) I have merely come to that site within prakriti whereby the three gunas are ever so delicately jostled out of their perfect equilibrium and precipitate mahat, which then evolves into ahamkara, the first rude perception, the first dim ego, which then bifurcates into the subjective and the objective, in the latter of which, as I recall, the five tanmatras, subtle and potential, give rise to the relatively coarse paramanu and sthula-bhutani—atoms and molecules! The subjective equivalent would be (as I conceived it) the chittavrittis, the eddies of consciousness it is the purpose of yoga to suppress.

I fear I was a bad sannyasin, for all the flattery and tutorial zeal you and Alinga and Vikshipta lavished upon me, because I was never able quite to let go of my chittavrittis—I was afraid of the void beneath them. For what is life, this illusion which we live and wish to sustain, but this very same skin of fluctuating awareness, of unsteady and no doubt unworthy nibbles and glimmer and halted thoughts and half-sensations? Isn't this, this thin impalpable skin of color and flicker, this and only this the ecstasy of existence that we wish to prolong forever, to prolong beyond that palya after which even the shining protons of the diamond-strewn Buddha Field fall into decay? The terrible unending stillness of samadhi was for me indistinguishable from death, and I dreaded falling into it inadvertently while in some asana—I was terrified that moksha would swoop down and render me blank. In these last several weeks I have often reflected upon you and conclude that you are not, as I may in a moment of female pique have implied, a fraud: no, truly you are a jivan-mukta, a living blank who simultaneously sustains the chitta-vrittis while locating his being beneath them, in that utter indifference which is purusha and the atman. Just so, the body of a man on death row mysteriously contin-ues its operations—its fluid exchanges and molecular haggling—even to the grotesque extent that on the eve-ning of his execution this body falls asleep and in the morning it consumes breakfast, a meal its enzymes and digestive juices are still busily attacking when the elec-tric current fatally surges through and melts all connec-tions. You *have* relocated your life, Master, and that is what I am still seeking to do.

When I came to the desert I thought my environment greatly simplified, but it was a seething crowded place compared with where I am now. In most directions there is merely the line where samsara makes its vast sad horizon with nirvana. Sattva, rajas, and tamas are all in such nearly perfect balance here that the merest smudge in the sky serves for a cloud, a single small yellow-breasted bird for a flock, and a trip to the local bookstore for an adventure, a pilgrimage. Your books and your posters are on display, and my love for you is slowly being restored to the love it was before reality intervened. For, yes, we do wish to live entirely in our chittavrittis yet cheat them by hoping they are not all there is, and any demonstration we can make of our ideality—loving a man on a poster, for instance—flatters this hope. The pleasure of love, you taught me, lies in love's stalling, in vajrolimudra. How you did wickedly delight in my dying again and again while impaled on your inflexible ungiving all-giving vajra, your darling thunder-jewel! For a woman, the equivalent of such nivritti—since our female instrument of love is the entire body, even to the eyelashes and the toenails—is removal, denial, betrayal even: love's expression must become absence and silence.

My absence you already have, the silence will follow this letter. I fear you will not greatly care. Mahima will make my void her plenum. There are many Shaktis. And the human hunger for a god will always reward those with the temerity—the inner density and vacuity—to call themselves gods. Something like that happens whenever a woman falls for a man. But the *suffering* a woman endures for the same mute Shiva, the same stony linga, over and over! My entire subtle body aches; I awake to this ache and fall asleep impaled upon it. Also, I have caught a cold, as I tend to when I travel. These ignoble constant sniffles and sore throats of ours, and twinges in the teeth—are they, do you suppose, scratches that as it were geologically remember prakriti's being extracted from purusha?

In all those blissful months, even while wimpy Yajna whacked my jaw and Vikshipta turned sadistic and the shots were ringing out during Durga's last stand, your spirit sheltered me and I felt no fear. Now I feel fear. Master, having already bestowed upon me the mudra of dama (your boon more generous than perhaps you knew), do not withhold your abhayamudra. *Fear not!*— what all the gods say, like so many suns burning through the mists of circumstance.

[unsigned]

December 13, 15, 18—while
a full moon comes and goes

Dear Charles—

The disgusting news that you are to marry Midge Hibbens knocked me for a loop, I confess. She babbled away blithely about it in the last of these tapes we've been exchanging—as of course you know. You know everything, it turns out, though I must say the image of you and Midge holding hands and God knows what all—heavy petting, let's call it—while listening to your poor betrayed wife's gushing taped confessions is one of the least appetizing images of courtship I have ever entertained. With her really remarkable insensitivity, Midge assumed I'd be *pleased* by her news! She said she'd been detecting all sorts of guilt in my references to you and this should ease it! She *had* mumbled a bit in her tape before the last one about her and Ed "having troubles" (of course leaving out that the main trouble was her wish to switch over to you), and in response to that I girlishly mentioned this dream in which you and I were making love, and it must have been in response to that that she popped her gladsome tidings. I do think she took a fright of jealousy from just my dreaming about you! Talk about possessive!! And not even in legal possession yet.

I wonder how much you really understand about Midge. She is crass, Charles. She is lively but not sensitive. In our sessions with Irving she has never shown the slightest grasp or interest in the philosophy and cosmology underlying hatha-yoga. As far as she's concerned it's just a slimming exercise—which she does need, granted—but as far as spiritual energy goes she might as well be doing aerobics to the Bee Gees. I'm sure she's wonderful in bed—any woman is, when there's a conquest to be made—but aren't you going to get *tired* of that brassy laugh, those unreal paprika-colored curls, the way she says "doggie" instead of "dog" and "din-din" instead of "dinner"? It wasn't just Ed who was the loudmouth in that couple—remember how we used to come away from their house with decibel headaches? Midge has the kind of mind that honestly thinks the sayings on barbecue aprons and big fat coffee mugs are cute. And whose house are you proposing to live in?— not ours, that would be a *sacrilege*, and their split-level is much too tacky for a man in your position—that shag-carpet rumpus room Ed put in the basement with all that pine panelling and shelves for his bowling trophies was fine for the yoga group but can you imagine yourself sitting down there of an evening in the Barca-lounger reading through their stacks of old *Smithsonians*? And what are your snobby MGH neurosurgeon friends going to say when Midge in one of those lurid loose splashy dresses she wears to confuse the weight issue breaks into her shrill giggle and asks the host if there's a little-girls' room where she can wash her hands? Darling, you're going to have a decibel headache day and night. I just can't bear to think of her in our *house* or even in our *garden*—she'll just put plaster toads and bunnies everywhere and *choke* the bed with marigolds and salvia—she has absolutely no eye—in fact I've often wondered if she isn't hiding color blindness, the way she dresses and the way her slipcovers go with her wallpapers—hideous! She *does* wear contact lenses, you know—one time doing Shirsasana one of them came out and we never did find it in the rug so it must have slipped back into her brain and may still be there.

I love Midge, of course. She has very little negativity, and for another woman that's a great plus, since we tend as a sex toward depression. Many's the time I went over there vaguely desperate and came away laughing, full of cottage cheese and fruit salad and white-wine silliness. It was like going to some unisex health club where you leave your intelligence in the locker room. But for a *man*, who wants a partner who can give him back some resonance at every level, it will be like living with Pearl at age twelve and a half, only not so pretty and with no prospect of growth. There is something sweet but *arrested* about Midge—she has always been so vain of her dainty hands and feet, in rather insistent contrast to mine especially—she was always having us compare shoes, and professing astonishment that mine were so much like rowboats, and always touching or patting me with her little stubby paws as if to call attention to them, with all their preposterous eye-catching clunky rings and really very *tawdry* fingernail polish, those plummy reds and baby pinks and even, I remember one Saint Patrick's Day, an unbelievable parsley green. And her feet, squeezed like rising dough into these poor creaking pumps—I mean, as women supposedly head into the twenty-first century, are bound feet what we need?

But I forget that you must be a man in love, enchanted, bewitched, and that even my most innocuous observation will strike you as sheer spite. Not at all— you two deserve each other. But before I leave the subject: Have you ever listened to her eat? *Listened*, I mean—she makes little happy humming noises with every bite, and pats her lips together in a kind of tiny applause all the way up from her stomach. Perhaps she makes the same noises in bed—that's for you to know— lucky you. For her, of course, you are a great step up— Ed called himself a security-systems analyst but he was really just a glorified electrician installing these futile burglar alarms, whereas you are in one of the hallowed professions—the *only* hallowed one, actually, since teaching and preaching and lawyering are all known now to be con games. I must say I can't *bear* it, imagining her humming and smacking her lips over you in the dark—your betrayals had become old hat to me and had male thoughtlessness and brutishness to exonerate them up to a point, but Midge inside that doggie piggie brain of hers *must* have known it was somehow not *nice* to steal a woman's husband while that same woman was trustfully giving and giving of herself on these tapes, those utterly confiding and trusting Maxells. Burn them, in all decency. *Not* in our fireplace—they'll stink and melt and stick fast to the andirons and the bricks. How about in Ed's old barbecue pit? One thing I *have* decided: you are *not* going to live with that hateful ridiculous woman in my lovely house with the view of the sea and the rocks and those English-style border beds I brought back from the absolute weed-patches that old Mrs. Pyncheon had allowed to grow up everywhere. You will *sell* the house and give me my *half* of the proceeds if in fact I don't have Ducky ask for *all* of it, 100%—women *usually* get the house, they were supposedly the *homemakers*—even your hatchet man Gilman will tell you that.

And what of little Pearl? Suppose the news gives her a miscarriage?

Later. Another day. Calmer now. Peace, Charles. I realize this morning that Midge is only rising to a higher level of socioeconomic energy and should not be blamed. And I suppose honestly there was nothing in my tapes to indicate that you weren't fair game, though a person with even a *little* sensitivity—but I can't rouse myself to even enough indignation to complete the sentence. What matters really and always has is *us*—you and I. I've taken time to think and meditate and just relax into the space I'm in, and I've decided I don't believe in divorce and will write and tell Ducky to make no terms at all. You and your roly-poly little suburban pudding can do whatever you want—retire to her rumpus room and leave adulterous stains all over the shag carpet. Your infatuation will wear itself out with or without my blessing. I'm doing you a great favor, blocking a marriage that no sane man, and certainly not my straitlaced thrifty Charles (you know how Midge *spends*—Ed was always bragging/complaining), would really want. No, what you really want is to skim from Midge that demonic erotic courtship energy women can produce for short spurts and then abandon her emotionally just as you did me.

Did you know that the Jains reckon time in palyas, a palya being "a period of countless years," and that 100,000,000 times 100,000,000 palyas equals an "ocean of years"? They say furthermore that the age before ours lasted 100,000,000,000,000 oceans of years (approximately) and saw people shrink from a thousand yards tall, with thirty-two ribs, to only nine and a half feet in height? The age was called the duhshama-sushama, which means Very Beautifully Sorrowful, and our age is simply the Sorrowful (duhshama) and will be succeeded by the last, the Sorrowfully Sorrowful (duhshama-duhshama). I give these facts (transcribing them from a book I obtained at the local bookstore, where I have a little charge account) to suggest the conceptual context in which I am presently operating, and to convey the tranquillity and serenity of my state of mind. You can see why the Jains don't like to inhale gnats—. from their perspective we are all just gnats, at best.

I have left the ashram. Midge's gloating gleeful news and some local disillusionments made me realize that this phase of my progress was over. The love that I left you for has been sublimated—literally turned into radiant etheric vapor at a location called Sahasrara a few inches above my head. Rare Sarah, I have now become. Where I am now geographically suits my rarefied condition. I can't give it away, lest Gilman come swooping in in a biplane with all sorts of writs and handcuffs. It is as near nowhere as you can imagine and yet *some*where, if you know what I mean. With its own little historical distinctions, export crops, and atmospheric flavor. The flavor is in my nostrils night and day and the atmosphere rests on my skin and keeps reminding me of the time in about 1970 or '71 (Pearl I know had begun at that Episcopalian kindergarten and was big enough so we thought we could leave her for a week with my parents—you hadn't had a vacation since beginning internship and were thin as a rail) when we flew to Saint Martin, the French side, because I thought I could practice my French, but their accent was quite different and everybody in all the shops spoke English anyway, and in the jet down we had daiquiris, and after our second ones, what with the rum and the relief at being away

from work, you got passionate and began murmuring
to me all the things you were going to do to me, all the
sexual things, and I kept nodding and giggling and
hoping the people in the seats around us couldn't hear,
and felt the rum heating up my face; and when we got
there, this perfectly darling little run-down and not
especially clean hotel off the main street in Marigot,
with filigreed wooden balconies and our room overlooking the quaint old cemetery full of whitewashed
broken tombs and the greeny-blue violet-striped sea
beyond, we did them all, we made a systematic job of
it, a little high every night on wine and the liqueurs that
were so cheap duty-free, and then in the mornings too,
after eating the slices of green melon and the crumby
hard rolls and the bitter good coffee the girl brought,
the nine-o'clock sun coming in through the louvers at
an angle making warm stripes on the straw rug beside
the bed, and then in the mid-afternoon too, after our
hours on the beach with the piña coladas for lunch at
the little thatched bar there, the sun now having moved
around and the room shadowy and cool with the stripes
from the louvers beginning to climb the wall over in the
far corner, and the noon's sunburn settling into our
shoulders and thighs, we worked through our list, everything you had said in the airplane; and though some
of the things we had never done before and when it
came down to doing them you were shy of hurting or
abusing me I made you go through with them, I
thought you should have everything I could give because you'd been working so hard and were so boyishly
thin and this was our holiday. Dear Charles, after the

first nights I smelled of your semen all the time, my hands and face and between my breasts where you came that way once—nothing, not the saltwater at the beach or the soap in the shower could wash it off, this faint lingering semi-sour smell of *you* somehow worked into my pores; I wondered if other people, the slim black girls in the wristwatch shops and the waiters bending over us at the evening meal with its hibiscus on the table and little candle-bowl guttering and even the staring men hanging around at the old cement dock, could smell it—I was terrified they could but also I *liked* smelling that way, just soaked in your seed, floating along in this little faintly rancid cloud of sex smell, there in the sunshine where nobody knew us. We worked your list through, we did it all the ways we could think of or had read about in books and I felt so *married* to you, so yours, exuding this spunky aroma and aching a bit in the intimate places. I never have known why I didn't get pregnant that time, my cycle was right and we took no precautions, I was sure we would go back having started a little brother for Pearl but it wasn't to be—how odd when the time we *did* make a baby was one of those awful almost virginal times when you came much too soon and I didn't come at all and we both felt embarrassed and inadequate afterwards. That week in Saint Martin I loved you so much for *trusting* me with all that seed of yours, the sperm all furiously thrashing and swimming to reach my egg, my egg that I was made to carry, my whole intricate body and spirit simply its package and wrapping really, you didn't hold it back as some men do to give a woman and themselves pleasure, for us it was more than pleasure, there was a rigor to it, a duty, a ruthless and thorough mutual exploitation, a union at that solemn level where I unwashably smelled—that funny helpless hollowish smell semen has—and where I would always be yours. So, with the atmosphere of that week in my mouth and nostrils and soft on my skin all day where I am now you can see why I don't believe in divorce and brush away Midge as the bothersome gnat she is.

Days later. Prolonging the sad pleasure, the Beautifully Sorrowful. I do enjoy writing to you, old dear. Maybe it's your silence I enjoy—no scolding word about the state of the drapes or dust in the bookcase or about the house going to pot inside while I dug in the garden or wasted half the day at yoga. You hated my yoga, but maybe Midge will lead you along the Eightfold Path. Really, it's just stretching exercises and an attempt to still the mind, to quiet the ego and let something other than its clamoring be heard.

Now I wonder if my reactions to you and Midge haven't been selfish and non-non-attached. After all, I *did* leave, and can't really imagine coming back. We've had our Krishna-Radha week in Marigot. How old were we? I would have been twenty-six, and you twenty-eight. The perfect age to play at being gods. If there is—as various patriarchal religions keep suggesting—a divinity in whoredom, I touched it that week. I wasn't just me, I was *you*, your sukra and my rajas indivisible. You got so brown, I remember, all but your cute pale tight fanny, and your body was like something harder

than flesh, your chest leaning above me flat and hairless
like a—what? A primitive lean-to, a piece of slanty attic
roof that a child likes to huddle under while it rains.
That must have been behind the dream of mine that I
suppose Midge played for you. She really *has* come
between us, hasn't she? In a way the Arhat never did.
He belonged to my subtle body and you to my gross
earthly sthula body—my real body, I suppose you'd say.
I felt big enough for you both, if I can claim that without appearing immodest.

Charles, I can't express how serene and benign I feel
about you and me. Parting is an illusion. Loss is an
illusion, just as is gain. We shed our skins but something
naked and white and amara slithers out and is always
the same. I think I eventually will go to Holland and
help Pearl bear our grandchild. These Dutch brewers
have at least the charm of money—guilders, isn't it,
over there? It all—*sa grossesse et tout*—seemed a little
soon, but then everything does, I suppose, from being
born to dying. I've dropped a note to Ducky asking him
to try to work it out with Gilman. Did it bother you to
hear on the tapes that I had a flirtation of sorts with
Ducky, before he knew that he was gay? Poor Gloria,
how terrible to realize that your supposed feminine
charm is an unloaded gun, so to speak. There was something *challenging* about Ducky for a woman and I suppose that was it. Anyway, your flings with those flat-
heeled nurses (how *can* you medical people who know
so much about the body's ins and outs still get excited
making love?—or does that expertise make it more so?)
did bother me, however lightly you took them. They

were klishta. They sullied me and you—wounded us, really. Things can't always be undone, it would seem. There is a *grain* to prakriti, an arrow of time. We get tired. Do remember and remind the despicable Gilman that whether or not this divorce goes through is to me a matter of utter indifference. Having known the Arhat's divine love I am not in the market (unlike needy old you) for any further attachments. I need to be still and feel now I have acquired the means to be still.

As I wrote you last spring, I have the Price salver and teapot and the Peabody flatware and candlesticks and Daddy's Milton and Donne and Herbert and Vaughan and Marvell. You *can't* begrudge me those, and I've willed them to the Houghton Library in any case. The stocks that I impulsively sold on the advice of Irving's astrology I *do* apologize for—who would have thought the market could keep rising the nonsensical way it has? It's the terrible trade imbalance—the Japanese and Arabs and Germans have to do *something* with all their deteriorating dollars, and so they toss them back at us. In compensation, you can have the New Hampshire land— I don't think the Loon condos are going to come that way in this century—and I lavishly waive more than half of the assessed present value of our house and the Cape property. I would think the former would be worth a million now, with its view, so it should be easy to figure what you owe me if you and Midge have such poor taste as to want to live there, with my ghost sneaking around every corner, rose clippers in hand. I *certainly* can't picture even so gross a duo as you two humping away in our old fourposter, so when you sell it point out to the dealer that the carving is by William Lemon of Salem and the gilding by Daggett of Boston—these names add *hundreds* to the value. The Chippendale dining table and matching eight chairs with the diamond-and-scroll back splats came from the Perkinses and should go eventually to Pearl, along with the carved sea chest that accompanied Daddy's great-granddaddy back and forth to China countless times and the dear little blackened salt-and-pepper shakers handed down through Mother's mother's mother's people the Prynnes. The Worth things are of course yours, though I confess I would *love* to have, here in my lonely cottage by the sea, the flame-stitch wing chair I used to sit in waiting for you to come home, stitching away at those hateful to-be-mono-grammed place mats your tiresome Aunt Hilda inflicted on us as a wedding present—of the twelve, I think I did only three plus half of one more *W* over the course of twenty-two years. In most wing chairs I feel slightly repressed but that flame-stitch one had just the right gentle grip. Where I am now, the winter days are about the length of spring days in New England, and for that first half-hour of the dark as I sit reading zoology or cosmology or just staring into space I catch myself listening for the grinding sound of the garage door sliding up, in obedience to its own inner eye.

Ever,

S.

Glossary

abhayamudra the gesture dispelling fear

abhinivesha the will to enjoy; the will to live

abhyasana practice

adipurusha the Primal Man, the universal life-monad that manifests itself through pure, self-contained consciousness

advaya the state of absolute unity; non-duality

agni fire; *(cap.)* god of divine fire and spirit of Soma

aham the ego; "I"

ahamkara the uniform apperceptive mass emergent from *mahat*, not yet personal but with a dim consciousness of ego

Airavata a celestial six-trunked white elephant ridden by Indra

ajiva "non-spirit," not vital, *i.e.*, matter

Ajna the sixth *chakra*, located between the eyebrows; *(without cap.)* command

aklishta undefiled; pure; clean

alinga *prakriti's* original state of perfect, uncharacterized equilibrium

amara immortal

amaya non-deceit

amitabha immeasurably radiant; *(cap.)* the celestial Buddha who dwells in the Land of Bliss in the West

amitayus immeasurably long-living; *(cap.)* Amitabha

Anahata the heart *chakra*; *(without cap.)* the unstruck sound

Ananta "endless"; the endless serpent with one thousand heads, upon whom Vishnu sleeps, as from his navel

blossoms Brahma the creator; the archetype of the un-
conscious and the underworld

apakva unripe

apsaras a celestial dancer, who performs to delight the
gods

Ardha-Shalabhasana the Half-Locust position in *yoga*

Ardhanarishvara Shiva and Shakti in a united, androgy-
nous form

arhat "deserving one"; a Buddhist monk who has
reached a high level of enlightenment

aropa attribution of qualities to the object, that is, subdu-
ing the beloved's physical, biological, and psychological
aspects to an ontological perspective

artha material success; wealth

arthamatranirbhasam svarupashunyamiva empty of itself

asana a posture in *yoga*

asanga without attachments; non-attached; *(cap.)* the
founder of Buddhist tantrism, *c.* 400 B.C.

ashram a place of religious retreat

atman the Self, or true self, not to be confused with *aham*
or *buddhi;* virtually synonymous with *purusha*

avatar an incarnation of a Hindu deity, especially
Vishnu

avidya unknowing; ignorance

ayoni not born from the womb; without origin or
source; eternal

bhaga womb; vagina; good fortune, happiness, excellence

bhanda vessel, pot, dish; the body as a vessel for the
truth, as distinguished from *brahmanda*

bhava being; birth; divine emotion

bhaya fear

bhoga physical enjoyment

bindu point; sperm

bodhi enlightenment; illumination

bodhisattva enlightened being; on the scale of achieved
holiness, lower than Buddha and higher than an *arhat*:
in the Buddha Fields, the two Great Bodhisattvas,
Avalokiteshvara and Mahasthama, flank Amitabha

Brahma the Creator; with Vishnu and Shiva, one of the

trinity of major deities and much the weakest: only one temple to him exists in India, at Lake Pushkar

brahman holy power derived from chanting the Vedic hymns; the metaphysical ground of being; *(cap.)* ultimate reality, pure consciousness and spirit, akin to *atman* and *purusha*

brahmanda the universe; Brahma's creation; the macrocosm as a vessel for the truth

Brahmavaivarta Purana a fourteenth-century epic

Brahmin a member of the priestly caste

Buddhatvam yoshidyonisamsritam "Buddhahood is in the *yoni*"

buddhi intelligence

chakra center; *lit.*, wheel or circle; energy centers located in the subtle body

chittavrittis eddies or fluctuations of consciousness

Dakini the *shakti* of Brahma at the Muladhara *chakra*; *(without cap)* the tantric consort of a god

dama gift, boon

darshan "view"; audience with a saint or *guru*

Dhammapada "the path of truth"; a collection, in Pali, of Buddhist aphorisms, compiled in the third century B.C. *(dhamma = Sanskrit dharma)*

dharma virtue, in accordance with cosmic law

dhyana meditation

digambara "sky-clad" or "space-clad"; naked; one of two main sects of Jainism

dombi the "washerwoman"; *(cap.)* Shakti as a low-caste courtesan

duhkha dissatisfaction; pain

duhshama sorrowful

Durga "difficult of approach"; Shakti in her aspect as the goddess of war and destruction

dvandvanabhighata the cessation of trouble from pairs of opposites

ekagrata "single-pointedness"; the state of concentration whereby the *yogi* eliminates distractions and gains control over his restless consciousness

Ganesha the elephant-headed god of auspicious beginnings; deity of wisdom and patron of literature

gauri-pattan "platter"; receptacle in which stone *linga* stands; female sexual organs

Gopis the wives of the cowherds among whom Krishna was reared

Gotama the family name of Buddha

granthi a knot of obstruction in the *nadis*, encountered by Kundalini in her ascent

Guanahaná the Lucayan Indian term for San Salvador, wherever it was

gunas qualities; the three modalities of *prakriti*: *sattva*, *rajas*, and *tamas*

guru "heavy"; a religious teacher

Hakini the *shakti* of Paramashiva at the Ajna *chakra*

Hanuman the monkey-god, thought to manifest divine energy on earth; the general of the army of the monkey-king, Sugriva, allied with Rama in the *Ramayana*

hatha "sun" *(ha)* plus "moon" *(tha)*; violent effort

Hinayana the "abandoned ferry" or "lesser vehicle"; the original, more austere form of Buddhism

Hling kling kandarpa svaha a mantra that accompanies sacrificial offerings: "Oblation to the lord of creatures and to that within him which causes him to create; may we gain knowledge, joy, and power"

ida the lunar subtle channel or *nadi*, ending at the left nostril

Isha the presiding god of the Anahata *chakra*

iti iti "it is here, it is here": the path of worldly enjoyment

jiva the individual spirit; the vital soul

jivan-mukta the "living liberated" who, though having attained *moksha*, remains on earth

Jumna a sacred river flowing from the Himalayas into the Ganges

Kakini the *shakti* of Isha at the Anahata *chakra*

Kali the goddess of time, of destruction and disease and rebirth; the "black one," the malign aspect of Shakti: depicted with a protruding red tongue and a garland of skulls, she is beloved of the lower castes and the object of blood sacrifices

Kaliyuga the Iron Age; this present era of decay and diminishment

kalpana the imagination

kama sexual desire

karma action; the principle of causality; the moral accumulation of actions in one life which determine one's fate in the next; the entire endless cycle of reincarnation

karuna compassion

klishta defiled; afflicted; unclean

Ko veda? Who knows?

krodha wrath

Kula the all-transcending light of consciousness, a phase of Kundalini; also, a kind of *yogini* that dwells in *kula* trees

Kundalini "coiled up"; the serpent of female energy dormant at the base of the spinal column; *(without cap)* this type of energy and the *yoga* performed to awaken it

Lakini the *shakti* of Rudra at the Manipura *chakra*

Lakshmi the wife of Vishnu; goddess of good luck and plenty, and personification of beauty

lila play

linga mark, sign, emblem; the subtle body and subtle space; light, spirit, consciousness; the male principle, symbolic of Shiva; phallus

lobha greed

ma "mother"; reverential title addressed to women

Mahabindu "the great point"; the Transcendental Void; the ultimate goal of Kundalini

Mahaparinirvana "the great state beyond *nirvana*"; death

Mahasukha the Great Bliss

mahat "the great"; the energetic, unself-conscious mass that appears when *prakriti* departs from *alinga*

Mahayana the "Great Vehicle"; the later, more supernaturalist and syncretist form of Buddhism

mahima the ability, allegedly acquired by an accomplished *yogi*, to swell to such enormous size that one can touch the moon (other such powers are: *anima*, to become small or invisible; *laghima*, to become so light one can walk on air or water; *garima*, to become as heavy as the world; *prapti*; *prakamya*, to enjoy things infinitely;

ishitva, to master all things, including death; *vashitva,* to subdue or bewitch by magic)

maithuna   coitus

makara   dragon

mala   necklace

manana   reflection

mandala   "circle"; sacred design

mandir   meeting hall; temple

mani padme   the jewel in the lotus; the mind in *nirvana,* the *linga* in the *yoni*

Manipura   the third *chakra,* located at the solar plexus; the "gem city"

mantra   sacred sound or word or sentence; incantation

manus   man

mara   death; *(cap.)* Buddha's tempter

maya   cosmic illusion, dependent upon *avidya;* magic

moksha   liberation; release from delusion; ultimate enlightenment

mudra   yogic gesture or finger position

Muladhara   the root *chakra,* located at the base of the spine

Nachiketa   the son of Vajasrabasa, in the Veda called "Katha"

nadi   a nerve or channel of the subtle body, through which astral and pranic currents flow

naga   snake

nagga   naked

namaste   a greeting, meaning "I salute the god within you"

nayika   "devout woman"; deified love-object in yogico-tantric *maithuna*

neti neti   "not this, not that": the path of asceticism

nirgundi   box-elder tree

nirvana   "without wind"; a state of being beyond *duhkha, karma,* and *samsara,* sought by Buddhism as the ultimate beatitude, on the plane of the unconditioned

nitya   eternal

nivritti   withdrawal or quiescence of the senses or mind; total arrest of process

niyamas   disciplines

ojas, ojas shakti psychic or hormonal energy, manifested as a subtle radiance when sublimated

Om a mystical syllable incarnating the essence of the cosmos, the Whole, the *brahman* and the *atman*

padma lotus; the female genitals

palya a period of countless years

parakiya rati another's wife

Paramahasukha the Supreme Great Bliss

paramanu atoms

Paramashiva Shakti and Shiva in coitus

parinama development; evolution

parinirvana "the going beyond nirvana"; Buddha's death

Pashchimottanasana the "stretching the back" *asana*; also translated "climbing westwards," as the *shakti* enters the head from the *sushumna* in the spine

Patanjali the author of the classic text on *yoga*, in the third century B.C.

phalatrishna "thirst for fruits"; the desire for ego-satisfaction and -extension

pingala the solar *nadi*, ending at the right nostril

prakhya vivacity; mental clarity and serenity

prakriti matter; Nature

prana life-force; breath (one of five types)

pranayama discipline of respiration; breathing exercise

prapatti passive surrender

prapti the power to obtain anything at will, including knowledge of the past and future

pratiloman against the grain

pratyahara withdrawal of sensory activity from exterior objects

prem loving being: a mode of address

prema love

puja "invocation"; worship; cult

puram city

purnabhisheka ritual copulation practiced in "left-handed" tantric *yoga*; the *shri chakra* or *chakra puja*

purusha eternal cosmic spirit, from which *prakriti* emerged; Self, one with *atman* and *brahman*

Radha Krishna's deified lover

Rahula the son of Buddha and Yashodhara

rajas the *guna* of motor energy and mental activity; passion; dust; menstrual fluid; female secretions: *fig.*, the "lotus seed"

Rakini the *shakti* of Vishnu at the Svadhisthana *chakra*

rasa flavor; essence; mercury, the essence of Shiva; bliss; sap; juice; sweat

rasamandali "circle of bliss"; Krishna's dance with the Gopis; orgy

ressentiment French term used by Nietzsche for resentment as the basis of "slave morality"

rishi seer

rita, ṛta "course"; the rhythmic order whereby Varuna maintains the universe

Rudra the storm-god; presiding deity at the Manipura *chakra*

sachchidananda being-consciousness-bliss: triune attribute of Brahman and of highest human realization

sadhana realization, in tantrism

sahaja "the innate"; pure spontaneity, arrived at by transcending the dualities, in tantrism

Sahasrara the seventh *chakra*, above the crown of the head, its lotus of a thousand petals shedding illumination

samadhi the ultimate contemplative state in *yoga*, closed to stimuli, in which an object presented to the mind is seen in its true light, without distortion, as if *arthamatranirbhasam svarupashunyamiva*

samanya rati ordinary (consort) woman

samara a dry one-seeded winged fruit, often in pairs

samarasa the beatific experience of unity, obtained through arrest of breath or of semen

sambhogakaya in tantric Buddhism, the subtle "body of bliss"

samsara existence; the cosmic process; the round of birth and death, destruction and renewal

Sankhya an ancient philosophy, supposedly founded by Kapila, distinguished from *yoga* by its atheism and its emphasis upon metaphysical knowledge, rather than meditation, as the means to *moksha*

sannyasin   pilgrim; holy man, sworn to itinerant poverty; the fourth and ultimate stage of the model male life, the three preceding being *brahmacharya*, celibate studenthood; *grihastha*, husband and householder; and *vanaprastha*, partial withdrawal, as to a forest hermitage

satori   enlightenment, in Zen Buddhism

sattva   the *guna* of luminosity and intelligence

satya   truth

Satyavati   the daughter, called "Fishy Smell," of King Vasa and a fish, and the mother of the great poet and *rishi* Vyasa

Savitri   the Vedic sun-god

shakti   power; energy; *(cap.)* the consort of Shiva, bringing the dynamic principle to his immutable foundational consciousness; the feminine creative principle throughout the cosmos, worshipped in many forms, *e.g.*, as Parvati, the ideal wife; Kali, the destroyer; Durga, the terrible; Shri, the bringer of prosperity; Lakshmi; Shashthi, protector of children; and Shitala, the personification of smallpox

shanti   peace

Shirsasana   in *yoga*, the Headstand

Shiva   "auspicious"; the destroyer in the Brahma-Shiva-Vishnu trinity, Brahma being the creator and Vishnu the preserver; the god of pure consciousness, with the *linga* as his symbol

shri   holy

shri chakra   "holy circle"; ritual copulation in a temple setting

Shuddhodana   "having pure rice"; Buddha's father

Shudra   a member of the artisan or worker caste

shunya   the void, of an adamantine essence and therefore called *vajra*; a girl of low caste, or courtesan

Siddhartha   Buddha's given name

smarana   recollection

Soma   intoxicating plant juice consumed by the Vedic

priests and worshipped as an immortality-bestowing god

sthula gross; material

sthulabhutani molecules

strivyatireka love

Sukhavati the Land of Bliss

sukra semen

sukshma subtle; etheric; immaterial

sushumna the central subtle channel

sutra "thread"; a concise religious text

Svadhisthana the second *chakra*, located in the genital region

svarupa proper or essential form: *sahaja* is the *svarupa* of all things

tamas the *guna* of inertia and resistance, produced by matter, passion, and clouded consciousness

tanmatras the five subtle elements or energy nuclei produced from *ahamkara* and giving rise to the *paramanu* and *sthulabhutani*

tantra "loom, weave"; scriptures advocating anti-ascetic forms of *yoga* emphasizing Shakti-worship, visualizations, mandalas, and the "five boons": *madya* (wine), *mamsa* (meat), *matsya* (fish), *mudra* (woman or parched cereal), and *maithuna*

tapas "heat, ardor"; asceticism

Tat tvam asi "That thou art," meaning that our innermost nature is the same as ultimate reality, *purusha*

tena tyaktena bhunjithah "Accept the quota set aside (for you) by him (God)"—from the Vedas

tikka beauty spot applied between female brows, to ward off evil eye and to symbolize third eye of wisdom

ujjana sadhana against the current

Uma "peace of the night"; Shakti in her benign, wifely aspect, representing feminine creativity and heavenly wisdom

vairagya detachment

vajra thunderbolt; *linga*; urethral meatus

vajrolimudra the "thunderbolt posture"; the yogic technique whereby semen is retained and *rajas* are absorbed

Vamachara the "left-handed," more overtly sexual practice of tantric *yoga*

Varuna   a Vedic deity, the god of the waters; presiding over *rita*

vasana   the subconscious; the source and repository of latencies, the *vasanas*, in the cycle *vasanas-vrittis-karma-vasanas*

vayu   air; *(cap.)* the Vedic god of winds

Vedas   the four canonical collections of the hymns and prayers of the Aryan people who invaded Northwest India c. 1500 B.C.; the oldest Hindu sacred writings

vidya   wisdom; science; metaphysical knowledge

vikshipta   scattered attention; uncenteredness; a merely provisional and occasional state of concentration, undisciplined by *yoga*

virya   "heroism"; strength, potency

vishesha rati   extraordinary consort

Vishnu   the god who in the Hindu trinity takes most interest in human affairs and is most widely worshipped: of his ten incarnations, Krishna and Rama are best known

Vishuddha   "pure"; the fifth *chakra*, located behind the throat

Vrindavan   the idyllic realm where Krishna copulates with Radha and the Gopis

vrittis   eddies, fluctuations; *chittavrittis*

yajna   sacrifice

yamas   restraints

Yashodhara   "upholding glory"; the name of Buddha's wife

yoga   "yoke, link"; a philosophy and method of uniting the mind with the essential Self, the *atman*: defined by Patanjali as "chittavritti-nirodhyah"—the settling of the mind into silence

yogi   male practitioner of *yoga*

yogini   female practitioner of *yoga*; a type of forest fairy

yoni   vagina; womb

yuganaddha   a state of unity obtained by transcending the two polarities of *samsara* and *nivritti* and perceiving the identity of the phenomenal world and the absolute

About the Author

JOHN UPDIKE was born in 1932 in Shillington, Pennsylvania. He graduated from Harvard in 1954, and spent a year in England on the Knox Fellowship, at the Ruskin School of Drawing and Fine Art in Oxford. From 1955 to 1957 he was a member of the staff of *The New Yorker*, to which he has contributed short stories, poems, and book reviews. His fiction has won the Pulitzer Prize, the National Book Award, the American Book Award, and the National Book Critics Circle Award. Since 1957, he has lived in Massachusetts.

BECH IS BACK

Famous for his writer's block, renowned author Henry Bech is now fifty years old. In this collection of stories, Bech reflects on his fame, roams the world, marries an Episcopalian divorcée from Westchester and—surprise to all—writes a book that becomes a smash bestseller. All the while, he looks at life with a blend of wonder and cynicism that makes us laugh with delight and wince in recognition.

THE CENTAUR

Winner of the National Book Award, this novel is set in a small Pennsylvania town in 1947, where schoolteacher George Caldwell yearns to find meaning in his life. Alone with his teenage son for three days in a blizzard, Caldwell sees his son grow and change while he himself begins to lose touch with his life. Interwoven with the myth of Chiron, the noblest centaur, and his own relationship with Prometheus, this is one of Updike's most brilliant and unusual novels.

THE COUP

Kush, the imaginary African nation, a large, land-locked, drought-ridden territory, is ruled by Colonel Hakim Felix Ellelloû. The good colonel has four wives, a silver Mercedes, and a fanatic aversion to the United States. But the Ugly American keeps creeping into Kush— with all sorts of strange repercussions.

COUPLES

An artful, seductive, savagely graphic portrait of love, marriage, and adultery in a small Massachusetts town in the 1960s.

"Stylistically brilliant."
WILLIAM KENNEDY

MARRY ME

Updike's classic portrait of intimacy and infidelity in the suburbs.

". . . so smooth and miraculously intact that it is irresistible."
THE BOSTON GLOBE

A MONTH OF SUNDAYS

The Reverend Tom Marshfield is literate,
charming, sexual, and his outrageous
behavior with the ladies of his flock
scandalizes his parish.

"A tour de force . . . readable, clever."
CHICAGO TRIBUNE

OF THE FARM

When Joey Robinson, thirty-five-year-old
advertising consultant in Manhattan, returns
with his new second wife and stepson to the
farm where he grew up, it is an adventure.
For three days, a quartet of voices explores
the air, relating stories, making confessions,
seeking solace, hoping for love.

PICKED-UP PIECES

A selection of critical essays and humorous
pieces by the novelist.

"Brilliant, gentle, self-deprecating yet sure of
his view, John Updike is a graceful, inventive,
joyous and affectionate writer."
THE WASHINGTON POST

PIGEON FEATHERS

Nineteen short stories in a bestselling collection.

"So full of fire and ice that it almost breaks through to some 'fourth dimension' in writing."
SAN FRANCISCO CHRONICLE

THE POORHOUSE FAIR

In Updike's first novel, the setting is a poorhouse—repository of the old, the infirm, and the impoverished—on the day of the annual summer fair. The time is the future, in our century. Crotchety John Hook, with his ninety years of memories . . . the administrator Stephen Conner, caught between his own sense of mission and the old people's human perversity . . . his young assistant Buddy, a trifle too eager to please. The people are Updike's own, vividly realized, entirely unforgettable.

PROBLEMS

Updike's masterful collection of stories that illuminate and reflect the lives we lead.

"Radiant, dazzling."
THE BOSTON GLOBE

RABBIT, RUN

Rabbit Angstrom, a former high-school basketball
star, is the typical product of the world
which he —and each of us—finds baffling.
The world, its myths, and its realities are
exposed in the lives of Rabbit, his wife,
his mistress, even his minister. In their imperfect
vision of themselves, in what they themselves
cannot articulate, Updike challenges an image
of life still cherished in America.

RABBIT REDUX

Harry Angstrom, known to all as Rabbit, finds
his drab life shattered by the furor of the late
sixties and by the infidelity of his wife, Janice.

"A superb performance, all grace and dazzle
. . . a brilliant portrait of Middle America."
LIFE

RABBIT IS RICH

Winner of the Pulitzer Prize and the American
Book Award, RABBIT IS RICH brings back
Harry Angstrom, now a Toyota sales rep and in
good shape. He is at last ready to enjoy life,
until his son Nelson returns from the West, and
the image of an old love pays him a visit. New
characters and old populate these scenes from
Rabbit's mid-life, as he continues to pursue, in
his erratic fashion, the rainbow of happiness.

ROGER'S VERSION

A born-again computer whiz kid bent on proving
the existence of God on his computer meets
a middle-aged divinity professor who'd just as
soon leave faith a mystery. Then that computer
hacker, Dale Kohler, begins an adulterous affair
with the professor Roger Lambert's wife. Roger
himself experiences longings for a somewhat
trashy teenage girl. In Updike's acclaimed
novel, love and sex and God and faith and
modern life are explored with style, passion,
and incomparable skill.

TOO FAR TO GO:
The Maples Stories

Seventeen short stories, spanning twenty years,
that trace the decline and fall of a marriage,
but also a story in many ways happy, of
growing children and a million mundane
moments shared.

TRUST ME

Twenty-two stories of husbands and wives and lovers.

"As always with Mr. Updike's writing, there is the dazzling variety of perception to which his restless and inquisitive imagination transports him. . . . We certainly can trust him—we are in very good hands."
THE NEW YORK TIMES

THE WITCHES OF EASTWICK

In a small New England town in the late 1960s, there lived three witches. Alexandra Spofford, a sculptress, could create thunderstorms. Jane Smart, a cellist, could fly. The local gossip columnist, Sukie Rougemont, could turn milk into cream. Divorced but hardly celibate, content but always ripe for adventure, our three wonderful witches one day found themselves quite under the spell of the new man in town, one Darryl Van Horne, whose hot tub was the scene of some rather bewitching delights. Basis for the major motion picture starring Jack Nicholson and Cher.

	ISBN	Price
BECH IS BACK	20277-9	$2.95
THE CENTAUR	21522-9	$3.95
THE COUP	24259-9	$4.50
COUPLES	20797-8	$4.50
MARRY ME	20361-1	$2.95
A MONTH OF SUNDAYS	20795-1	$3.50
OF THE FARM	21451-6	$3.95
PICKED-UP PIECES	23363-4	$2.95
PIGEON FEATHERS	21132-0	$2.95
THE POORHOUSE FAIR	21213-0	$3.95
PROBLEMS	21103-7	$3.50
RABBIT, RUN	20506-1	$3.95
RABBIT REDUX	20934-2	$3.95
RABBIT IS RICH	24548-9	$3.95
ROGER'S VERSION	21288-2	$4.95
TOO FAR TO GO	20016-7	$2.75
TRUST ME	21498-2	$4.95
THE WITCHES OF EASTWICK	20647-5	$4.50

These John Updike books are available at your local bookstore or call toll-free:

1-800-733-3000

to use your American Express, MasterCard, or Visa. To expedite your order, please mention Interest Code "MRM 9." Postage charges are $1 for the first book, 50¢ for each additional book.

To order by mail, send check or money order (no cash or CODs please) to: Fawcett Mail Sales, 8-4, 201 E. 50th St., New York, NY 10022.

Prices and numbers subject to change without notice. All orders subject to availability of books. Valid in U.S. only.